IMMORTAL NEXUS

AN IMMORTAL STORY OF TRUE LOVE, FAMILY, AND COMMITMENT

Book 6

The Immortals Stories Series

by

Linda Ashton Trott

Tagger Press

Copyright

Dedication

I am dedicating this book to my husband, who without, it would have been impossible to complete this work.

A huge thank you to Lee Burton of Oceanside Editing for being my editor. He continues to help me improve everything I write. He is a very good teacher and editor.

A big thank you to Dawn Hughes for being my continuity editor, keeping the timelines straight and the details consistent.

Thanks to you, the reader, for purchasing this book. I hope you enjoy it! If you do, don't forget to leave a review.

Contents

What did you miss?

This is what you missed in Book 5 – Immortal Hunt

- Wild parties
- Tiny House Project gets started
- Lora and Andrews go through their transformation
- Time travel
- More immortals are found
- Spelunking in volcanoes
- An engagement
- Pirates
- Meeting a coven in Ireland
- Traveling to another dimension

1—Carlow, Ireland

Lora

It was an epic night, bringing all those souls back from the pocket dimension where they had been trapped. The power of the magic still vibrated through us, sparking off and sizzling.

We six immortals had succeeded in reviving the ancient magic their ancestors had relied on. Through the energy of sexual connectivity, we had opened a vast portal to another world and brought thirteen men and women back home.

It was an epic night indeed. My great-great grandmother, Innogen, also released Esperanza from her prison and took her place in the occult store. Now I would forever be able to communicate and learn from her. I couldn't wait. There was a large part of me that was more interested in returning to the vast room where we did the magic, just to be there where it happened. But I had to take care of the physical right now. I was starving after all that work and jumping through dimensions.

"Are you pregnant?" asked Gwen.

"Oh!" I said, snapping back from my reverie. "I don't know."

"I think I am," murmured Gwen.

"Oh, that's wonderful!" cried Falon. "Congratulations, Gwen and Andrews!"

"What!" said Andrews. "Did you say pregnant?"

"Gwen was ripe for a child," said Mark. "She just needed a potent male."

"Yes, my love," said Gwen. "You put a baby in me."

"Now what?" asked Falon.

"Oh my God," said Andrews, feeling a little stunned.

"I vote for sleep," said Mark. He took hold of Falon's hand and led her back to their room.

"Bye, all!" called Falon over her shoulder.

"Come here, lover," said Gwen, pulling Andrews into her arms. "Let's go get something to eat in our room, eh?" Gwen and Andrews left as well, leaving me and Rick alone in our room.

"You did it, love," he said, nuzzling me.

"We did it," I said. "But what do we do now?"

"Are you pregnant?" he asked shyly.

"I don't know. It's very possible with all the intense sex we've been having. It's nice, not having to wear protection anymore. I used to hate having to ask those questions: Are you clean? When were you last tested? Do you have condoms?"

"Yes, it's certainly one of the more enjoyable perks of being intimate with an immortal. We don't catch or pass on human diseases. In fact, even having sex with you as a human I wasn't at risk, nor were you. Pregnancy is another situation though. Why don't we go get some food and a test?"

"Sounds like a plan."

The streets of Carlow were quiet with most shops closed, but "our" pub was open so we went in to get some food.

"Welcome back, you two," said the barkeep. "It's rather late, isn't it?"

"Yes, but we were hungry after a very long hard day. Would you have anything to munch on?" I asked.

"Well, I believe there is some bread just out of the oven, and some stew leftovers and a wee bit of lamb as well. Let me put some plates together for you."

"Thank you!"

In no time at all, two heaping plates were placed in front of us filled with the savory smell of roasted lamb and the heavenly scent of a fresh loaf of bread with a pot of cream butter, plus two cold pints to go with it.

Rick and I spent no time talking but dug into the wonderful food, groaning with pleasure while we were chewing. Eventually, I pushed back from the bar with my plate empty, smiling like a fool and moaning about an over-full stomach.

"Oh my God, that was so good!" I said at last.

"I agree," said Rick.

"I'm going to miss this place."

"Why?" asked the barkeep.

"Well, we'll be going home to Canada tomorrow."

"Then you'll have to come back for a visit, now don' ye know," said the barkeep.

"Oh, we will, you can count on that!" said Rick. "I want your recipe for the stew."

"Ah well, that there's a family secret, I'm afraid."

"I couldn't bribe you, eh?" asked Rick.

"We may be able to come to some sort of a deal," said the barkeep, with a finger sly to his nose.

Rick and I then returned the long way to our hotel room.

"Hun, I think I need to go check on the witches and see how they are doing," I said. "It's going to be a shock for them to suddenly be in the twenty-first century."

"Okay, can we do this tomorrow morning? I'm kind of more interested in getting you between the sheets, *mamacita*," Rick replied.

"Hmmm, I like the sound of that," I answered. "Let's stop on the way and get that test."

There was one drugstore in the area and it was unfortunately closed. So the two of us went back to the hotel. I stood in the hallway a moment as Rick unlocked the door to our room. We could hear murmurs coming from all the other rooms where our friends were staying. It didn't sound like anyone was engaged in anything more than pillow talk.

As Rick pushed open the door, our room was welcoming, cool and quiet. He took my hand and led me to the bed, where he slowly stripped away my clothes and then got down on his knees and put his ear to my belly.

"Hello in there," said Rick. "If anyone is listening, I want to introduce myself. I'm your papa."

Tears came to my eyes at the tenderness with which he touched me and kissed me. I'd never had a partner who was so caring about their child, let alone their unborn child.

"Little one, I will protect you with my own life. I love you and I cannot wait to meet you."

"Ah, Rick, that's so sweet," I said.

"To have a child with you would be the *pièce de résistance* of life."

"For me too," I said. "I would love to raise a child with you. I just need to tell my mortal children that their siblings won't get older the same way that they will."

"We will cross that bridge when we get to it," Rick said. Standing up, he took his own clothes off and uncharacteristically dropped them on the floor. Picking me up in his arms, he walked to the bedside, placed me down on the sheets and laid on top of me.

"All I want to do right now is hold you and love you," he said.

What he did was worship me. It brought tears to my eyes again as he kissed me tenderly and held me gently.

"Is something wrong?" Rick asked.

"No, my love, nothing is wrong. It's just all so right now."

"Not yet, we are not married."

"Well, that will have to be planned now that we are finished with this latest adventure."

"And it will. But for now, let me love you."

I felt the whisper of his lips cover my skin in kisses and the flutter of his breath as he passed over all of me. The small delicate sounds vibrated in me, stirring the resting tiger that was inside, awakening and stretching as if to be ready.

The more Rick did, the more that tiger revved up, until I was alternating between small growls of pleasure and purring in happiness. Rick was gentle with me, maybe because I might be pregnant, or perhaps just because that was his mood. But our lovemaking was not urgent, or fast, or hard, or any other over-the-top, excited ways. It was smooth, and sexy, and held a great deal of reverence.

When we came back down from our shared climax, he spooned me and held me like a treasure until we both fell asleep.

2—Going Home

The following morning, Falon knocked on Lora's door to see if they were awake.

"Just a minute!" came a voice from inside. Footsteps padding to the door could be heard and then the latch being undone.

"Yes?" asked a groggy Rick.

"Good morning. We were wondering if you would like to join us all for breakfast at the pub?"

"Oh yes, let me wake up Lora, and we'll join you downstairs in say, thirty minutes?"

"Got it."

Falon went down the hall and knocked on Gwen and Andrews's door as well. This time a bright-eyed face opened the door.

"Hello?"

"Good morning, you're up! Would you like to join us all for breakfast at the pub?"

"Absolutely, we're just packing and we'll meet you downstairs shortly," said Andrews.

"So you've adjusted to your shock?" asked Falon.

"Mostly, I'm very happy that we are pregnant."

Falon returned to her room. She and Mark finished packing, then went downstairs and checked out. Sitting in the front foyer, Falon looked around.

"This is a delightful area for a vacation, don't you think?" she asked.

"Yes, it's full of history and ancient ruins. I'd go for an adventure holiday where we could explore castles. Maybe get one of those tours that takes you around by bus."

"Oh, that is a great idea. Let's plan one in the near future."

"Absolutely."

Gwen and Andrews were downstairs first. They checked out too, then joined Falon and Mark in the foyer.

"So what are your plans next?" Andrews asked Mark.

"I'm not sure. We still have several project ideas on the table," said Mark.

"Like what?" asked Gwen.

"Like getting more history of Group 35 and 36, finding other groups of immortals, Lora and Rick's wedding, and now your baby."

"Ah yes, our baby," said Andrews, with a big goofy smile on his face.

"You don't sound excited," said Falon.

"I get waves of being a little overwhelmed. I never imagined myself as a father," he said. "But I'm very happy."

"He's going to make a wonderful dad," piped up Gwen. "Can't you see him giving Junior a horsey ride on his back?"

They all laughed at the image of strong, silent, serious Andrews giving his young son a horsey ride.

"Go on, make fun of me," he laughed. "Get it out of your system."

"What's so funny?" asked Lora, coming out of the elevator with Rick.

"Ah, we were giving Andrews a hard time about being a cute, adorable daddy," said Mark.

"I could see that," said Rick, covering his mouth to hide his laughter.

"Okay, everyone," said Lora, "you'll be going home today, but Rick and I will be taking a bit of a side trip. I want to check on our travelers today to make sure they are getting what they need."

"Where do we catch the ride?" asked Gwen.

"I've got the 'tickets' upstairs in our room for you," Lora said for the benefit of the public. Come up to get them after breakfast."

"Let's go!"

It was a sunny day, medium temperature, and smelled of fresh rain on cut grass. It was truly a wonderful day to take a walk. They all rubbernecked as they walked through the streets of Carlow, stopping to look in shop windows, even going in and looking around at some. There were exquisite glasswork and pottery stores, stores that sold locally made sweaters from genuine Galway sheep wool, a well-known commodity. Irish sweaters were sold around the world, but to see them here was a treat. There was such a variety of colors, as well as the traditional undyed wool. The girls insisted on buying everyone a sweater. By the time they got to the pub, they had multiple parcels to carry.

They all ordered a full Irish breakfast with orange juice. When the food came the plates were enormous, with enough food for almost three people on each one. It was a good thing the guys could eat as much as a horse. The food smelled wonderful and they dug in with gusto. There wasn't a crumb left when they were finished, even though they asked for more potatoes and toast.

Back at the hotel, everyone checked out and then went to Lora's room with their luggage.

"Okay, guys, here's your ticket home," she said, as she opened the portal to the occult store.

The four of them walked through to return to Montreal. Once the portal was closed she and Rick checked out of the hotel normally and then did the same thing in an alley, so the hotel saw them leaving.

"Innogen, hello!" called Lora once they were inside the occult store.

"Lora my dear, welcome back. I saw your friends back home safe and sound—I opened up a portal right inside their house for them."

"Oh thank you, 3G, that saves them a taxi ride," said Lora.

"Is there somewhere you want to go?"

"Yes, I was hoping to check up on the thirteen witches that came through yesterday."

"Oh, no need. They are all just fine. We found some rooms in the ship that would act as individual homes for them while they get acclimated to the twenty-first century."

"That's wonderful. So they are living on the ship right now?"

"Yes, although they don't know what it is. To them, it's just a very strange looking place with amenities."

"Is there anything they need?"

"Not yet, the ship provides. But I'm not telling them that. My sister is staying with them, and I've instructed her on how to get food and clothes from the ship for them. My sister will see to their education. We made a deal, you see. She gets to bring them up to date in exchange for them going free and getting to choose their own lives."

"That is amenable. Well, you know where to find me. I'll be coming here often anyway to learn from you what I should have been taught all along."

"Good to hear. We'll set up a schedule of classes."

"That works, then I can plan around them," said Lora. "Okay, 3G, we'll go home now."

"Bye, granddaughter."

A portal opened before Rick and Lora that they could see their living room in the new house. Stepping through, they faced Mama Anita, who stood there with a shocked look on her face. When the portal dissipated, she nearly fainted, but Rick moved fast enough to catch her before she hit her head on the ceramic floor.

"Ricardo, what was that?"

"I'll explain later, Mama, let's get you to a bed to lie down for a rest."

"No, no! Ricardo, don't keep secrets from me." Rick glanced at Lora and she shrugged.

"It's okay, Mama, it was magic. I'm a witch," said Lora.

"Okay, you two, start at the beginning. I want a full explanation now. I cannot protect you if I don't have the whole truth."

"Ah, Mama, you don't need to protect us," said Rick.

"Oh course I do. You have a secret that needs protecting, and from your children as well I can imagine."

"Well, my kids have always known I'm a witch, Mama. I just don't usually practice in front of them," said Lora. "Actually, they don't believe me and think it's some kind of weird thing their mom does."

"Still, I believe you, and I need to understand and know. Please, Lorita," said Mama. Lorita was her special name for Lora.

"Very well, let us unpack first."

"I will do that. I've made brunch for you. I will serve it on the pool deck first."

There was no stopping Mama Anita when she had a plan. Even if they had told her they just had a big breakfast, she'd still want to feed them again. It was the time of day after all, and Mama Anita always liked feeding her charges. She'd been taking care of Rick since he was a small boy when she started working for his parents. She wasn't about to stop now that he had a family of his own. She had three new young charges to look after.

"Okay, Mama, we'll be right there," said Rick. "Where are the kids?"

"Oh, they went to the pool next door," said Mama. "They are getting to know the neighbors now. They are supposed to be home by 4:00 in the afternoon to get cleaned up for dinner."

"Excellent," said Lora. "Thank you, Mama."

"No problem, *chica*, this is what I do," said Mama, smiling.

Rick and Lora walked out to the pool deck and sat on the deck chairs. It wasn't very warm outside, but it was pleasant in the sunshine.

"What will we tell her?" asked Rick.

"I can explain about my magic. We just don't tell her the whole story."

"Do you think she'll need the whole story eventually?"

"Perhaps, but we'll cross that bridge when we get to it. Life is becoming more complicated now, isn't it?"

"Yes it is," said Rick. "I didn't have these problems to deal with when I was alone and it didn't really come into conversation with my first wife. I didn't know I had these problems to deal with. Eventually, it would become obvious that I wasn't aging, and without meeting you I would not have known what was up."

"That's an interesting thought exercise to work through. What would you do? Hmmm."

Mama Anita walked out of the house carrying a tray and put it down on the table close by.

"Here you go, kids. There are some sandwiches and fruits for you to nibble on. I'm going to go unpack your bags and get the laundry on. Then I will come back for the explanation, si?"

"Si, Mama."

They spent a half hour picking at the food, because they weren't terribly hungry. When Mama Anita came back, she scowled at them like they were children worthy of a scolding. Then she removed the tray and came and sat back down expectantly.

"Mama, what I am about to tell you cannot be said to anyone else, do you understand?" asked Lora.

"Si, *chica*, I understand."

"I am a witch. Not in the movie sense, but I have inherited supernatural abilities through my family line that come from my great-great-grandmother, named Innogen. I am still learning much of what I am able to do. I was never taught by my mother, because her mother had shunned magic and all that it represented. I grew up with a talent for picking numbers and finding things, as well as knowing who was right for each other. I was an excellent matchmaker. I recently discovered my heritage, and have been learning a lot. One of the things I have learned is how to create a portal to a place called the occult store. This is what you saw us coming through earlier today. The portal takes us to another dimension where my 3G lives. She has agreed to train me, so you'll see me use that portal frequently now. Unfortunately, the rest of the world won't understand. So we have to keep it a secret, or risk becoming the subject of a news story, or worse, a government plot to capture us."

"Lora, do your children have this ability?"

"I don't know, Mama Anita. You know that's a good question."

"It seems to me that if the skills are inherited, you may have passed it on to your daughter as well?"

"It could have gone to any of them, male or female. In our world, there is no gender for a witch. A witch is a magic-wielder."

"How could you find out?" asked Rick.

"I could ask 3G."

"3G?" asked Mama Anita. "You used that term before. What does it mean?"

"My three times grandmother."

"Oh, si!"

3—Being a Parent

Andrews

"I don't want to fly home to Houston, I'm still exhausted after that ritual," said Gwen once we returned to Montreal. "Can I stay with you? I've already checked out of my hotel."

"Of course. I would be delighted for you to stay with me. It will give us time to talk about what happened. But I've got to warn you, my condo isn't what you would call feminine."

Her first expression when she walked in was oohs and aahs. Small wonder. My condo looked very cool. It was a very large two-storey condo near the top of the building. It was big enough for two. It had three bedrooms, a large kitchen with open-concept dining and living areas. The living room had an electric fireplace that actually gave off heat without any smoke. It was quite posh.

I made a good living, so when I purchased the property I could afford to hire a professional decorator to come in and do the whole place. The multi-level condo had glass surrounding the main level and the views out over the harbor and downtown Montreal, leading the decorator to set "my style" as industrial modern. So everything was in grays, white, and black with steel and concrete and dark gray flooring. There wasn't a "soft" edge to anything or a soft corner.

"This is exactly what I expected," Gwen said. "Power and male. It's beautiful, Andrews, really beautiful, and the views are amazing."

"Yeah, I love the view. I sit here many evenings just staring out at the city," I said. "Come and sit in my favorite spot and I'll grab us a bottle of wine."

She sat relaxing on the sofa with a glass of wine, looking out over the city. I sat beside her and started rubbing her feet. She cooed in pleasure.

I felt the need to talk about Gwen being pregnant and to find out where we stood on that. I wasn't sure, even though it was exciting.

"Do you want to talk about things?" I asked.

"I guess we should," she answered. "Let me start. While this may be a question after the fact, do you even want to have a child with me?"

"To be very honest, I have never thought about children. I'm still getting used to not being single," I said with a smirk.

"I expected that. If it's any consolation, neither have I."

"So what would you like to do, Gwen? Do you want children?"

"I'm not sure. I realize that's not the best answer, but it was honest." She smiled.

"Now that the shock has worn off, I'm kind of interested, maybe even excited," I said. "Would the child be immortal?"

"Yes, born so."

"Is there any chance the child would inherit anything from me?"

"I expect he'll inherit at least half of you, why?"

"I'm sorry, I don't do guile well, and I'd rather just be up front about my shortcomings."

"You have no shortcomings, not as far as I'm concerned."

"That's nice of you to say, but I'm not normal."

"Define normal, I dare you," she challenged me.

"As far as I can remember, I've been able to smell things I shouldn't be able to, things other people cannot smell."

"Like what?"

"Like when a woman is aroused. It's a very specific smell, and my nose picks it up immediately. It's what made me such a good sex games partner. I knew when someone was actually aroused by the game, and when they weren't. Comes in handy, so you can stop or change the game before anyone has a chance to get angry."

"So can I. It's an immortal thing. So perhaps you were immortal all along."

"I don't think so. Remember, I lost my arm. They had to sew it back on."

"We can grow new limbs, but it takes a long time, and it's very painful. It's quite possible that they reattached your arm before your body could do the repair itself. Let me look."

Gwen took off my shirt and examined where my arm was reattached. There was a thin line all the way around my bicep.

"That's it? That's the scar from basically an amputation sewn back on?"

"It's gone now because of the transformation. Initially, the scar was like a thick rope, but then it started shrinking and fading."

"That strongly suggests that you had immortal genes. Your body was healing itself when a human body would not."

"I didn't know. I had a cast on the arm for eight weeks, and they never did a check up on the arm until they removed the cast.

By then, it was healed really well. They even mentioned that they were surprised how quickly it had knitted together, and chalked it up to good genes."

"Now that you are fully immortal, all your scars have vanished."

"Yes, and somehow that is upsetting to me."

"Why?"

"Because they're sort of a badge of honor. It shows I survived something, what I survived. It was an important moment in my life, it defined me for so many years, the pain and recovery."

"You'll remember all that, it's embedded in your mind, it won't go away. So you don't need the scar to remember it by. The scar only tells others what you've been through. And since you'll only be baring your beautiful body for me, it won't matter, because I'll remember too."

"Now that you put it that way... come here, you vixen so I can bare the rest of me for you."

"Nope, said Gwen as she placed her hands flat on my chest. "We still need to finish this conversation. Where were we? Oh yes, getting used to not being single. Are you sure being immortal isn't bigger?"

"Immortality hasn't seemed to faze me. Perhaps because I'm used to looking at only the present. I'm not concerned with forty years down the road. I'm who I am right now, and that's who I am. I guess that when I still look like this in twenty years, it will be noticeable. But many of my friends don't show their age either. Black men and women rarely look their age. Fifty-year-olds routinely look in their thirties, and seventy-year-olds look in their fifties. So I think I have a while before that will have an impact on me. But being in a relationship, that is not something I ever thought I would have."

"We can always keep it casual between us. We don't have to be a couple," said Gwen.

"Would you be okay with that? I don't think so, especially with a child of mine coming."

"I have been alone for much longer than you, Andrews. Like you, being a couple was not something I was interested in. You are different though, and the more I'm with you, the more I want from you. I think I'm addicted to you. I find myself very surprised by this."

"I can say the same thing. Since we hooked up, the thought of anyone else is so far from my mind. I can only think of you and what we do for each other," said Andrews.

"Addiction is a real thing for immortals. We become addicted to the venom," said Gwen.

"Setting that aside, do *you* want to have a baby?" asked Andrews.

Gwen was silent for a moment, thinking.

"I want to have your baby," said Gwen. "I'm not convinced I would feel the same if it were anyone else's."

"Then how do you want to do this, Gwen? Do you want a partner? Do you want a baby daddy? Do you want a husband? Do you want a mate?"

"Hmmm, I don't want a baby daddy. I want a partner, but not necessarily a husband, and I think we're mated whether we like it or not."

Chuckling because that mirrored what I felt, I said, "I feel the same. I want you to know, I feel excitement at the thought of being a father. It's a feeling I never thought I would have. And the more it sits in my mind, the more I love the idea. I just don't know if I'll be a good one."

"I think you'll be a tremendously good father," said Gwen, as she wrapped her arms around me. I reciprocated and we sat there giving and taking the energy that passed between us. Feeling her body against mine made me feel I could take on the world as long as she was there. I believed in myself because she believed in me.

4—Hired by Aliens

Andrews

Last night, while Gwen and I were still in Carlow, I fell asleep thinking about where this journey for me started. My night was full of dreams that replayed the sequence of events that I went through. Those dreams haunted my thoughts today while I was working. It's not that I believed I made the wrong decision, but certainly that my decision had led me to the here and now.

I remembered that first day so clearly, because it happened shortly after an interview I did for a magazine was published. The office had become very busy with phones ringing just about every twenty minutes. Our phones had never rung that often before. It seemed like the world had suddenly found us. Ah, the power of the printed word. A well-placed profile article in a well read magazine used to be the best way to get noticed. Just a few years later, most people got their news from social media, not magazines. I don't know if the article would have had the same impact.

The magazine was a business magazine, and they were doing a whole issue on security. Hence we were interviewed—well, just me, actually. The writer was a cute girl wearing a very short, tight skirt and top. I didn't take her very seriously, but it was a shot, so I wasn't going to waste it. After all, looks can be deceiving.

One of those phone calls was from Mark Chisholm. He'd wanted to speak to me about hiring our company. Since he was in Houston, we arranged to meet at his office the following week. I was sitting in the conference room waiting for the meeting to start when his aide brought in breakfast and coffee and some magazines. One of them was the magazine I was interviewed for. She told me Mark would be with me in ten minutes. Curious, I picked up the magazine and started reading—about myself.

PROFILE: AGP Security

Security Magazine sat down with the newly minted CEO of AGP Security for a conversation.

Andrews Andrews knows a lot of people. "When I say I know a guy, chances are I really do," he laughed.

Andrews is a specialist. He specializes in connecting the right people for the job. "I have a number of other specialties too, from multiple SCUBA licenses to multiple black belts in a variety of martial arts."

He is a pretty good cook, very well organized, and as a male specimen, well, let's just say he is gorgeous. Everything is in the right place, and well defined. Now Andrews isn't a beefy guy—his muscles don't have muscles—but if he had a Speedo on, you would not be able to take your eyes off him.

Feeling my face getting hot, I looked up from the page. It was a little embarrassing to read this in a magazine that specialized in security. It wasn't very professional, and I was surprised it was left in the story. My prospective clients don't care if I looked good or not. I was a touch annoyed by the style of her writing, but I wasn't given any options or control over the content in the story. *I'd better find out what else she said*, I thought to myself, resuming.

Andrews' doesn't know his ancestry. "I didn't know where I came from, because I was adopted," he said. "My parents, though Caucasian, gave me every opportunity to explore my 'blackness' and to discover my culture. I took advantage of that as a youth, getting into rap and urban culture, but I found I had too many aspirations to stay contained in a 'hood.'"

Before Andrews Andrews left high school, he decided he was going into the military to learn as much as he could about everything he could find. Joining the army, he vaulted through the ranks into Special Forces, earning medals and commendations for sharpshooting, explosives, and tactical.

"I jumped ship to the Navy to learn about ships, submarines, and ended up being a chopper pilot, licensed for a number of craft," said Andrews. "That is also where I got my SCUBA training, not some fancy South Pacific hotel resort. My last military post was with the Marines, and then I rose to be a Raider. My training with them included some highly classified aircraft, as well as tactical training. When I left military service, I was twenty-five years older and had a heap of special skills, knowledge, and experience.

Again pausing, I looked up to see people scurrying around outside the conference room. Something was going on, and there was still no sign of Mark Chisholm. *Well, at least the writer started talking about my background*, I thought. It was at least more to the point and showed that I bring a lot of skills to the table.

At the age of forty-four, Andrews is in his prime. He looks more like he's in his mid-twenties.

SECURITY: Why did you start your own security company?

"When you leave the armed forces, you need to focus your mind on something or lose yourself in the trauma of what you've been through," said Andrews. "It made sense to use the skills I had accumulated. The decision to start a private security business was easy, especially when I approached my fellow ex-Marines and they were in."

SECURITY: How many former Marines did you bring into your business?

"Two. James Grisham was my go-to guy," answered Andrews. "He had similar training as me, but he was a weapons specialist. There wasn't a weapon he didn't know about, real or prototype, and not one he hadn't personally used at least once. He also had a personal interest in photography, which like all things he did, was professional level to the max.

"Another of my former guys is Geoffrey Parsons, who became my other partner. Geoffrey had a stint in espionage as well as being a linguist with seven languages. Like me, he had SCUBA licenses, and martial arts training. But he was a pro at disguises and blending in and being invisible. If you need to infiltrate something, he is your guy. Each of them had something I didn't.

"I knew those guys like the back of my hand. We had survived shit together, gotten out of more scrapes than I can think of, and our skill set complemented each other's. Where one was less knowledgeable, another was an expert."

SECURITY: How many tours did you do?

"I did four tours, then I was discharged due to injury," answered Andrews. "I'd lost too many friends, and my 'pack' had already stopped running around because they were married or all becoming fathers. We called ourselves a pack of wolfhounds because we were really good at sniffing out the enemy. But it just wasn't fun anymore."

SECURITY: How is business going?

"It has been a slow process getting the business running," said Andrews. "There are a lot of security companies. We had to find a way to stand out, so we decided to specialize in difficult cases. Our tagline is "Nothing is too difficult to secure!""

"Mr. Andrews?" interrupted a voice. I looked up from the magazine and Mark Chisholm was standing over me.

"Yes, sorry, Andrews Andrews. What can I do for you?" I answered back, putting down the magazine.

"It's a good read," said Mark. "When I went shopping for a security company, your tagline set you apart. Can you live up to it?"

"I believe so," I answered. "My team is small, but we have a very detailed and wide set of skills specifically useful in this type of work. Plus, I have access to people outside my organization with even more specific skills that enhance what we can accomplish."

"I believe you," said Mark. "The article was a good primer for an interview. My own background check confirms all your stories and details. You are legit. So I'd like to hire you."

"Thank you, sir. What do you need AGP Security to secure?"

"I run an international conglomerate with fingers in many different industries," said Mark, indicating that we both take seats again. "We are widely diversified. Our business is old, having been started by my grandfather, and I'm the third generation to run it."

"That's quite a legacy, sir."

"Yes, a serious responsibility too," said Mark. "I'm not allowed to fail." He paused there with an expression on his face that closely resembled a man about to be hung. *Strange!*

"Anyway, I believe that my interests need to be protected. In particular, my family."

"Why don't we start with an all-around assessment of your work, life, activities, and such, and see where there are holes that need to be filled and security issues that need to be addressed," I said. "I don't like jumping into a project until I've done the recon first."

"A thorough man. I like that," said Mark.

I left his office with a newfound confidence. Getting that contract meant it would even out our cash flow and we could begin growing. But first, I'd meant what I said about doing an assessment of his business. The first thing would be to get my guys doing a full sweep of his background, the business, and any associates. We needed to know what we were dealing with. What kind of industries he "had his fingers in" as he said. I wasn't going to take on anyone involved with organized crime or anything shady or illegal.

Geoffrey started the deep dive into his background and he soon discovered some interesting anomalies. The most intriguing piece of information was that Mark Chisholm hadn't existed three years before. That rang all kinds of alarm bells for me, considering what he had said in the initial interview.

While I wasn't opposed to separating Mark from his money, I wanted to know what the hell I was dealing with. Thankfully, the deep dive into his background was CIA-level thanks to Geoffrey. He even managed to recover a sample of Mark's DNA and had that run in a private lab where they did the kind of tests that weren't quite legal.

The tests uncovered something we weren't prepared for. Mark's DNA wasn't human. It had an extra strand of DNA—three instead of two. *Huh!* Okay, was this just an aberration or was he some kind of alien?

Yet when Geoffrey had the DNA run at a lab, even with cross checks, nothing came up at all. No birth, no death, no nothing. That wasn't possible. He had to have existed somewhere to be here today.

James had an idea of trying to trace his work history further back. That led us to the discovery of the hotels and companies he owned, his sister, and New York City.

While his holdings were real, the title of them had recently been given the name Mark Chisholm. He was centered in Houston by the time we met, but earlier it was New York that seemed to be a nexus for Mark. It's where he first surfaced as an individual. Breaking into the data banks of the hotel, we found his job application, which was part of the cover. So he had been an employee before the family bought that hotel. *Interesting.*

Chisholm's job application to the hotel said he was from Houston. So that's where Grisham's investigation went next. In

Houston, he found a family connection to a shipping company that had offices in Montreal and Greece. He also uncovered that the family had been purchasing hotels in New York, Houston, Montreal, and Greece.

The family was filthy rich but lived very modestly. There were four children in the family, all on the board of directors for the shipping company. But there was one son who appeared to be a black sheep of sorts. There were reports of him being "sent away" to New York. *Hmm, a tie?*

When Grisham reported back to me that he might have found something, I told him to do what he needed to do to get definitive answers. We needed to know who we were working for.

Grisham returned to Houston a week later with a fantastic report, but it was all backed with information, photos, and dates.

"You are not going to believe this, boss," said Grisham.

"Go ahead and tell me anyway, James," I said.

"The family in Montreal was headed by a man called Nicholas Antoni. He immigrated to Canada in the mid-1800s, running his shipping business from the old port. Nicholas died in 1890, and was succeeded by his son—also called Nicholas—who ran the company until 1960. He was then succeeded by a son called Nicolas, who still runs the company today. His firstborn son, Nicholas, is set to take over next year."

"Hmm, that does sound rather suspicious. Go on."

"There are three children. Nicholas is eldest, then Gwen, then Zisis. About five years ago, his son Zisis disappeared."

"What do you mean, exactly?"

"Well, by all accounts he left Montreal and vanished. Neighbors say he was sent to New York to work in his dad's business there. But there is no record of a Zisis Antoni leaving Canada or entering the United States, and no record of an application for citizenship or a work visa. The kid just disappeared."

"Interesting."

"That's where Mark Chisholm surfaces for the first time. I'm pretty sure that Zisis Antoni is Mark Chisholm, but for the life of me I don't know why. Anyway, Mark completed a job application at the hotel that he eventually purchased. How did he do that? He apparently had lots of money. I was able to follow Mark through a series of purchases and connect them all to Mark Chisholm of Houston—who is this guy who hired us."

"Good work, James."

"What does it mean?"

"I don't know yet," I said. "But I will."

There was one thing my military training honed in me to a sharp point: my bull-shit indicator. I was smelling bullshit and I needed to get to the bottom of it.

My opportunity came a few days later when Mark called me with a small job. It would give me a chance to see how he operated and what sort of security he would need.

"Hey, Andrews, I am taking a trip to Atlanta in a few days to discuss a merger or takeover of sorts with my sister," Chisholm said over the phone. "What it will be is entirely dependent on how the prospect copes with our offer. I'd like a background on a company called…" and Mark went on to give me a list of names in the company and the company details he had.

"Sure, when do you need this report?" I asked.

"Is the end of the week too quick?" Mark answered.

"No, I don't think so. This is pretty easy stuff. But I do have a question for you about something entirely not related."

"Shoot," said Mark.

"Who is Zisis Antoni?"

Crickets…

"Mark?"

26

"Yeah, I wish you hadn't asked me that, Andrews," Mark replied.

"Why not?"

"It's complicated," said Mark. "Look, I cannot have this conversation over the phone. Please come to the office and we can discuss this."

"Are you in Montreal?"

"Yes, I'm staying at the Queen E, room 1407."

"Fine, I'll be there in fifteen minutes."

Mark met me at the main door of the hotel and escorted me to his room, closing the blinds before sitting down.

"Andrews, what I'm about to tell you is confidential and secret. It cannot leave this room."

"I understand cloak and dagger, Mark. But I work for you, and that means I need to know who I am working for. I cannot put my guys in jeopardy because I don't have all the facts. I need to know who the hell you are. If you're into organized crime, I want nothing to do with you. Do you understand?"

"Yes, I do. If it's any consolation, we're absolutely not organized crime."

"So what are you?"

"Very old."

"What does that mean?"

"Our family, it's very old."

"What does that have to do with it?"

I sat there while Mark inhaled and then exhaled a long breath. Clearly what he was about to say was difficult.

"If I tell you, I need to swear you to secrecy, on your life—the same for your employees."

"Wow, Mark, that is heavy. I'll have to make the decision once I hear it."

"I cannot do that. I need to have your sworn oath that you will keep the secret before you hear it."

I thought about it for a while, Mark was patiently waiting. *What was the downside to agreeing? That the secret somehow led to a heinous crime and I was beholden to keep it? What was the upside? I'd get a quirky client? I wasn't sure. It seemed like an important thing, but was it? It was to him.*

"Okay, Mark, I will swear to keep this secret to myself, and let no one know it on penalty of my death. I surely hope it's worth it."

"I'll double your rate for you," said Mark.

"That'll help. Now what is this secret?"

"My family is not human. We are a race of beings with a very long lifespan, and because of that, we have to change identities about every ten years to make sure we don't raise suspicions."

Crickets from me this time. *Did I actually hear him say he was not human?*

"What? Come again?"

"We're aliens. We look human, we're not. We've been on this planet for tens of thousands of years. I'm 150 years old or thereabouts."

"You're an alien?"

"Yes."

"From another planet?"

"Yes."

"You've got to be kidding."

"No."

"Seriously?"

"Yes."

"I'm afraid I'm going to have to have proof."

"That can be done."

"Now."

"Okay." As I watched, Mark stood up and walked across the room and stopped in front of me. His eyes started turning red, like they had a light behind them, and a pair of fangs grew out of his mouth between his lips. He lifted his hand palm up and pulled a pocketknife from his pants pocket and sliced open his wrist lengthwise before I could move. By the time I reacted to the injury, it was already closing up in front of me. Within seconds, there was nothing there, no scar, only the few drops of blood from the initial cut.

Stunned, I sat there and stared at the place on his wrist where the injury was made. I'd never seen anything like it. It wasn't human. It wasn't human ... crap.

"You're going to have to triple my rate!" I said, coming to a conclusion. "You're a vampire!"

"No. We are not vampires. They don't exist. Yes, I can triple your rate."

Swallowing hard against the feelings in my throat, I asked: "So who is Zisis Antoni?"

"It was me while I lived in Montreal. My family settled in Montreal in the early 1800s. I was born there. Because the persona of my father was a Greek shipping magnate, we all had Greek names at the time.

"I met and fell in love with a woman and wanted to have a relationship with her. My father and I argued, I lost, and I had to leave her. My parents sent me to New York to get me away from her. There, I assumed a new identity, got a job, and started a new life. Unfortunately, three years later, she came to New York."

"No! Are you talking about the same woman you met in Montreal?"

"Yes."

"Jesus Christ in a bucket. Holy fuck! I mean, excuse me, but that's unreal."

"Yes, it is. But there it is. She now knows, of course."

"That you're an alien?"

"Yes."

"That must have been a tough conversation. "

"The first time, yes. I don't know about the second time yet."

"The second time?"

"She doesn't know I was Zisis. I still have to tell her."

"Oh, you're fucked, dude. So fucked. Wait, how doesn't she recognize you?"

"Yes, I'm afraid I am rather fucked. We can alter our appearance slightly as needed."

"When will you tell her?"

"It is one of the reasons I'm going to Atlanta. She will be there. I'm hoping to surprise her with a visit and then lay it all on the line."

"I wish you good luck. Geez, I don't want to be in your shoes, nuh uh."

Mark sat there with a faraway expression on his face.

"Mark?"

"Yeah."

"Is your father the same man that has held ownership of the shipping company since the 1800s?"

"Actually, it existed long before that. Our family has owned the company since it first launched in Greece in the 1600s. We brought it over to Montreal in the early 1800s. Records are sparse before the 1800s because of regularly occurring warehouse fires. My father is very adept at being his own 'son' for about ten years, then minimizing his public appearances until he 'dies' and his 'son' takes over. A change of fashion, and new hair styles helped hide the fact it was the same person, and any resemblance was accepted. He's been doing this for a very long time. My mother and he are never seen in public together, so it's not a problem. My siblings and I do the same. We disappear and reappear as someone else in a different place. Gwen keeps using the same name because she likes it."

"You know, you guys are going to have a harder and harder time staying hidden today with all the electronic surveillance and electronic identification."

"Yes, I know that. It's one of the problems I'm working on for the family."

"How many are in your family?"

"My immediate family has five members. The extended family is about a hundred and twenty-three people. The extended family includes members of the original group who left the ark ship thousands of years ago. With the exception of my immediate family, all of them live in a compound in Oregon. It's one of the reasons I hired your firm."

"I see. Does your entire family need protection, or just you and Falon?"

"I'm looking for security independent from the family," said Mark. "I want to protect my interests, my—hopefully to be—mate, and friends."

"To provide you with the best service, I'll need to read my guys in or they will start to question why they're doing things. Some of which will be generating fake data—that's a giveaway. They need to be read in—eventually."

"Then I will have to trust you, that you know when they need to know."

"Thank you, Mark, for this opportunity," I said, standing to leave.

"You're welcome. I'm glad to have you on board."

"I'll be in touch with the next step," I said. I left the building and was walking back to my office thinking to myself, *"How the hell am I going to tell the guys this?"*

5—Let the Kids Know

Lora

It was on my mind, with Rick and Anita coming into my life, and the increased use of magic that I was doing, that I needed to sit down with my kids and make sure they were okay with all this.

Yes, they knew I was a "witch," because I had told them all since they were all very little, but had I ever explained what that was? I wasn't sure. I knew that they all knew what my magic room was, what I did, but frankly, there were no real big events or things happening.

Mostly what I did was small spells for friends, things like luck or love. I never got into the pentagram-drawing, coven-involved, magic. In fact, I was a sole practitioner and didn't have a coven.

Before I finalized all the details of getting married, I needed to sit down with them. Sunday morning was my first opportunity. We had a wonderful brunch together and the kids were helping clear the table.

"Kids, could I have a few minutes of your time before you go off and do your thing today?" I asked them as they were clearing plates.

"Sure, Mom," said Minni.

"I guess," said Trent.

"Do I have to?" asked Pascal.

"I would appreciate it," I answered. "It's about the wedding."

Sighing dramatically, Pascal sat at the table and crossed their arms demonstratively, while the other two sat down too. I joined them at the table.

"Okay, where do I start?" I asked rhetorically. "You all know I'm a witch, right?"

"Yes, Mom," came the chorus.

"But what does that mean exactly?" asked Minni.

"I'm glad you ask," I said. "It means that I come from a very long line of people, mostly women, who have magical, or supernatural, abilities. I haven't done much in my life, because I just didn't know how to. Teaching oneself is difficult. But there has been a big change in my life. I've located and met my great-great-grandmother and she has been teaching me."

"Great-great-grandmother?" asked Trent. "How many grandmothers do we have?"

"Well, living, only one. My mother is your grandmother."

"If she's not alive, how did you meet her?" asked Pascal.

"Her name is Innogen, and she is alive," I answered. "She just isn't in this realm of existence."

"Mom, you're getting confusing!" said Minni.

"Okay. You know how in sci-fi movies they talk about alternate universes and dimensions?"

"Yeah."

"Well, they do actually exist. Innogen is trapped in one of them. She was trapped there by her sister many years ago."

"Why?" asked Trent.

"Because they had a disagreement on how to do something," I said. "But that is not important. What is important is that Innogen is now training me, and she will be coming to the wedding."

"How?" asked Minni.

"I have to do a special spell so that she can come here." I waited for more questions and comments. All three fell silent for a minute.

"How is this different from what you used to do?" asked Minni.

"First, my magic is becoming more visible now. This ritual will happen in front of everyone. Only people who know about my magic will be at the wedding. Second, my magic is getting bigger."

"I didn't really believe you were a witch, Mom," said Pascal. "I never saw you do anything that was magical. At least, I don't think so."

"What did you think it was Pascal?"

"I dunno, magic tricks?"

"Remember that time Mom decorated the house for Trent's birthday in a few minutes and we wondered how she had done it so quickly?" asked Minni.

"Yeah. That was magic?" asked Pascal.

"There is no way she could have done all that decorating without magic."

"Oh."

"There have been lots of little things like that over the years," said Minni. "Mom, what can we do to help?"

"Mom, will I be magical?" asked Trent.

"You're not a girl," said Pascal.

"That doesn't matter," I answered. "Trent, you might be magical. We'll only know if you try, but you likely won't come into your powers until you're older, though."

"What about me, Mom?" asked Minni.

"You would have come into something by now if you were going to. We should test you. But that's another day and another discussion," I said. "I want to make sure, today, that the three of you are good with all this magic business."

"Do we have a choice?" asked Pascal.

"No, just as your sexuality isn't a choice, it just is. My magic just is. I didn't wake up one morning and decide to learn how to be a witch."

"Huh," said Pascal. "I understand that, Mom. Okay, I'm good with this. You're magical, I'm non-binary, and my siblings are typical. We have a cool family. Is Rick magical too?"

"No. But that is—"

"Another discussion for another day," interrupted Pascal. "I get it. Wait to be told."

"I'm good with it too, Mom," said Trent. "It makes you the cool mom in school."

"Honey, you cannot tell people at school though," I said.

"Oh, why not?" he asked. "I may have already told some people."

"Did they believe you?" I asked.

"No, they laughed at me."

"Well, then, leave them ignorant, okay?"

"Okay."

"Mom, I'm delighted that you found your grandmother. I know how you've struggled without a mentor. I hope we can learn together."

"How did you know that?" I asked.

"I would occasionally hear you late at night working in your office trying to do stuff. I was more aware than you realize Mom."

I didn't have anything to say to that, so I just said, "Okay, kids, that was all I wanted to say."

The three of them got up abruptly and kissed my cheek as they flew out of the kitchen, off to do who knows what. I felt better for having had this discussion though. It would help solidify their beliefs, and make it easier for them when we had to tell them about Rick, myself, and the other immortals.

6—Planning the Wedding

Lora

We'd been in the new house for a few months. Work started on the remodeling projects as soon as Anita moved in. We thought the kitchen had to be done first, so that's where we started.

So far, things were progressing very well. Anita had been able to take advantage of the outdoor kitchen for cooking while the indoor kitchen was being torn up. It should all be done before the wedding.

We had the house completely repainted a creamy white to freshen it up. The decorator we hired and Anita had been godsends. They put everything we moved away somewhere, ordered and installed appropriate furniture where needed for storage, and hung all the artwork, some of which Rick brought up from Atlanta. The house was starting to feel like a home. The rest of the extensive remodeling we planned to do could wait until our lives were less busy.

That was important as Rick and I decided to have the wedding at the new house on June 13th. That was just fifty-two days away! So I needed to finalize the details.

I had to send the invitations out. All I wanted was to have the party. *Let's start with the party*. Who would I invite? Just immortals? Family? Friends? *How do we mix all those people?*

How many people could we safely have here? I looked at our backyard through the kitchen doors. I could envision five tables of eight. So I had room for forty people.

Rick and I, Anita, and three kids.

Falon and Mark.

Gwen and Andrews and his three staff and plus ones, so eight there.

Duffy and three crew plus ones, another eight.

Justin plus one

That was twenty-five people. I wasn't inviting any outside immortals, but perhaps the witches and Amarlyis would like to come.

I needed to talk to Rick about this, but he was busy with Escalata II. Justin and Rick hoped to have their soft opening by mid-October. That would give them about two and a half months to work out kinks in the scheduling of staff, the menu, and layout before the grand opening on New Year's Eve. It was going to be a New Year's Eve party. It should be a big bang.

I wanted my 3G here, so I needed to speak to her about how I was going to manage that. Murmuring the incantation to open the portal, I walked through to the occult store.

"Innogen? Are you busy?" I called.

"Yes, dear," came her voice a few moments later. "What can I do for you?"

"Innogen, I'm planning my wedding, and I would like you to be there—my mom and grandmother too if that is possible."

"Your mother lives still. She's gone back to Ireland. Your grandmother is not on your plane of existence. However, because she forsook her magical abilities. She cannot reach them to contact me. I've been trying these past months."

"So it will be just you, then. Can you come to the wedding?"

"Yes, but that will require some strong magic for me to materialize at your wedding, and even then it would not be for very long, maybe an hour or so."

"Long enough to officiate? That will work. I'd like you to bind us."

"I'd be honored," said Innogen. "So let's work on the spell you'll need together. Like the pocket dimension I lived in, you'll be creating a pocket within your world that I can materialize in. Others will see me as well, but I cannot interact with anyone. I will be a disembodied soul."

"I see, so the location where I create the pocket will be important. You need to materialize in the correct place because you won't be able to move around?"

"Correct, granddaughter. So the incantation is *'facere bulla tempore ad hanc animam,'* which translates to 'create a bubble in time to receive this soul.' You need to place eight crystals in a circle, with four of them at the cardinal points, and the other four equally divided. The circle must be contained by pure salt, and the ground must be sanctified."

"Got it," I said as I wrote notes. "Do I use the usual spell to sanctify?"

"Yes, that will do," answered Innogen. "Now here's the important part: this spell must be cast at precisely midnight. It will last an hour only and will dissipate automatically."

"I can only cast it when I need you to be there?"

"Yes, I'm afraid so. The timeframe is quite restrictive. So perhaps your wedding will take place at an unusual time."

"I don't see that as a big problem. There just may be a few logistics to work out," I said. "Is there anything else I need to know?"

"Let me think," said Innogen. "Oh, if anyone crosses the circle, they may be pulled into the dimension with me, or they may kick me out to some other dimension. That wouldn't be good."

"No, not at all. Okay, I need to make sure the circle is unbroken," I said. "I guess I'm having my wedding at midnight!"

"If you have any other questions, let me know, granddaughter."

"I will, thank you!" I returned to the house to see Mama Anita staring at me as I popped out of thin air.

"Oh, *chica*, that startled me!" said Anita.

"Sorry, Mama, I went to visit my great-great-grandmother."

"Oh, that is good news. I am hoping to meet your grandmother at the wedding," said Anita. "*Chica*, can I help you with the planning? It would be fun to have such a happy affair here at the house."

"Mama, you read my mind! I need your help. But you won't be doing the cooking! I'll have it catered so you can be at the party. You are family."

"*Chica*, I want to cook!"

"Well, then I'll let you and Justin battle it out for who gets to cook what."

"What plans have you got so far?" asked Anita.

"None, I've just started."

"Well, let's roll up our sleeves. Do you have a date yet?"

"Yup, June 13th," I said. "Rick has left the wedding to me because they are so busy with the new restaurant construction."

"*Chica*, well let's divide the jobs between us. Have you got your favorite colors and flowers?"

"No, I don't. And I'm not that creative when it comes to things like that."

"I think it should be green—to go with your eyes," she said.

"That would be pretty, but there aren't any green flowers."

"No, the flowers are white, and all the greenery is a background."

"Oh, I like that, Anita," I said. "I could use the same theme on the invitations too, and the tables, and decorations."

"Yes, so let me get busy on that for you while you send out the invites."

"That won't take me long, so I'll arrange for the serving places too. What's next?"

"I'll find a florist and rent furniture. Leave it to me. I am good at throwing a party."

"I bet you are!"

"This is why I should be cooking. I can bring in people to help, and then we can make all the favorites and ethnic dishes we want."

"Hmmm, that's good reasoning, Mama. You're right. Getting Justin and Rick to cater the wedding now would be an added stress neither of them need. But Rick won't let anyone else make the wedding cake. That I do know."

"That is fine, because I'm not a baker," smiled Anita. "But I can make a wonderful assortment of some of the finest Cuban and Mexican dishes."

"Okay, Mama, you've won me over. Come up with a menu—let's say fifty people. We'll do a buffet to make it easier."

"Fifty? That's all?"

"Unless you know of people on Rick's side who could come?"

"Si, I know where some of his family is. I will contact them for you. His parents should be here."

"I agree. I guess the only thing left is to pick out clothes. And we'll need music. What else do we need for a party?"

"Food, alcohol, music, that's enough. The rest will happen organically," said Anita. "I'll see if I can find a talented bartender for the event. Oh, can I bring my cousin Carlos up? He's as good a cook, if not better, than me. He wants to start his own catering company. He would be able to help me with the wedding."

"That's a wonderful idea, Anita. Make that happen."

"Let me get to work!" she said, as she walked away with a huge grin on her face.

This job would be enormous without her help. I plan on getting my kids to help too. I called them downstairs.

"Kids, as you know Rick and I are going to have a wedding here on June 13th." There were excited squeals from all three. "I need your help for the most important part."

"What can we do, Mom?" asked my eldest.

"You three can help Anita plan the decorations. So we'll need a place for the altar, people to sit, and where we can put five tables in the back yard. We need a color scheme, and to choose flowers. Anita says white flowers with lots of green."

"Mom, that will be fun, we can do that." said Minni, my eldest.

"Now, there is a little twist," I told them. "We're going to have the ceremony at midnight."

"Midnight, do we get to stay up?" asked my youngest.

"Of course! I wouldn't let you miss it for the world. Minni, I need you to keep me up to date on all the plans every day. If there is any problem, let me know. Okay?"

"Yes, Mom." The three of them went into the kitchen and started coming up with ideas. Minni suggested they first ask Anita what they were going to need. I knew they were going to be fine with a little supervision.

With a date set, I started making the invitations online. It was easy to do. In a couple of hours, I had the invitations designed and sent out to all the people I was sure of.

Next would be hiring the decorators. I found a small company that did intimate party decorations, and would have tables, chairs, dishes, glassware, and cutlery. I called them.

"Intimate Catering, Mya speaking."

"Hello Mya, my name is Lora. I'm planning my wedding."

"Oh, how exciting! I can help you with that."

"We're going to do it at home in our backyard, June 13th."

"Oh, that is fast!" she said. "What do you need from me?"

"I figure there will be about fifty people, so I need tables and place settings."

"Do you want linens with that? How about chairs and covers?"

"Yes, and anything you can think of."

"Okay, Lora, let me work out a basic quote for you and we'll go from there. Do you want decorations?"

"Yes, and I'll get you to coordinate with my housekeeper, as she is the keeper of all the plans."

"Very good, her name is?"

"Anita, at this phone number."

"I'll include centerpieces, a head table, and enough seating for fifty."

"Thank you, Mya."

Two things started—well, three. *Invites out, what's next?* I consulted my list. Invites, check. Caterer, check. Tables, check. Decor, check. 3G, check. *Dresses! Clothes.* We needed clothes for the kids, Rick, and myself. I was going to make Minni my maid of honor. Pascal and Trent would be the ringbearers. It should be adorable. They didn't know yet. Anita deserved a dress too. I needed to go shopping. *Perhaps I can enlist Falon.*

"Falon speaking."

"It's me."

"Hiya, what's up?"

"I need to get a wedding dress!"

"Oh my God, yes you do. Have you decided on a date yet?"

"Yes, June 13th."

"That doesn't give loads of time, Lora."

"What are you doing right now?"

"Nothing of any consequence. Just going over some plans for the next Tiny House Project."

"Oh, where are you doing that one?"

"It's here in Montreal again. We keep getting demand, so we keep buying parcels of land to use."

"It's a good thing you do."

"As long as we keep getting donations. We'll need to have another gala soon."

"Let's wait until after New Year's—perhaps February would be a good month to land the Gala permanently?"

"That's a good idea. I'll work on that. Greggory will have some ideas. So shall I pick you up, or are you going to meet me downtown?"

"I'll come to you. Give me an hour and I'll be there."

I let Anita know I was going out, checked on the kids and then I was off, driving down the Trans Canada Highway toward town. By the time I parked, Falon met me at the front door of the building. We took the Metro down to St-Hubert Street, which was renowned for its boutiques and shops for wedding and formal wear. It was also known for fabrics, but we weren't there for that. There must be thirty stores on St-Hubert that specialized in designer gowns. Usually, I could wear off-the-rack, so that was what I was hoping I could find today.

The first shop was suitably snooty. They basically turned their noses up when they saw what we were wearing. I looked at the woman and said, "My husband can afford to buy your whole store, so don't get snooty with me, ma'am."

"I'm sorry, miss. What can I do for you today?"

"I need a wedding dress, of course."

"Off-white, cocktail length?"

"No, white, full length. Why are you making judgements about me before you even know me?"

"I'm sorry, we don't usually get brides as old as you."

"Okay, that does it, you just lost a sale. Too bad for you. Come on, Falon. This store is obviously too young and too rich for us."

We left without another word. We went through three other stores with similar attitudes until we came to a little out-of-the-way shop that was run by just one designer. In fact, she was selling her own designs.

As soon as I walked inside, I felt welcomed and knew this was the place. The owner of the shop introduced herself as Natallya and served us; she was the designer too. We were directed to a comfy lounge room with a big fluffy white sofa, served tea and biscuits, which were yummy, all the while models walked by us wearing some of her creations.

I fell in love with a dress that was simple but elegance personified. It had a sheer net top layer that covered the big skirt. The netting was embroidered with a vine and leaf pattern that was modern and draped gently down the folds of the skirt, adding motion to movement, while still covering the bodice sufficiently. Natallya asked me what size I wore, and I told her a six. She clapped her hands in delight excitedly.

"That dress just happens to be a size six. So why don't we help you with it?"

They put me up on a pedestal and stripped off my clothes down to my panties.

"You need a proper bra for this dress. What is your cup size?" asked the dresser.

"Uh, I'm a D cup." They brought a bra that was so comfortable I didn't feel it.

Unfortunately, the bust was not big enough. I heard the dresser tsk-tsking behind me as she tried zipping me up.

"I'm afraid the bust needs to be altered, but the rest of the dress fits like it was made for you," she said after giving up.

"Don't worry about this, Lora," said Natallya. "I will modify the bust for you and it will fit flawlessly. You won't know I made any alterations. Now how tall do you want the shoes?"

"I can handle five inches," I said, but I didn't want to. "I'd rather go barefoot."

"How tall is your beau?"

"Oh, he's six-four."

"Oh my! Flat shoes won't do. You must be adorable together! You're so tiny and he's so tall!"

"Lora, the dress has a really beautiful train. Maybe you should wear shoes for the beginning of the evening, and then take them off?" suggested Falon.

"Okay, let's do shoes, but I'll need you to give me a way to shorten the dress."

Natallya picked out a bejeweled pair of dance shoes in white satin and rhinestone with five-inch heels and a one-inch platform. I felt like Cinderella wearing them.

"This is the dress. I don't want to look any further. Now, how much is this?"

"This dress, shoes, veil, and the undergarments is $22,000. That includes the alterations."

I choked a little. I'd never spent that kind of money before on a single outfit. "Oh gosh. I better check with my bank. Just a minute please."

"Of course. I'll give you some privacy."

"Falon, call Rick for me please," I asked, because I couldn't reach my phone.

"Here you go," she said, handing me the phone.

"Falon?" asked Rick.

"No, it's me, honey. Sorry to bother you."

"You'll never bother me, beautiful woman. What do you need?"

"I'm trying on a wedding dress."

"Oh good. I was going to remind you of that. Did you find one?

Yes I did, Rick, but it's twenty-two grand."

"So?"

"So that is too much money."

"For you, no it is not. Get it if you love it. But only if you love it. I want nothing less for you. Then I will go and buy the jewelry to go with it."

"Thank you, my love." I handed her phone back to Falon.

"What did he say?"

"He said go for it." Falon skipped a step and went to get Natallya.

"We'll take it," I said, when the shop owner returned. "Now we need a dress for my eldest daughter, and one for Falon. Falon and my daughter will be my bridesmaids."

"Let's do Falon first. But let's get you out of the dress so my seamstress can make the adjustments. When do you need the dress?"

The seamstress took careful measurements of my dress—I thought of it as my dress now—while I was wearing it, before helping me slip out of it. Smiling quietly at me, she nodded and took it away to the back.

"Um, June 13th is the wedding," I said, returning my attention to Natallya.

"That's fine, we can do that easily."

"Falon, what do you want as a dress color?"

"Emerald-green," I answered for her. That is her best color." The process started over again, this time with the models wearing different colors. When a dress came through very similar in style to my dress I said, "Stop. I love this one, and the color is amazing."

The dress had a simple, elegant design, in a true emerald-green satin. It didn't have the train, but it too was a trumpet shape, and it slit up the back. The front had a sweetheart neckline.

"This dress is a size eight. Is that good for you, Falon?"

"I don't know. Let's try." Again, the dresser and an army of girls came to help Falon remove the clothes she was wearing and get into the gorgeous dress. First, they pulled it up from the floor and it got stuck on her hips. Then they put it over her head. That worked, except it bunched up at the hips. Natallya walked around her several times, making small noises and pinching the fabric as she was assessing the fit of the dress.

"I don't like this dress on you," she said after a few minutes. "It is the wrong shape. I would rather put the right shape on you. May I try another dress?"

"Of course." They got Falon out of that dress and Natallya brought another, the same color and fabric but a different style. This one had a plunging neckline and fit looser around the hips.

It fit Falon much better, especially with her small waist. It looked like it hugged her body without being tight.

"That is better!" said Natallya and me together.

"I like this one," said Falon. "What is the price?"

"It is $2,500," said Natallya.

"Excellent price. I'll take it and some shoes to match please," I said.

"Thank you. Lora, and for your daughter?" asked Natallya.

"I want her in amethyst. She's almost fifteen now, so something a little grown up but not revealing. Classic. She wears a size four."

The models started a new show of purples and eggplants, and fuchsia and a wide variety of gown styles. For Minni, I settled on a style similar to my dress but without a train, and a shorter length. I'd bring my daughter back later for a fitting.

"Tell me, do you also do men's tuxedos?' I asked.

"I do," smiled Natallya. "I love dressing men. They're so beautiful when dressed well."

Falon and I smiled at each other. This designer was about to have the most beautiful wedding group to dress ever. I was going to make sure all the immortals dressed with her.

Walking back to the metro, I could not resist walking into that first snooty store and letting her know what she missed out of.

"Hi, remember me? Yeah, well, we just laid down about $75,000 with another designer just up the street. So boo-hoo for you. You really should be nicer to potential customers," I said as I turned on my heel and walked out of her store. Her mouth was agape and drooling as I walked passed her.

When we got back to Falon's office, I picked up my car and drove home. I arrived at the same time as Rick and we met at the front door.

"Did you get the dress?" he asked.

"Yup, and you are going to die when you see it."

"I'm hoping to," he said, with a lascivious look on his face.

"Oh, I'm going to send all you immortal boys to the same designer. She's going to give us a deal on four men and two boys. I am going to get all the ladies to shop there too. She's a new designer starting out and her work is fabulous."

"I'm always happy to help a new designer. We should use her for our gala wear as well, and perhaps whenever we need special garments. She can become our couturier of choice."

"I love that idea, Rick!" I cried. It would be like having our very own family designer.

7—A Hook-up

Margaret

Back then, I was always a responsible person, always. I fastened my seatbelt, I always looked both ways before crossing the street, even at the lights. I always returned my library books before they were due. I always paid my bills on time.

So why wasn't I responsible *that* night?

That night was three years ago. I went out with some friends; we went barhopping. Not something I usually did on a Tuesday night, but this night was a special celebration for one of the girls.

Because it was a party, I dressed up. I was wearing a cherry red fitted knit dress that was off-the-shoulder, and it hugged my ample curves like a second skin. My girlfriend assured me that it looked sexy and great, but I wasn't so sure. I was much more comfortable in tailored clothes, not fitted sexy clothes.

When I came out of the bathroom after changing with my auburn hair in a tight bun still from work, she marched me back in and redid my hair in a messy updo. There were locks hanging down and curling everywhere. But again, she said it looked less severe.

The main reason I didn't go out during the week was I hated waking up feeling like death warmed over and not out of any goody-two-shoes need to behave. I liked drinking and dancing a lot. I just didn't like the hangovers in the morning. And I definitely didn't want to have to deal with my boss when I was hung over! He was difficult enough for me to deal with, even when I had slept a sober eight hours the night before.

So what was with me that night?

It was that guy.

Oh my God, he was beautiful. I looked into his eyes for a second and I couldn't look away. So stereotypical, I know, but that was what happened. I left behind my friends without so much as a "see you later," in favor of going with this guy.

We were in fact not at a bar, we were between bars. The group of us were walking down the boardwalk next to the sea, getting fresh air. Leaning up against a streetlight, I was enjoying the wind coming off the water. I heard voices approaching and opened my eyes to see this god walking toward me. He was alone.

He really looked like a god. Perfectly formed, and his skin almost glowed. I had a thing for gorgeous black men. I must say he was yummy. My friends knew this, so they were always trying to hook me up. But this one, *my my*, he exuded a sexuality I had rarely seen before. He was like a big hunk of dark chocolate amongst all the powder puffs. One of my friends spotted him and leaned toward me and pointed him out. Soon, they were all speculating on who would go home with him.

I hadn't thought it would be me. But there I was, the one drawn to him. I was tethered just as assuredly as if he had lassoed me. I found myself standing up to walk toward him.

He stopped in his tracks and was staring directly at me. Meanwhile, the girls behind me were whooping and hollering and making catcalls. It was embarrassing. But the god smiled at me and I felt my insides melt. He took a step toward me and I felt my knees buckle. His next step seemed to have crossed the distance of about fifteen feet to catch me before I ended up on the ground.

"Are you okay?" asked the god, with a melodious voice, deep and resonating in my head. I felt the infrasound of his voice reverberating inside my ribcage.

"Um, yes," I started. "I think I'm fine. I flipped my ankle over," I lied.

"Let me help you. There is a bench just over there." And with that, he literally swept me off my feet, carried me to the park bench, and set me down gently, sitting beside me.

"Thank you. My name is Margaret. Margaret Thistle. My friends call me Marge," I said, holding out my hand.

"My name is Abeo," he answered, taking my hand between his. Of course, that had me all flummoxed. My throat went dry and I cleared it, trying to be able to speak again.

"May I get you something to drink? Some water perhaps?" asked Abeo.

"That's not necessary. I'll be fine, thanks."

"Nonsense, I'll be right back."

He left me on the bench, ran across the street, and ducked inside a building. Quickly, the girls came over.

"What are you doing?" asked one.

"Nothing, I tripped and he's gone to get some water."

"Well, we'll see you tomorrow, Marge," said another.

"No, I'm coming with you."

"No, you're not. He's gorgeous, and you're going to stay with him," said the girl of honor. "Oh, here he comes. Girls, let's vamoose!"

Abeo had a couple of bottles in his hands.

"Here you go. I hope plain water is okay. It's all they had."

"That's great. Really, I'm fine."

"Can you still walk?"

"Yes. I'm fine."

"Would you walk with me?"

"I'd like that, yes." So he helped me up and we continued along the boardwalk together.

"It's a beautiful evening, don't you think?" he asked.

"It is. Before I saw you I was enjoying the breezes from the ocean."

"Are you from Halifax?"

"No, I'm from Montreal. I have been working here for about a month on contract. I'm actually finished up in a couple of weeks, then I'm going home."

"Come dancing with me," he said as a statement rather than a request.

"Alright."

Next thing I knew, Abeo had taken me into the next bar, found us a table, then gone for drinks.

"This is scotch and the other is called a Ladyslipper," he said, when he got back.

"Oh, I haven't had that cocktail. What's in it?"

"Sweet sherry, creme de cacao, and chocolate extract with a dusting of cinnamon," he answered.

"Umm, that sounds delicious. I'll have that." Sipping the drink a little, I discovered it was indeed delicious, smooth, and sweet. "Oh, I like this. Thank you."

"So, Margaret—you don't mind if I use your full name, do you?"

"No, not at all. Marge makes me feel like the *Simpsons* cartoon."

Abeo laughed and looked into my eyes. He took my hand and stood up, clearly on his way to the dance floor. I took a big gulp of my cocktail and followed.

As we danced, I looked into his eyes. They were warm and inviting. He made me feel at ease and very relaxed. Or maybe it was just the drink, I'm wasn't sure.

A slower song started and he pulled me in and held me close to his body. His breath just outside my ear as my chin rested on his chest.

"Margaret, I would love to take you," he murmured into my ear. It sent shivers all the way down my body. *Oh my God.* My knees almost buckled again. I hung on to him.

Startled with the instant invitation, I fumbled over my thoughts. How do you answer that?

"Well, perhaps let's get to know each other a bit more?" I suggested.

"That wasn't a no, was it?"

"No, it wasn't a no," I said. Oh God, it wasn't. I was just delaying.

"Well, if it isn't a no, then why delay? We can get to know each other on the way, and at my place."

I had no argument with that. *Nothing.* But my body was answering. Oh geez, was it ever. My body was pretty much singing, it was tingling so much. *Did I bring condoms with me? I don't remember.* Pregnancy wasn't an issue because I had an IUD. *Am I good to leave now?* Before my brain could reason my way through this mire I heard my mouth say, "You're right. Let's go now, but wait, I don't have condoms with me."

"That's okay," he said, casually.

I downed the cocktail in one shot and turned to follow Abeo out. Turns out, the girls were in the same establishment. I saw them all at a booth lassoing their hands above their heads and crowing.

"Marge, are you going to play?" one called out at me. The other five women turned their heads toward me. Some had looks of shock on their faces, others were smiling like the cat that had just swallowed a canary.

I was not known for doing such impulsive things. For me, being spontaneous required booking time in my calendar first.

Waving them off, I continued. *Let them think what they want. I'll hear about it tomorrow at the office.* I slipped my hand through Abeo's elbow and we made our way through the crowd and out of the bar.

"Where is your place?" I asked, once we were free of the loud music.

"I'm staying in a hotel right now."

"Oh, which one?"

"Novotel. We can walk."

"Why are you in a hotel?"

"I'm only here for a short time as well."

"Do you travel often?"

"Yes, my job takes me all over the world. I tend to rent apartments in the cities I do business in, but it's my first time here so I don't have furniture, only clothes. So until I find an appropriate place to live, I prefer a hotel. Novotel gives monthly rates, and they have small apartments for long term guests."

"Oh, that's a great idea. What do you do for a living?"

"I'm a banker and a pilot."

"Two careers, how interesting." Not really, but I was trying to be polite. I imagined being a banker was nothing but numbers all day long, *snooze.* "Um, what sort of banking do you do?"

"International banking," he said. "We work with companies that are global, and my job is to bring funds from one country to another for various reasons. What do you do?"

"Oh, I'm nobody, " I answered. "I just work as an admin. Not very interesting at all. May I ask how old you are?"

"I'm a man of indeterminate age," he said, smirking.

"What does that mean?"

"I'm older than I look."

I chuckled. It was a typical answer from a woman. "Okay, I get it. You don't want to say. So let's ask some personal questions."

"Of course, go ahead."

"Are you clean? I mean disease. I've got to ask that of a guy who is basically asking for a hook-up."

"Yes, I'm clean. I've always been clean. You?"

"Never caught anything, and I make sure I'm tested monthly if I'm active."

"Good practice."

"Are you married, engaged, or otherwise committed to one individual?"

"No, I'm single and have been for many years."

"Why?"

"Why am I single? Or why for many years?"

"Yes."

"I prefer to be single because I travel a lot. For many years, because the last relationship suffered greatly, and I don't want to go through that again."

So he's hiding from a serious relationship, I thought. "Do you like animals?"

"Yes, but again, I don't have them because I move around too often. It wouldn't be fair to them to always change residences."

"How often do you move?"

"Monthly, sometimes more often. It depends on the complexity of the deal I'm working on."

"How long do you expect to be here?" I asked, just in case he was someone I wanted. to see more than once.

"About two to three months, I expect," he answered.

"When you said you were here a short time, I thought you meant a few days, not a few months."

"Yes, I see what you mean," he said. "When I think in contrast to living somewhere, it's a short time. Ah, here we are." He opened the front door of the hotel for me and followed me into the lobby. He pointed over to the elevator and led me that way. We took it up to the penthouse floor and walked down the short hallway to the end. When he opened the door, I gasped at the size of the room. It wasn't a room at all, it was a huge suite. So this guy had some serious money.

"Nice room."

"It has a very nice view too. There is a fully stocked bar, so would you like another cocktail?"

"Yes please. I'll have a vodka martini please. Do you have any munchies to go with that?"

"No, but I'll order some in a minute." He made me my martini, then ordered some tapas for two.

We sat down on the sofa together. He put on the fireplace and I was gazing out the window.

"Why don't you get comfortable," he suggested. "Perhaps taking off your shoes will let you curl up and we can chat."

That seemed like a good suggestion, so I slipped off my shoes and curled up on the sofa facing him with one arm over the back. There were two seats on the sofa, so he was close. He put his own arm over the back as well, and caressed my arm gently. His touch was soft and not demanding.

"You intrigued me at the bar," he started. "Your eyes were what I saw first."

"Really?" I asked. "You saw me in the bar?"

"Yes, that's when I first noticed you. When I saw you leave, I followed because I wanted to meet you."

I was watching his face as he spoke. He didn't seem stalkery.

"The first moment I saw you, I noticed how handsome you were. In fact, you have beautiful features. I'm sorry if I stared, but I was captivated." I was blushing a little. I could feel my cheeks getting warm.

"May I kiss you?" he asked.

In answer, I leaned into him and he met me halfway. Our lips touched softly. An electric shock went through my body, leaving every nerve ending at attention. *What a first kiss!*

Separating, I said, "Did you feel that?"

"Yes, I felt the shock." Then he kissed me again. I felt his tongue gently ask for permission to come in. I opened my lips in invitation. I felt his hand which was caressing my arm slip through my hair and cup the back of my head allowing him to press his kiss harder. He pushed into my mouth and explored gently. I tried to focus on breathing through my nose, but soon I was unable to think of anything else other than the kiss that was happening, and how turned on I was getting. Every fiber of my body was getting zinged repeatedly. Every part of my body was becoming very sensitive.

As the kiss continued, my nipples got hard against my dress, creating little turrets that tried to poke through the fabric. I was feeling heat between my legs, and the coil inside was tightening ever so slightly. His hand, holding my head, traveled through my hair applying balanced pressure to his questing tongue. His soft lips enveloped mine and took over so that my brain shut down completely.

His other hand, the one I thought held a drink, cupped around my breast and I felt a finger or thumb gently rub the nipple that was standing out. He slowly slid my dress lower, exposing me. When he saw I was not wearing a bra, he gently cupped my breast and planted a light kiss on my nipple. Then he tweaked the nipple and made it so hard it almost hurt.

Breaking the kiss, he leaned back and looked at me. "You are a good kisser," he said. "I love how responsive your body is."

"You're pretty good yourself," I countered. His eyes looked like swirling whirlpools, but that must have been how dizzy I was feeling. No blood in the brain. He took my turgid nipple between his teeth gently and sucked on it, causing me to squirm in response, and my nipples to harden and start to hurt. But they didn't hurt, it was so erotic.

"Would you like to remove your dress?" he asked.

"Your turn," I said.

So he pulled off his turtleneck, exposing a well-formed chest of dark chocolate unmarred by a single mark or hair. His own nipples, surrounded by dark, almost black circles, were standing up, and I took one of them in my hand and returned the gesture. He grunted and bit his lip as his nipple also became turgid. I leaned over and sucked on it until he too was groaning in pleasure.

He reached over and slid my dress completely off. Again, he smiled and moaned with the discovery that I wasn't wearing underwear.

"Tell me, is it your custom to not wear undergarments?"

"Yes, I don't like wires. They are exceedingly uncomfortable. Besides, my breasts are full and firm enough I can get away without. As for panties, thongs are uncomfortable when you have a full ass, but I hate panty lines more. So I prefer to go without."

He draped my dress over the back of the sofa and pulled my ankles toward him and opened my legs. He leaned down to my mound and looked at me before making contact, as if to ask permission.

"Please," I said to him. I opened my legs a little more.

He started with his hand, slipping his fingers into my slit and caressing me from front to back. He spread my lower lips and found that bundle of nerves that were so charged at the moment, his first touch nearly undid me.

I tried to watch, because the sight of his delicious chocolate skin against mine was truly erotic. I felt like I was being sexed by a god. He gently pressed down on my nub, moving his finger in a circular motion, winding me up like a toy. The pleasure caused my head to stretch back, and my eyes to roll.

Just when I thought I couldn't go any tighter, he took that bundle of nerves between his lips and sucked on me like a teat. A climax exploded out of me as his sucking released the coil. He added a finger or two to my vagina and that made me climax again, releasing a little less energy, but now my body felt loose and open. He was rubbing that spot inside that just got me going so much I wanted to scream.

Few hook-ups spend the time on the girl's pleasure first. It was usually just a get in, get hot, and done. So this was delicious—getting spoiled by a man who was into pleasuring me for a change. My eyes were closed and I was living in that feeling. When I felt him withdraw, I whimpered in disappointment. When I opened my eyes, he had removed the rest of his clothes and stood before me in all his glory.

He picked me up effortlessly, and carried me into the bedroom and put me down on the king bed. He cupped my mound, slipping his finger between the lips again as he moved onto the bed beside me. He leaned down and kissed me while his fingers slid into my vagina and felt the wet of my excitement.

"You are perfectly wet. May I take you?" he asked.

"Yes, take me. Wait! Condoms."

"No need. I do not catch diseases and I cannot transmit them," he said. I heard him, it sank in, but it confused me. But I was so far gone, I didn't care.

He lifted my hips up a little to line up his cock and I felt him press it against my opening. He was hot and swollen, and ready.

He guided himself into me, and a long moan escaped my lips as the lovely feeling of being filled up suffused through me. This joining was like coming home. When he was fully inside, I could feel the tip of him deep in me wiggle and dance. I squeezed him and he gasped lightly.

"You've strong muscles!"

"Yes, the better to hold you with." I felt kind of proud of that. It was all the exercising I did, I guess.

He started to move inside me, pulling out slowly and then pushing back in slowly. It was a delicious movement, allowing for me to feel every inch of him go in and come out. Each time he plunged back in, he was a little harder and longer. On the fifth or sixth stroke, he suddenly hit the end of me, causing me to cry out in pain. But it didn't hurt, not the way a normal injury would hurt. It was a pain that felt good.

"I'm tipping you," he said.

"Um, what?" I asked incoherently, because my brain wasn't really connected.

"I'm tipping you—touching the end of you. Are you okay?"

"Ummm, yeah, just fine, better than fine actually. Tip me some more, harder."

"Are you sure?"

"Oh yeah, very sure."

He started thrusting harder and his cock bottomed out with each thrust, hitting the end of my channel and touching that secret place no one ever goes. Nothing was better at climbing that excitement ladder than having that secret place nudged and touched. *Nothing.* The coil in me was tightening at a fast rate now. It wouldn't be long before I wouldn't be able to hold back. I opened my eyes a peek and saw his rutting face. It's usually not pretty on a man, which was why I kept my eyes closed. But his face was different. His eyes were open and watching me. They were definitely swirling like tornadoes. His mouth was closed but it looked like he had buck teeth because his lips were pushed out. The look on his face was intense as he was clearly close to climax too.

"Take me harder!" I screamed.

He changed in tempo, going faster. "I'm going to lose control in a second," he warned me.

"So am I."

We came together as my orgasm exploded out of me. So did his. He spilled his seed into me as he pushed to the very end of my channel. I could feel him right at the end, his cock jumping with every squirt. My eyes were closed again as I drifted on a blissful orgasm, but they snapped open when I felt a pinprick on my shoulder. His head was on my shoulder, and he lifted it up just as I felt another orgasm take me and another, and another. I felt giddy and lightheaded as my body shuddered over and over until I felt like wet noodles. Not a bone was left in my body and I lay there limp and spent.

He collapsed on me and I think I passed out. When I came to, I was cleaned up, and he was spooning me, with his arm protectively across my belly.

I opened my eyes and saw that it was getting light out. *Huh! The whole night had passed.* I started to straighten out my body and he stirred.

"Good morning, pretty lady," he murmured behind my ear.

"Good morning. That was the very best, most awesome sex last night. Thank you."

"Would you like breakfast?"

"Nah, I should probably get going. I'll need to change before going into work."

"That's too bad. I was hoping to spend the day with you."

Oh, that's a fine offer. Dare I skip work? "I could call in sick, I suppose."

"Would you?" he asked. "I want to pleasure you some more."

How could a girl turn that down?

"I'll tell you what: I'll go and get breakfast and let you get dressed and think about it," he said. "If you're here when I get back, we can have some more fun. If you're not, well, it's just not meant to be."

How does one walk away from some of the best sex they have ever had?

He was up and out of the room in about five minutes, leaving me in bed. And that's when I started to remember: *How could I have been so irresponsible last night? No condom! Staying the night! Oh wow, at least I'm not hungover.*

I called the office quickly and let them know that I wasn't feeling well today, and probably wouldn't be in.

Getting off the phone, I felt naughty by playing hooky. But I was also feeling excited. Abeo returned with a trolley filled with food, juice, and coffee. When he saw me there, he smiled a big wide smile.

The day went by like a dream. We didn't spend the whole day in bed—pity. Instead, he took me out and we went to out-of-the-way fooderies and sampled delicious morsels from other countries. We walked along the boardwalk and watched whales play in the ocean. We had a picnic by the sea of succulent seafood perfectly prepared. Then we returned to my apartment and made love like I've never done before.

He worshiped my body and cared for it. I had never felt so languid after an orgasm, nor so completely spent. It's like he fulfilled me in every way. It was a fantasy, it wasn't reality—it couldn't have been.

When I woke the next morning, expecting to roll over and feel his sublime body next to mine, the bed was cold, the covers pulled back, and he was gone.

Was it a dream? I asked myself. *Did it happen? In the bright light of day, it feels surreal, like it happened in my head and somehow I was delirious. Perhaps I did have a fever yesterday.*

I got up and dressed, went to work, and got on with my life. The memory of that twenty-four hours faded even though my body held on to the physical memory. I would take the memory out every now and then, dust it off, and treasure it. I could have fallen hard for that man.

8—Another Chance Meeting

Margaret

Another business trip to Halifax happened three years later. I was having lunch at a café by the boardwalk watching the ships come in and out of the harbor. I was meeting a friend for lunch and she wasn't there yet. She said she needed to talk. So I would listen. So far, it was just a liquid lunch.

People were passing by the café outside the fenced-in area and I wasn't paying attention to who it was until I heard my name being called.

"Margaret?" asked a voice. "Is that you?"

I looked up and blinked into the light. I recognized that face. "Abeo?"

"Yes! It's me. I'm in town again."

"Wow, you look wonderful! You haven't changed at all in three years," I said, appraising him.

"So do you. What brings you down here at this time of the day?"

"I am meeting a friend for lunch. She needed to talk. How about you?"

"My bank's office is around the corner, so I often stop here when I'm in town."

"That's nice. How long are you here this time?"

"A while, can we get together later?"

"I have nothing booked this afternoon. Want to play hooky again?" I asked, referencing our last encounter. His eyes instantly became hooded and a slow smile pushed up the corners of his mouth.

"I would like that very much," he said with a breathy voice. "Come with me."

"I can't. I'm waiting for someone, really."

"When is your friend supposed to be here?" he asked.

"Like, ten minutes ago. I'll text her and see what happened."

A reply came back from her two minutes later: "Sorry! got another offer. see you tomorrow."

"Bitch!"

"Bad news?"

"The 'friend' I was supposed to meet bailed on me at the last minute, and wasn't even going to tell me."

"Some friend."

"Yeah, well, not really. Just a work friend, but still! You don't do that to people. I don't do that to people. So, now I don't have to wait anymore," I said, standing up. Once I paid for my beverage, I walked out of the café and joined him on the boardwalk.

He took my hand and slipped it through his arm and led me in the opposite direction of my office. We turned a corner and he pushed me up against a stone wall and pushed his body against mine, holding my hands at my shoulders. Looking deeply into my eyes, he kissed me like he had never kissed me before. It was slow and gentle at first, then insistent and hungry, and after he had thoroughly claimed my mouth, he broke away. I was out of breath and breathing hard.

"I needed that," he said, panting.

"Do you often shove girls up against walls when you haven't seen them for a while?" I asked.

"No, and I'm sorry if I was wrong and taking liberties."

"You weren't wrong," I said. "I needed that too. But I want more than that." His eyes looked like they glowed at that point. The sunlight was reflecting off the windows across the street and into his face. It was a little freaky, but it passed in a moment.

"Let's continue down this street. My office is close by."

It was a four-storey building on the edge of the port district. The building was gray stone and had tall, narrow windows wrapping all around the first floor. The sign over the door said A. Dixon & Assoc.

"Who is A. Dixon?" I asked.

"Me," he said. "I chose a Western name for the business that would be easy for people to say and remember."

"Oh. And the associates?"

"I have two business partners. They live in the other cities that we do business in."

It was a wonderful space on the inside. The windows were framed in natural wood, and the floor was a slate looking material, again natural looking. There was a reception desk in front of two offices that were walled off in glass. Abeo led me to the one on the right.

I walked in and put my bag in one of the chairs in front of his desk. He walked over to the wall and hit a button, and the glass around the office suddenly went opaque. It was completely screened while allowing light to still come through. Nice technology. Then he came back to me and offered to help me with my jacket.

"What's going to happen here?" I asked him.

"What would you like to happen?"

"I have two answers for you."

"And they are?"

"Sex and conversation."

"We are at least on the same page. Which would you like first?"

"Conversation."

"Come sit with me. Would you like a beverage?"

"No thanks, unless you have scotch."

"I do." He poured a finger of scotch for both of us and brought the glasses to the couch that was lining one of the glass walls.

"How soundproof are these walls?"

"Not very, I'm afraid. But there is no one else that works here, in spite of the other desks. It's just me."

"So the other desks are for show?"

"Basically, yes. We want to appear small, but not too small."

"Ah," I said, taking a sip. It was a good scotch, very smooth. I could feel it as it slid down my throat and warmed me up. I felt it release some of the nerves I felt too. Why was I nervous? Now that I was sitting close to him, I could smell his manliness, the musk that was him. It was alluring, and captivated my senses. I felt myself close my eyes and inhale deeply. As the musk hit my nose, I felt a shiver run down my spine and my sex squeeze in anticipation.

I had dreamed of that scent for three years. I had doubted my memory of its veracity, and thought myself losing my mind once or twice. The memory of our nights was the stuff of legend, and as such, it was difficult to keep it clear in my head without thinking it was just a dream.

But there it was again. As strong as ever.

So much for conversation. I wanted so much more. When I opened my eyes, he was watching me closely. He had removed his tie and jacket and opened a couple of buttons on his shirt. Involuntarily, my hand lifted and landed on his chest. I felt his warmth through the fine fabric, likely silk, and his skin twitched slightly. I hadn't taken my eyes from his. I was letting my fingertips give me feedback.

When I felt the muscle contract, I knew he had started to lift his own hand. It landed on mine. He pulled it up to his lips and kissed my fingers one at a time. Each kiss sent a tingle running up my arm. He pulled on my arm more to bring me closer. I had to stand and move myself closer. Our knees were touching. He put down his glass and placed that hand on my knee, then ran that hand slowly up my leg until it got to the edge of my hem. I had put on a jacket and skirt suit this morning. The skirt was tight enough that when I sat down it rode up on my leg to mid-thigh. He delicately ran one finger under the hem, back and forth across my leg. Each time it went farther on the inside of my leg, another wave of shivers took me. The heat was building up in my body quickly.

I reached down and slipped off my shoes. While I was bent over, Abeo slid his hand around my ass and held on firmly.

"I adore your curves. You've the body of a sensual woman ripe with fertility."

"Well, I don't know about fertility, because I have an IUD, but the curves I've got."

I gently pushed his shoulder backward until he was lying down on the couch. Kneeling on the floor, I leaned over him and kissed the skin that showed through his shirt while my hand undid his belt and pants. Sliding my hand down his torso, I felt the ripples of the muscles as they reacted to my fingers. When I reached the top of his pants, I stealthily ran a finger underneath the edge like he had done to my skirt hem.

Remembering what was lurking inside, I licked my lips unconsciously. He pulled himself out of his pants, and his glorious penis was standing erect and proud. I stood and hiked up my skirt and straddled him. He watched me while we lined up our bodies, his head with my vagina, and the look on his face was precious.

We were both holding our breath for that moment. His head nestled in my opening, which was now very wet, and he moved himself back and forth until it fit like a notch. While I was watching his eyes, I sank down on him in one motion, taking him inside me in one step, pushing him to the very end until he tipped me. The sharp pain that accompanied that made me twitch, but then the pleasure replaced it.

The moment he slid home, we both groaned in unison. Deep and melodious, the sound was coming from his chest and my throat. My body shuddered in near completion because of the intensity of the pleasure just from that joining.

I sat still for a few minutes, reveling in the feeling of him filling me all the way. *I remember this*, my body said. *This is the way it's supposed to be.* I tipped my head back and my posture was as erect as his penis, putting pressure downward to ensure full penetration. I might have lost awareness, lost in the sensations instead. Suddenly it seemed he was speaking to me.

"Oh, Margaret, how I have missed you and this connection," he said. "I had thought it was just another hook-up, but it was so much more. I could never completely forget you, and now I know why."

"Mmm?" I murmured, reconnecting my mind to my body. "What do you mean?"

"Our bodies know, they sing together."

I looked down at him and smiled with carnal knowledge. "Let's make them yell, then."

I started to rock my hips, moving around on him, feeling him make contact with every centimeter of me inside. When he reached my sweet spot, I couldn't help myself, I moved with harder motions, more aggressively rubbing him against me, building up the excitement and the wave. He joined me in rocking and soon I was riding him like he was a stallion, the pressure building and building as I moved him in and out and around and around. He started twitching and I could feel him get harder and lengthen as we both approached an epic climax. When it came it was not loud, nor boisterous, but quiet and deep. We both let go together, and my body shuddered as the waves of pleasure took me as I slowed down on my rocking. His body gripped and tensed as he let go, his seed spilling into me with the force of a hose. I could feel him fill me.

I planted my hands on his chest to support me as I bent over slightly. A fine sheet of sweat coated my skin and his as I sat there panting a bit. His hands grasped my shoulders and pulled me down to him. He rested me on his body, my head just coming to his shoulder. I could feel his breath on the top of my head as he rested his chin there.

"Margaret, that was … I have no words. Thank you."

"Margaret is not currently available. Please try again later," I joked.

Abeo chuckled quietly and wrapped his arms around my waist.

9—Nuptials

Lora

Everything is under control. Breathe, I kept saying to myself. *Everything is under control. Breathe. Everything is under control. Breathe…*

I'd been saying this to myself for the past half hour. I didn't believe it yet. What a morning! Today was my wedding day. If truth be told, we did remarkably well. The kitchen remodel finished up two days ago, all the painting was finished, and all the contractors had pulled out and the house was clean and set up. Anita had worked so hard to make this happen.

Everything was supposed to be under control. But this morning I woke up to the sound of tractors and big machines and trucks outside.

I looked out the window to discover that the empty lot next to us was busy with construction people. Apparently, the lot had been sold and they were breaking ground today.

I went out and asked for the foreman. I calmly, in a businesslike manner, explained to him that this day was my wedding day and that it was happening here. That I had all kinds of deliveries happening today and people coming. I couldn't have this noise happening all day long.

He was unsympathetic. Completely unsympathetic. The big machines rolled over the ground, rattling dishes, plates, everything. Anita was in the kitchen busy cooking today—in fact she was using both the indoor and outdoor kitchens. She had several people helping her too. I was expecting Mya today with all the tables and setup. My daughter Minni was waiting for her so they could work together decorating everything.

Everyone was told it was going to be an evening wedding. So they knew that they had today to prepare.

I wasn't expecting the DJ until around 8:00 p.m. He would have ample time to get his lights and sound set up around the pool. He chose the top of the waterfall cliff to set up his table. So we turned off the water so he could go up there. To our surprise, he told us that he built a rig that would straddle the water like a bridge, so the water would still run. It was going to look very cool.

The florist was supposed to arrive around 3:00 p.m. to deliver all the flowers for the decor as well as the wedding.

My problem was that there were so many big trucks and equipment on the street in front of our house, and the street was filled with mud. The deliveries couldn't get to the door without going through mud. It's not like guests could park down the street and walk through all the mud either!

I was sitting in the kitchen having coffee and breakfast with Rick. His only task today other than marrying me was to make the cake. He could do that in his sleep.

"Lora, relax, we have time. I'll go and 'talk' to them, okay?" he told me.

"Can you influence them to leave?"

"Yes, I can."

He picked up his cup and went out the front door. He wandered over to where the foreman was speaking to several workers and went over what were clearly blueprints for the house next door.

I opened a window in the living room and listened.

"Good morning, gentlemen."

"Good morning, sir," said the foreman. "I'm sorry but you cannot be over here right now."

"I understand. I just wanted to ask you if you knew that my girlfriend and I are getting married today."

"I heard. Congratulations, sir. We're so sorry this is happening on your wedding day. But we didn't pick the date."

"I understand. But it is a Saturday. Is there any way you can delay until Monday? What's a weekend on a schedule?"

"The customer wanted to break ground as soon as possible. Head office chose today."

"I understand. I'm sure you can find it in your heart to delay this one time?"

"Sir, I wish I could."

They weren't going to give up on this. As I was listening, the tears started falling uncontrollably. I had always wanted a wedding and now it was going to be destroyed with trucks and mud and torn-up ground. I left my perch by the window and marched out to where Rick was trying to speak sense to them.

"You are ruining my wedding day!" I wailed. "It's my wedding day! Are you really going to leave me with the memory of mud and trucks and noise drowning out our vows and music?" I sobbed and my breath caught. "Are you really going to destroy the happiest day of my life because you … what … can't wait until the next business day?" I sobbed again. "Who starts to dig a house on a Saturday?" The tears were streaming down my face and I must have been an ugly crier, because the foreman paused. He looked at me and he almost spoke. "What would you do if this had been your wedding day? What would your wife have done? How would she have felt?" I rounded on him with my question, pointing at his wedding band. That finally crumbled him.

"Okay, ma'am, we'll stop. I'll call a stop to work. Okay?"

"Really?" I sniffed and hiccupped. Rick walked up behind me at that moment to witness the end of my breakdown.

"Yes. No one deserves to have their wedding day ruined. We'll get going as soon as we set the plan. We won't tear up any ground and we won't leave any machines behind today. We'll be starting very early on Monday though."

"Oh thank you!" I ran up and hugged him. I felt him look down at me and pat me on the shoulder. "Okay, miss. We'll be gone in an hour."

"You know," started Rick. "That's going to cost them a lot of money. Perhaps I should offer to cover their payroll for the day."

"Can you?"

"No problem." Rick turned around and went back to the foreman. I stood and watched him while he spoke to the man for a few moments. Then the foreman smiled and they shook hands.

I walked back into the house with Rick and we sat at the kitchen table again. I think he burst out laughing first, then I followed him.

"I've never seen you use tears before to get someone to do something," he said.

"I've never used tears before, no. I didn't realize they worked so well!"

"Oh my, as soon as you came out of the house, he was putty. There was no way he was going to deny this tiny, very upset little bride crying her eyes out."

"Well, I'm just glad something worked!"

Finishing up breakfast, I checked on everyone's progress. We were doing the wedding sort of backwards. The "reception" would start before the ceremony. That way people who had to leave could. People should be arriving around 7:30-8:00 for cocktails and hors d'oeuvres. Mya had a talented barkeep who was working the kitchen outside. He had turned it into a bar, and was stocking it with the basics, but he had created a cocktail for our wedding too.

The dresses and tuxedos were being delivered today at 2:00 p.m. True to their word, all the immortals had their dresses and tuxedos made and/or fitted by Natallya, the young designer who did my dress. I think we gave her enough business to pay her bills for a year.

Anita had arranged for someone to do all our hair and makeup. That was happening at 1:00. So I had about two hours to myself before all mayhem broke loose. Time for a shower.

A long hot shower is a wonderful luxury. I got out relaxed, centered, and peaceful. I burned some white sage and infused my room with the scent to keep me relaxed. When my bedroom door was tapped, my daughter came in to tell me that the hairstylist was here.

I went downstairs to tell her to do the kids first, then Falon who happened to walk through the door too, and Gwen, who would be there soon.

The stylist brought extra hands with him, very smart, and set up in the laundry room. It was out of the way, with counters and access to water. So he was happy. I looked outside, and sure enough, all the trucks and machines had left and the street wasn't a muddy mess. Thank the goddess. The last thing we needed was mud everywhere for people to track into the house. The designer, Natallya, was arriving soon, and it would remain clean when she brought in all the clothes.

The wonderful scents coming from the kitchen made me wander in to see how the food prep was going. What I saw was amazing. There must have been ten chafing dishes ready to be filled with food. Anita had made at least seven or eight entrees and sides with specialties like Cuban beef cigars, which were a thin pastry wrapped around a spicy empanada filling. She had mojo potatoes and chicken, both Cuban specialties. Of course there were sriracha pork tacos and Cuban rice. On the Mexican side, she had a steak dish infused with cilantro and lime, and enchiladas, as well as a shrimp and avocado Ceviche, which is

Gulf shrimp marinated in lime with cilantro. Somehow Anita also managed to make several dozen tortillas as well, to scoop and eat with.

My mouth was watering indeed.

It was my turn to get coiffed. The kids were done, and the designer was making sure they got dressed. Falon was done, and was just waiting to put on her dress till the last moment. The guys were all under the instruction that they had to be dressed by 6:00 for some photos.

Gwen arrived with Andrews, and they got right to doing what they needed to do. Apparently, I had nothing else to do for the rest of the day. Between Gwen and Falon, they finished making sure everything was ready, set up properly, and waiting for guests.

Six o'clock came around and we all congregated in the main foyer for some photos. Mya helped us with a photographer too. There were all kinds of photos on the circular stairs—with the kids, without, with everyone, and without. The photographer had us walk around the house, and whenever he saw a pretty picture, he took one.

Minni came and got my attention just before 7:00. "Mom, Amarlyis is in our room upstairs."

"Oh yes, that was the prearranged location for her to open a portal so the witches could come to the wedding. They should all be coming downstairs just like other guests."

Sure enough, there was chatter on the staircase as the witches started coming downstairs. It was important that they arrived before the ceremony, so they didn't cross the ritual circle. I was relieved and happy to see they were all wearing modern clothes. Amarlyis must have taken them shopping for dresses for the wedding. The men were also tailored in nice suits for the occasion. In fact, the group of them looked smashing.

"Minni, please take over the role of hostess for me and show them around."

"Will do."

By 7:30, all the guests had arrived. Minni acted the perfect hostess, directing everyone to the bar to get a special cocktail and then to find their seats. Any gifts were left in the foyer by the stairs for later.

Rick found me in the kitchen looking over the food. "Hun, everyone is here, so we can let the guests know," he said. "I've spoken to the DJ and the bartender, they will be packing up and gone by 11:30 p.m. We can run music and drink for anyone who is still here after the ceremony."

All-in-all, there were only two people who were not aware of my magical status, and that was Justin. He brought Greggory as his plus one and he didn't know either. I'd get Rick to draw them both aside to speak to them.

I went out to the party area and took the mic and got everyone's attention.

"Good evening, everyone. Thank you for coming and sharing this special day with Rick and me. This will be an unconventional wedding." Everyone chuckled.

"Lora, we know you two, nothing about you is conventional, hun!" cried Justin.

"To most of you, it's no secret that I am a witch. I have had my feet in the magical world since I was a girl. Tonight, we are having a very special ceremony. Not only will it be our bonding ceremony, but I will bring forth my great-great-grandmother from a magical dimension to perform the ceremony at midnight.

"So party now! The DJ will be here until 11:30 to spin tunes for you. Please help yourselves to the amazing food our very own Anita has prepared. It's all traditional Cuban and Mexican dishes in honor of Rick's family."

Rick and I walked around the tables and talked with everyone. When we got to Justin and Greggory, we sat with them for a few minutes.

"Justin, are you okay with my witchiness?" I asked.

"Lora, it doesn't faze me at all if you're a witch. I believe in magic," responded Justin.

"I'm okay with it too," said Greggory. "When you work for Falon and Mark, you see enough weird things to know there is much beyond our knowledge. I am fascinated to see the ceremony you will be doing."

"Guys, it's so nice to have you here. Enjoy your evening," said Rick. We left that table to continue to visit with everyone before grabbing food for ourselves.

People were dancing and having a good party. At ten minutes to midnight, I snuck out to the foyer and set up the crystals and salt. When everything was ready, I called everyone inside, and encouraged them to stand around the foyer and on the stairs to get a good view if they liked. I also warned them to not get within five feet of the salt on the floor.

Just before the grandfather clock struck midnight, Rick came to stand by my side. Falon and my three children stood outside the circle but close to us.

I began my spell to sanctify the ground. A hush came over everyone as they witnessed the candle flare about twenty inches tall, and a glow came over the area as I spoke the incantation: *Facere bulla tempore ad hanc animam.*

As my spell finished, a shimmering happened, and beams of light shot up from the crystals straight up through the roof. There was a gasp from everyone as we watched, the space between the beams filled in with an opaque film.

Suddenly, Innogen was there, in her ceremonial gown smiling widely, standing inside a crystal cave that sparkled with light.

A collective "wow" happened around us. Rick and I held hands and faced Innogen.

"Ladies and gentlemen, friends and family, we are gathered tonight to bond this man and this woman in marriage," said my great-great-grandmother.

"It is not every day that one such as I can perform this ceremony from beyond. I am deeply grateful to my granddaughter for wanting to learn so that I can be here for her.

"Marriage as we know it, is a life of two individuals who swear to be loyal to each other, to love each other, and to be each other's backup. It's important that this duty be evenly shared and equally shouldered, else the marriage will not last. Inequality breeds mistrust."

"Do you, Ricardo Benal, take this woman to be your mate, more than marriage, more than wife, for all the eternity that you share?"

"Yes, with all my heart, I do," said Rick.

"Do you, Lora Emily O'Reilly, take this man to be your mate, more than marriage, more than husband, for all the eternity that you share?"

"Yes, with all my heart, I do," I said.

"Then, by the power given to me by the universe, and by the faith of my goddess, I bind you together so that none may break you apart. I give you the strength to always come back to each other, and the gift of always finding each other. My dear granddaughter, my dear grandson, you were chosen for each other by fate. Congratulations!"

As Innogen spoke the wedding verse, her hand was winding a magical cord around our wrists and hands, indeed binding us together. Once she finished, the binding sank into our skin and vanished.

Everyone cheered and clapped for us. As I watched Innogen's form fade away, she mouthed that she loved me very much, and the crystal cave dissolved. She knew she would not be able to stay long, because the power it required to materialize was immense.

After my Innogen vanished and the light circle collapsed, everyone took an audible deep breath. The first person who approached me was Gwen.

"Oh my, that was magical, literally, but figuratively too. Beautiful, you two. Congrats," she said, hugging me. Andrews was shaking Rick's hand.

"Everyone!" I yelled. "Now it's time to party! Please join us for more food, drink, and dancing outside!" As everyone milled out of the house, they stopped by the six of us, congratulated and hugged us, and then went outside to rejoin the party in progress.

I turned to my family and motioned them to all come in close. We grasped hands together. "My dear family, I want to thank you for being here for this, for helping, for working so hard and for being my family. I feel so blessed."

"Lora, Minni, Pascal, Trent, I am so happy the four of you came into my life—mine and Anita's life," said Rick. "You have made it special beyond reason. I hope to live a very long time with all of you." I nudged him before he said too much.

"Mom," said Minni. "You are a beautiful bride, and I'm happy you found Rick too. You deserve to be happy."

"Ah, sweetheart," I started, and ended up pulling her into a hug and crying down her back. "Thank you," I whispered. My other two weren't sentimental, but I got big hugs from both of them.

"Okay, you guys, you can stay up another hour, and then it is off to bed, okay?"

"Actually, Mom, can I go now?" asked the youngest. "I'm tired!"

"Of course you can, honey."

"I'll take him up to bed," said Anita. "You go and join your party."

Rick and I walked out to the pool deck, and a roar of cheering erupted from our closest friends as they all clapped their hands and whistled. The party was well under way; everyone was dancing to the music Andrews had put on. Even the witches were getting into the party vibe. Mark had taken over bartending, so the alcohol was flowing and everyone was a little tipsy, but no one was overdoing it.

It was a wonderful party and lasted well into the morning. By the time the sun was coming up, it was down to the six of us: Mark, Falon, Gwen, Andrews, and Rick and me.

"So who's next to get married?" I asked my friends, looking pointedly at Gwen and Andrews.

"Who knows?" said Gwen.

"Well, thank you for sharing this day with us."

"Oh," started Andrews, "we wanted to let you know, we're building a house up here too. Not too far from Falon and Mark. We bought a lot down the street. The house should be ready by the spring."

"Oh, that's exciting!" I said. "It will be good to have everyone close by."

With that news, they all left and we were alone.

"Wife," said Rick. "Let's go to bed. I want to make love to you as the sun comes up and celebrates our union."

"Husband, you'll need to carry me, I'm afraid."

"That's not a problem. In fact it would be my pleasure," he said, warmly.

Rick scooped me up in his arms and carried me up the circular stairs to our room. It was the perfect movie ending to a nearly perfect day.

10—Consequences

Margaret

It had been two months since Abeo and I reconnected. This time it was not just a hookup. It was the best sex, being pampered and loved, of my life. I still thought he was a god, I was sure of it. No one was that good.

He was in town for six weeks, so we took advantage of that and saw each other every night. We were so strongly drawn to each other it was impossible to deny. He picked me up for lunch some days, tantalizing the girls in the office. We were officially labeled a "thing" on the third lunch date.

Glorious nights, with a man who seemed too perfect to be real. But then came the day he said he was leaving to return to Zurich for another project. I knew it would happen eventually, but in all honesty I think I pretended he would want to stay. I cried for two days. Stupid me, crying over a man.

Oh, but what a man!

I had a regular routine check-up with my family doctor scheduled, but I'd decided to cancel it. Then, just last week, I started feeling crappy. Every day I felt nauseated all day long. Finally, after puking my guts out for a week, I took myself to the emergency room. I was sitting in the exam room waiting for a doctor to return. The curtain got pushed aside as he returned with a sardonic expression on his face.

"Margaret, you're pregnant."

Silence. *I was suddenly very cold.*

More silence.

"Margaret? Did you hear me?"

"Ya, ya, I heard you." *The doctor just gave me the diagnosis: pregnant. Not an illness, not cancer, not anything that could be "fixed," pregnant. I was pregnant! How? I had an IUD for God's sake. This wasn't supposed to happen.*

"Margaret? Are you okay?"

"How could I be okay?" I asked. "You just told me I was pregnant!" *I can't have a baby! How will I care for it? I have a career, I have a life. What will I do?*

"These things happen when you have sex," said the old man, with attitude.

"Thank you for that misogynistic sarcasm." *Turd!* "You're a guy, you don't understand the betrayal I feel right now."

"Betrayal? What for?"

"Because I don't want children! I specifically had an IUD put in so that I wouldn't get pregnant, you moron!" I was screeching, I knew it. I went to the emergency department because all week long I had been puking my guts out all day long. It had never occurred to me that I could be pregnant. *How the FUCK did this happen?*

"Margaret, calm down, and I'll explain."

"I don't want to calm down, and stop treating me like I'm an idiot! I know how it happened!" *Jesus fucking Christ!*

"Well you keep asking how, so I can tell you."

"I … KNOW … how I got pregnant. The question is WHY did the IUD fail?"

"It didn't. It's only 99.8% effective. You were very unlucky, in this case, 0.2% that it didn't stop fertilization. Now, it's very rare. I am collecting data for a study on pregnancies that happen during contraception. We are trying to get a more accurate picture of occurrence. Would you feel up to some questions?"

"Questions about what?"

"Who you had sex with."

"What relevance will that have? Isn't one man the same as the next? Don't you all have penises that squirt semen filled with little sperm that fertilize an egg? I'm not comfortable with these questions. So no."

Fuck! Fuck! Fuck!

"You were the one who had sex," said the doctor.

"Don't be all high and mighty on me. I thought I was protected."

"Well, since you're here, let's do an ultrasound on the fetus and see how it's doing, eh?"

"Fine." *Fuck! Fuck! Fuck!*

A nurse brought in a machine cart and set it up next to the bed. The doctor spread some cold jelly on my belly and used a wand to see inside my womb. There it was, the IUD, still in place. Beside it were two objects about the size of a bean inside a black circle.

"What is that?" I asked, pointing to the bean.

"That … is a baby."

"And what is the other one?"

"That is also a baby."

"Two babies? As in twins?"

"It would appear so. Not just twins, but fraternal twins," said the doctor. "Two separate embryos have been created. That means the man's sperm fertilized two eggs, or you had two partners that each fertilized one egg, which is doubtful. This is doubly interesting. We will need to remove the IUD of course. So I'll schedule that right away. Oh, you're about ten weeks along, if that helps identify the man or men."

"I've only had sex with one man in the past half year, so I know who the father is and the exact date of conception," I answered. "It was two months ago. I just don't know where he is. Wait, take the IUD out? Doesn't that mean continue with the pregnancy? I don't know yet if I want to do that. Do I have to remove the IUD yet?"

"Two months, you say? Hmm. Yes, well, if you decide to continue with the pregnancy, you need to remove it sooner than later. If you decide to abort, it will be removed anyway."

"Oh, well, go ahead then and do that—remove it."

Oh my God, I need to talk to someone. Who? Do I know anyone I trust that I can talk to about this? I am not close to anyone at work for sure. Not my parents, not my family. I don't have any friends I would say are close enough. except one. Lora O'Reilly, maybe. We were very good friends in high school. She had gotten pregnant and had an abortion, I remember. Maybe she would be good to get advice from. Do I have her number?

I picked up my phone and looked through my contacts. Nope, not in my list. Maybe I can find her on social media.

A quick check showed me there were lots of Lora O'Reillys in the world. It was going to take some time to narrow it down. I was going to have to find one in Montreal. This is not worth it!

Twins, me with twins. Do I want twins? Do I even want one baby? Should I give them up for adoption? That would mean I need to go through with the pregnancy. I could do that, just to not kill these kids. They didn't ask to be created, and they were created by a spectacular man. Hmmm, I wonder what they'd look like? They would be beautiful if his genes had anything to do with it. Two children. I wondered if they were both the same or one of each. It was too early to tell. I'd have to wait until it was too late to abort to find that out.

If I was eight weeks pregnant now, that meant that the first time we were together this time I got pregnant. What were the odds of that?

I know: 0.2%.

I wish I had kept his contact information. I threw it away because I was angry that he had to leave sooner than he thought he would. So angry. I was starting to fall for him. We were with each other every day for six weeks. The sex was out-of-this-world and he always treated me like I was special. We went everywhere and did all kinds of things together. I learned about his family, that he loved flying but didn't have many opportunities anymore other than business. He flew himself all around the planet for the bank.

We had six magical weeks together. And then he told me he had to leave. I cried for hours after he said goodbye, and then I got so angry I threw his information into the fireplace.

Oh, Margaret, you are so stupid sometimes, especially when you think you're being smart. The doctor was coming back in.

"Okay, Miss Thistle, we have you booked in OR6 for the removal of the IUD. The nurse will prepare you and take you upstairs right now."

"Okay, thanks. Then what?"

"You'll have three weeks to make up your mind if you are keeping the babies or not. After twelve weeks, it gets much more complicated."

"Thank you, Doctor, and I'm sorry for melting down on you."

"No problem, dear. Things like this happen weekly."

A nurse came in and had me remove all my clothes, put on two gowns and get back up on the bed. Ten minutes later, an orderly was wheeling me and a grocery bag to an elevator. He stopped outside a door marked OR6 and took the grocery bag from me.

"This will be at the nurses' station until after you are out of surgery."

"Thank you."

A little while later, another nurse came and checked on me.

"Miss Thistle, I presume?"

"Yes, that is me."

"We are removing an IUD?"

"Yes. It failed, and I'm pregnant."

"Oh, that's too bad. Are we aborting the pregnancy as well?"

"Um, I haven't made up my mind yet."

"Do you need to speak to someone about that?" the nurse asked.

"Yes, that would be helpful."

"I'll send someone to you." She left and walked to the nursing station and picked up a phone. An announcement over the PA system calling for a psych consult blared over the loudspeaker above my head. Five minutes later, a woman wearing street clothes approached the nurses' station, conferred for a few minutes, then approached me.

"Miss Thistle? I'm Dr. D'Agente."

"Hello, Doctor."

"I hear you have a difficult situation, a pregnancy in spite of an IUD."

"A double pregnancy. They're twins."

"Oh! Wow. Okay, well, the obvious question is have you changed your mind on wanting children since you had the IUD inserted?"

"Not really. I hadn't been trying to get pregnant."

"Now that you are, how are you feeling?"

"Shocked. All I'm feeling is shock, still. I don't know. Although I have been wondering what they'll look like. Whether it's two of a kind or different."

"Ah, that is the first step to acceptance, wonder. Once our minds start to accept that things are different, our mind starts to ask questions. Let me ask: do you have a support system? Someone who can help you raise twins?"

"No. I'm single and live alone. I sometimes have to travel for work too, and stay extended periods of time. I make a good living though."

"That would make having twins difficult. You really need both parents. Is the father not in the picture?" I shook my head.

"Twins are twice the work, sometimes more. And, with newborns, it often overwhelms two parents. With just one parent, I'm afraid you may not be able to cope without a support system. What about your parents? Are they in the picture?"

"My mom is. They are divorced. My mom still lives in the city."

"Could she help you?"

"I'd have to ask her. And that's a conversation I don't know how to have. Hey, Mom, I had sex with a guy, just fun sex, and well, ya, I got pregnant. And not just pregnant, twins! How do you like that? No, he's gone off to Zurich or somewhere."

"I see."

"Yeah, that's not going to happen."

"What would you like to do?"

"Is it possible to remove the IUD without stopping the pregnancy today?" I asked.

"Yes, that is possible. You would then have about two weeks to make a decision. You could come back and talk to me in a few days. I can help you work out this conundrum."

"Thanks, Doctor. I would like to do that." At that moment, another orderly came and interrupted us and said he had to move me into the OR.

11—Finding a Mate

Gwen

I woke up lying in Andrews's bed. I could hear him downstairs working in the kitchen. *He must be making breakfast for us*. I had time to reflect on my life, where it was going, where I have been. A new chapter was coming—with a mate and a child. How did I get here?

I was born in 1696. In the early days, my family took up residence on the northwest coast of North America with a village of indigenous people on Haida Gwaii. It was a beautiful fishing village nestled against the mountains and forests, with about two hundred individuals in multiple generations. They farmed and used the sea for just about everything. Accomplished artisans, their beadwork and sculpture is known today far and wide. But at that time, that particular village was very vulnerable to the sea and they didn't know it. Never before had they faced a tsunami. When it happened, it wiped most of them out.

I was the only survivor of my family, and I lived with the surviving villagers until I was deemed an adult. At the age of fifteen, I didn't feel like an adult. My parents had told me a little of our history, so I decided to make my way back to Oregon to find my own people. A warrior from the tribe accompanied me as far as the valley, but then returned back to his people.

My people lived under a mountain in Oregon. They were descended from the original group that left the ark ship so many thousands of years ago. When I arrived, my people welcomed me and made space for me. I was placed with a small family, who eventually adopted me as their daughter. I learned more of the history of our people from them. I learned where I came from, learned our language, and that our people were long-lived, even immortal compared to humans.

I didn't need a mate. I immersed myself in what it was to be an immortal. An opportunity came up for my family to travel to another city. The four of us got to Montreal in the early 1800s and saw there was a burgeoning trade happening with furs. My father, as I came to consider him, the patriarch of the group, set up offices for his Greek shipping company in Montreal that would take trade back and forth from North America to Europe. They made a lot of money bringing liquor back from the West Indies and spices as well. I was given the task of learning the laws of the land in every port we went to so that I could negotiate on behalf of the company. Obtaining a law degree at the university in Montreal let me into the world of men, and afforded me some power.

When father and mother had another child, he was given a traditional name in Greek, because that is where they said they were from. Zisis also came to see me as a sister. It was nice having a younger sibling again. It helped fill the hole made in my heart when I lost my little sister.

Heavily involved in the business, I was as happy as I could be. Mother worried that I didn't seek out companionship, but I had lovers, just no one that was going to mean anything to me. I took pleasure when I wanted it, and didn't look back. I've had hundreds of lovers in my life. When you've lived as long as I had, you need variety. The problem is, for me, sex with humans was ultimately boring. I wanted more, which is why I embraced the kinkier, darker side with humans. At least it was a turn on. The play took time, and had a buildup which let me experience orgasm, even if I couldn't bite anyone. It was so much better than the "wham, bam, thank you, ma'ams" I got from most men.

So, no one was more surprised than me to discover that I had feelings for a human male, and not just little feelings, but big messy ones that don't go away, as much as I tried.

The remarkable thing was that the feelings hit me like a ton of bricks the instant I laid eyes on him. I had to have him. At first, I mistook those feelings for lust as always, but the connection we made that first time touched me in a way I had not experienced before. But I couldn't get him out of my head.

My first experience with Andrews was so ... so ... compelling. Here was a human with great strength, who liked kink, and didn't deflate after two minutes. More impressively, he was built like we were, larger than humans. I'd had sex with only a few immortals before. We are endowed differently—our females are deeper and wider channeled; our men are longer and wider to fill us. Both males and females have fangs that deliver a potent aphrodisiac on climax. Immortal sex is violent, and long, with big finishes.

Andrews gave me that while being a human. Well, everything but the finishing bite. He didn't have fangs back then.

Other immortals were hard to find. In fact, I knew of no others outside of my family up until a year ago. Our council was made up of descendants from the original group, so we were all related to each other. You don't want to go there.

After our first sexual encounter, I kept overthinking my situation, because forming close ties was taboo. It wasn't really that possible with humans, and the council forbade us getting involved with humans because of the complications. Watching people you love grow old and die is one of the loneliest things you can do as an immortal. It's easier to be alone. As Elrond said to Arwen: "There lies only death for you among the world of men."

But I could not let Andrews go.

When Mark insisted on turning Falon, that opened up a possibility for me too. I could turn Andrews. This felt like our destiny.

And now I was pregnant! *Oh my, that was a surprise*. But I felt it happen. The moment we conceived. I could feel the difference and the instant change in my body. For immortals, it takes roughly ten months. Our babies tend to grow larger and longer. It was a good thing we were sort of indestructible.

Andrews had now completed his change to immortality. He and Mark mock-fought so that he could be bitten. Our venom was the key to changing a human into one of us. For males, we used combat to generate the venom. For females, we used sex. At least, that was the way it used to be done. Now, we've mostly dropped the rituals and a simple injection worked. But the ceremony of the transmogrification seemed important.

Children born to immortal couples are born immortal, but without their adult skills. They don't have their fangs, they cannot produce venom. An injection or a ceremony is required when they reach puberty to complete their development.

There was talk that if you gave an immortal infant venom after birth they would develop without requiring the booster at puberty. We didn't have any proof of that. Andrews might have been born to immortal parents, because he had great healing properties as a child. Those properties served him well while he was in the military.

Rick was a child of immortal parents, and he grew up with the benefits of being immortal. Somehow he was bitten by a male around puberty, because he had developed his fangs and not needed the ceremony. Unfortunately, he got no answers from his mother when he met her. That was something to ask him about. Who finished his transformation?

Pulling myself back to the present, I looked around. Andrews's apartment was definitely masculine, but it felt like being home, because he was here. But his decor left a lot to be desired. This apartment was ultra modern with very square and straight lines. I looked around a little and thought about the small changes I could do to imprint myself here. The colors were all gray and cold. I would like some color incorporated and some curves. I still preferred the clean lines of modernity, not being a fussy person.

I swung my feet out of bed and wrapped my bathrobe around myself. When I turned around, Andrews was looking into my eyes.

"Would you like some more coffee?" he asked.

"Yes, please. I'm coming down to get it." I walked with him downstairs into the kitchen. He stood at the counter pouring coffee for us, so I wrapped my arms around his shoulders and hugged him from behind.

"I love you," I said. "I haven't told you yet, but you need to know. I have never in three hundred years ever felt this way."

"I think I love you too," said Andrews. "I've never felt this before in all the years I've been alive. I can't not be with you. Every time we're apart, my brain schemes ways to see you, to touch you." He turned around in my arms to face me.

"I know what you mean. I can hardly focus anymore. It's a good thing I've got good people working for me."

I took a few minutes to think. "Andrews, just because I'm pregnant doesn't have to mean you are involved," I said. "I don't want to pressure you in any way."

"I've never thought about it. I was too old as a human to be doing that sort of thing, but the game has changed. I won't be trying to raise teenagers as an old man anymore."

"What does that mean?"

"I think it … I want this child. I want to be his or her father. Do you want a child?"

"After all this time, I do. More importantly, I think my body does. I think you impregnated me during the ritual because my body believes we're mates. It felt it was the right time and the right person. I felt it happen."

"How could you tell?"

"Immortal women don't get pregnant often, because we have to spread out the eggs we have, so-to-speak. So when one gets fertilized, we know it."

He dropped his hand down to my tummy and laid it flat on me, pushing in gently.

"Hello, little one. I'm your daddy. I'm going to take very good care of you and mommy until I see you myself."

My eyes teared up at the tender moment. I too laid my hand over his on my stomach, willing myself to feel the tiny embryo that was beginning its life in my body.

Andrews then knelt down and kissed my stomach. He pulled off my top and lay me down on the bed. Pulling off my pants, he lay down beside me and caressed my stomach, planting a tender kiss there. His hand slowly slid down my skin until it cupped my mound. His head followed his hand and he slipped his tongue between my folds for one little taste. That elicited a startled gasp from me.

"Let's get dressed and go eat. You're eating for two now, and I expect our child to be strong and big."

"Oh my God, I can just imagine pushing out a child of yours between my legs. It already hurts!" I teased.

I got up and got re-dressed. "You owe me, Andrews."

"I'll deliver," he answered me.

12—Keep the Babies

Margaret

I spent days thinking about this decision. How many times did I go back and forth? I don't know.

Ultimately, I was curious. Was that bad?

I wanted to see who these little beings were and who they would become. So I decided to have the twins.

By the time twelve weeks was upon me, I knew I couldn't terminate. Then it was a decision to keep the children or give them up for adoption.

Getting through the pregnancy was not that difficult, or so I hoped. Meanwhile, I had to tell people a story to explain it though. I just had to make one up that wasn't a hook-up.

Not that I was embarrassed it was a hook-up. But I still felt betrayed by my body.

I remembered the name of the bank Abeo worked for and tried calling him in Zurich. He was not there, of course. So I left a message for him to call me back.

It had been a couple of weeks and no phone call. I wasn't expecting a phone call, but it would have been nice.

The conversation with my mom went better than I expected it would. She was sympathetic to my situation and wanted me to keep the children, promising she would help as much as she could. Without her living with me, I didn't know how that would work, but I was still considering it.

I never found Lora, although I contacted the high school and asked the reunion committee to see if they could get a message to her since they had contact information about her. My decision to reach out to someone I no longer had contact with, was more in line with anonimity than anything else. We were good friends back then, and she's been through this decision herself. So that made her a good candidate to get an opinion from. But she didn't travel in my circle, so it was also anonymous to some degree.

Looking around my two-bedroom apartment, I realized it was going to get very crowded before a year was up. I needed to consider moving. Well, only if I decided to keep the babies.

I knew I definitely wanted to meet them. I had even started talking to my stomach. I had read somewhere that expectant moms did that, talking to their baby in utero like they could hear. But I suppose they could, and maybe they'd learn to recognize my voice. I found myself touching my stomach every now and then, as if I were touching them. *I feel a connection to them somehow, even at this stage. How is that?* I thought. *Does pregnancy do this normally?*

In my second trimester, I was starting to show a clear and present baby bump. *Is it bigger because it's twins?* I thought so, certainly earlier because they were twins.

My doctor had me going in monthly for ultrasounds. The last one showed great progress. The next month they should be able to see how they were developing and if they were different sexes.

My phone rang while I was in the bathroom. Trying to hurry up my body, I sprinted for the phone, which I had left on my kitchen counter.

"Hello?"

"Margaret, it's Abeo."

"Hello! I'm glad you called. How are you? Where are you?"

"I'm doing fine, thanks. I'm in Montreal, which is why I called."

"Oh, it's not because I left a message?"

"You left a message? No, I did not get that message, sorry."

"Well, confession time, I lost your contact information. I finally remembered the name of the bank and tried to call you there."

"Oh my," he laughed. "Yes, they would know me, but not how to find me. I am so sorry."

"That's okay, it was my own stupidity."

"Can I see you? Tonight?"

"I'd love that. I have a surprise for you."

"A surprise? How did you know I would call?"

"I didn't, but this surprise would have happened no matter what."

"Where are you right now?" he asked.

"I'm at home. Why don't you come over now?" I gave him the address and he told me he would be here in an hour. That gave me time to pick up my place a bit.

Once I was finished, I put on a dress that would disguise my baby bump a bit. I didn't want him to see it before I had a chance to tell him. A knock on the door had my heart racing. Checking myself in the mirror, I quick-walked to the door.

"Coming!" I opened the door and all the memories of what I thought of this man were confirmed. He was a god. *Oh my!* My vagina squeezed instinctively as I gazed at his face. I saw him gulp at seeing me too. "It's good to see you. Come on in." I stepped back and let him pass.

As he did, Abeo stopped and faced me, planting the most sensual kiss on my lips as his hand found the curve of my waist and slid down my hip to squeeze my ass gently. I knew what he was here for—no objections from my body on that score.

"It's good to see you again, too. I've missed you, Margaret. That's new for me. I haven't missed anyone before."

I closed my front door and walked into the living room. He was putting down his coat.

"Can I get you refreshments?"

"What do you have?"

"Some wine, beer, vodka, gin, and scotch."

"Why don't I make us some martinis?"

"Not for me, thanks. I don't really need it."

"Neither do I. Come here. What I need is to hold you," he said.

I walked into Abeo's arms and he wrapped them around me. He kissed me gently at first, but it turned into a demand that became so hungry, I was panting in a few moments. Releasing me, his eyes were hooded.

"I'd forgotten about your eyes. They are hypnotic, you know."

He took me by the hand and led me straight away to the back of my apartment where my bedroom was.

"I hope you don't mind. I don't want to waste time, I need you, something fierce."

I wrapped my arms around his neck, pulled myself against his hips and kissed him back with all the hunger I felt for him. His hard shaft pressed up against me in invitation. His hands found my breasts, which were hyper-sensitive due to being pregnant, and my nipples almost sprang up at his touch. He smashed them against my body and tweaked them until they hurt with longing.

He broke off the kiss. Lifting me up effortlessly by my ass, he placed me on the bed. Kneeling down in front of me, he slid his warm hands up my thighs until he found the hot wetness between them.

"Oh my," he groaned when he discovered that I was not wearing panties again. "Woman, you make me so hard." He pressed his hand down between my legs and cupped my mound as his lips found my mouth again in a hungry, deep kiss. He inserted some fingers inside my wetness as his tongue probed my mouth, both with urgency.

"Lie down, beautiful. Let me pleasure you," he said with a growl.

"I have some news for you first," I said.

"Tell me, please."

I looked him in his eyes, took his hand, lifted my dress until my stomach was bare, and placed his hand on my baby bump.

"You're pregnant? Mine?"

"Yes, yours. I've been with no other since that first time I was with you. For three years after that, no other man would be good enough. You've spoiled me for the whole human race," I said with a smile, meaning it as a compliment.

"Are there males of other species on this planet you would consider?" he asked cryptically, with a strange expression on his face.

That left me puzzled as he placed his ear to my stomach and listened for the longest minute.

"Margaret, I should apologize to you," he said. "I was irresponsible and should have used contraception. I didn't mean to get you pregnant. However, now that you are, do you want these children? My children?"

"Children? How do you know? I haven't told you they are twins."

"I heard two heartbeats. Twins run in my family."

103

"Come, make love to me, and don't spare the children, Abeo," I told him. "They are very well cushioned where they are."

Abeo laid me out on the bed, and worshiped me, first by taking off my clothes carefully, and then by kissing nearly every square inch of my body. He paid particular attention to my breasts, making sure they knew how important they were. Already getting larger, they were tender but highly responsive.

When he got to my mound, my body was already close to climax, and his tongue gave me the first orgasm of the night as it speared into me while his magical fingers pressed on my nub. I was squirming and my hips were jerking to the rhythm of his tongue fucking me. I was almost all the way to my second climax when he quickly stripped off his clothes. He was suddenly between my legs, his cock pressing into my vagina. Not entering yet, he looked at me with a question in his eyes.

"Take me, please, with everything you have."

"My pleasure, pretty momma."

He pushed gently past the lips of my vagina, past my g-spot and all the way to the very end, where he pushed up against the womb where his progeny lay sleeping. Or not. Suddenly, I felt movement in my stomach, like a flutter as if a butterfly was trapped there.

"Oh! Oh! Oh! I think your kids just woke up!"

"Really?"

"I'm feeling them move!"

He pumped himself in and out again, and I groaned in delight at being filled up so completely. He was tipping me, but he always did. He was so large for my body, he stretched me, but it was such a sense of connection. It felt like he reached all the way inside me and we were one.

The fluttering continued. With each thrust they moved like they were feeling him knocking on the door to their room. Each thrust brought me closer to climax. Each thrust reconnected our two bodies like they were meant to be. Then one thrust pushed me over the edge and my body crescendoed down from the long climb and I shuddered with my release as I felt him climax with me. His seed poured into me once more. We lay there connected. I felt that feeling of never wanting to be separated again. I felt a pinch on my neck and a sense of delight, pleasure, and euphoria hit me. It set me adrift, on the sensations of his cock inside and his fingers playing lightly on my skin, as another orgasm took me.

I heard him murmur something into my ear so softly I couldn't understand what it was, sweet nothings probably, as I floated away into oblivion. When the floating subsided and I came back into my body, I found Abeo sprawled on top of me. His weight felt insignificant somehow, even though he was very tall. I could feel that he was still connected to me, so I squeezed him gently.

"You're back," he murmured. "My cock has been reluctant to leave his favorite spot."

"You were trying to talk him into leaving, weren't you?"

"I thought maybe I should lie beside you and hold you, but he's a greedy pig and would not leave."

"So who's in charge?"

"He is." We both laughed.

"I don't mind. I kind of like the feeling of you lying on me. It feels comforting somehow."

"Not heavy?"

"Surprisingly, no. Not heavy at all. In fact, it's just right. I feel our connection, physical and spiritual. The physical is your cock, making two into one. The spirit is you lying on top. I feel your heart."

"Oh my, Margaret, how I have missed you."

13—The Past in the Past

Andrews

I was making Gwen and I some breakfast. She came to stay with me at the condo after Carlow, and she hadn't left. That was wonderful, because we had the chance to talk about the baby, the future, and what we were to each other. We professed love to each other, and let me tell you, it's strange to be in your forties and finding love for the first time.

I'm going to be a father! This was going to change my whole life. My life—wow, it had been unconventional. I decided I needed to tell Gwen all my secrets before we started this family. She needed to know.

"Do you want to set the balcony table for breakfast, or would you prefer eating indoors?"

"How cool is it?" she asked as she got up and opened the glass doors. "Oh, it's a wonderful morning. Let's eat outside."

She came back in and got everything, including the coffee pot, and took it outside. I followed her with the plates.

"Oh, this looks divine! I haven't had waffles in ages. Thank you for cooking this."

"My pleasure. I don't often have someone to cook for, but I love doing it. Usually, it's me and a newspaper at the corner café."

We ate in pleasant silence for a few moments, watching the sun rise. I decided to dive in.

"Gwen, I know we agreed that our past is in the past, but there is one event that is recent history and I still work with the woman. I need to tell you about it. I want to have no secrets between us."

"Are you referring to Lora?"

"Yes, how do you know?"

"I could smell her arousal around you and vice versa. I figured there was history. But since she and Rick are married, I presume it is water under the bridge."

"It is, but I still wanted to tell you."

"Okay, tell me after dinner."

"Deal."

After work, I got back to my place before Gwen, and barbequed a couple of nice steaks, with corn on the cob and baked potatoes for dinner. Pulling a nice red wine from the fridge, I opened it and let it get to room temperature and breathe.

When Gwen got home, I had the patio all set up: the table was set, patio lights on for ambience, and the dinner was perfect. We even danced to the soft music that was playing until it got too cool outside to stay. So we came in and put on the fireplace.

"So what is this big bad secret you have to tell me?" asked Gwen once we were seated comfortably.

"It's about my past."

"Okay, but you do understand, we all have pasts. We all have had trysts, some meaning something, others not. It's what happens when you live."

"Yes, but this was recent, and I think I need to tell you."

"Go ahead, then. Understand, it doesn't change a thing for me, how I feel, or what I want," said Gwen. "But I want details."

"Thank you. Really? Okay. It happened a couple of years ago, when Mark and Falon were in trouble from Mark's council. Mark had tasked me to clear out Falon's hotel room and move everything to a more secure location. Lora was with me because she had been staying with Falon."

"Go on."

"Well, we drove back to the hotel together. As we packed up everything, we made sure there were no bugs or trackers. It was a long task. We were both tired and hungry when we got finished. Lora went to have a shower and I was waiting in the room in the dark, sitting in a chair. I was starting to drift off, but my thoughts were about her body in the shower. My imagination listened to the water and built an image of it sluicing over her head. She was a sexy girl."

"Go on."

"When I heard the water turn off, I jumped to alertness. She came out of the bathroom in a towel and stood there silhouetted by the light in the hall. She looked good enough to eat, and it had been a long time since I had been with anyone. My body reacted to her without prompting."

I paused for a moment to swallow and take a deep breath. This was harder than I thought it would be.

"She mentioned a movie title and wanted to play the game from the movie. I didn't recall it right away so I sat there silently. She sexy-walked toward me like a stripper, exaggerating each move so her body was shown to the best effect. She obviously knew how to strip. When she noticed my erection, all bets were off. She basically jumped me, and I was not an unwilling player. I gave her what she demanded, and it turned out to be kinky sex."

"What kind of kink?" asked Gwen.

"Rough, and multiple," I answered. Gwen growled seductively, and I sensed her own arousal.

"Did you give her what she asked for?"

"Yes, and then some. It was all very clinical to some extent. But then when people experiment the first time, it often is. They're exploring, not understanding what is coming. I have some experience in the kink she was interested in, so it was not a discovery for me."

"What was it?" Gwen asked.

"Hot. It was hot and sexy, and consuming. But I realized it was just sex, and it was not connected to any emotions on my part. I felt detached from the experience emotionally. Afterwards, so did she. She thanked me like I had brought her towels, and that was the end of it."

"You didn't answer my question."

"No, I didn't," I hestitated. "It was a triple penetration."

"That's extreme. Was it some sort of itch she had to scratch?"

"Yeah, exactly like that. It was curious. Once that was gone, the sexual tension we both had felt, dissipated quickly. We returned to being friends easily, and while attraction remained, it was never hot like it was that night."

"If I may, considering all your other experiences, this was nothing more than a very human need for connection after a traumatic event. We immortals go through the same feelings. The need to connect on a fundamental level, carnal and physical, is a drive to celebrate the life that was almost taken away. Warriors experience this all the time after battles. It's why there's usually an orgy after a significant battle throughout history."

I laughed, but her words hit home for me. "So you don't mind?" I asked.

"Mind?" she asked. "Of course not. That was nothing compared to the sizzle I had for you the first time I laid eyes on you."

"Oh my, yes, that was something. It was as if the skies parted and heaven shone down on your head. I was awestruck and flabbergasted. It wasn't sexual either, there was something stronger that hit me."

"It wasn't sexual?"

"Not at first. No. It was much more. It was like you were my home and I knew where I was supposed to be. I needed to go home to you. Then, I was driven by an overwhelming sexual need to have you completely."

"Huh, that perfectly describes what happened to me too. I wonder if that is common. Did that happen to the others?"

"I'm willing to say yes. From what Mark told me, his feelings for Falon were instant and all-consuming. He couldn't not love her from the moment he saw her. We seem to be drawn to our 'other' inexplicably, undeniably, and unrelentingly. Mark felt powerless over the pull Falon had on him. So much so, that he would risk everything again to be with her."

"Yes, he risked everything," said Gwen. "The family nearly killed him or her. They were furious with him. But eventually they realized there was no keeping the two of them apart. They made them jump through archaic hoops though, and insisted on stupid rituals. It was more of a test of her resolve than his. They had tested him, but they hadn't tested her. She was just a human, and they didn't know her at all."

"Why didn't they test me?" I asked.

"They don't need to. I've explained that you're my mate, and that there will be no other."

"Really?"

"Yes. Besides, my "family" is adopted. My natural parents were killed so long ago but they would be happy for me. To finally have found someone, to have an opportunity to have a family, to be happy."

"I love you, Gwen."

"And I love you with all my heart, Andrews."

14—Hiring Duffy

Andrews

Gwen and I had settled well into the condo. Fridays had become an important night for us, getting to touch base and tell each other about our week. We'd get home and cook together then light a fire and snuggle under the covers and tell each other tales. Our baby was growing well and we were five months into the pregnancy. The OB-Gyn looking after her was puzzled by the advanced development of the baby, but we just laughed it off. We weren't planning to have the baby in a hospital, so it didn't matter too much.

"Hmmm, so what story are we going to visit tonight?" asked Gwen.

"Did I ever tell you about Duffy?"

"No, I met him on our cruise in the Caribbean, right?"

"Yes, that's Duffy. He's another of my army buddies. He's about as indispensable a human can be. The man is multi-talented and has connections in all kinds of industries that are used for everything from spying to prospecting.

"We had just learned that an ancient order of vampire hunters was looking for Mark and Falon. I decided that we needed to recon their facility, and I needed a specialist for this, someone with the toys that would help us see inside. This is where Duffy comes in. When he left the military, he started his own business in Florida doing security and reconnaissance. He worked for some very big corporations and public figures as well as governments.

"I first met him during an operation we had in the Middle East. He was a specialist in surveillance and counter-surveillance. He had just about every gizmo you could imagine and some I didn't even know what they were. He had been responsible for getting us intel on a specific position with details about the underground facility. You see, there was nothing on the surface to see. But we had observed people entering a small building and disappearing. I mean their heat signatures disappeared off our instruments but they didn't exit the building anywhere. So we believed there was something underground.

"Duffy had some magical equipment that would allow him to map underground several hundred feet down. I have no idea how, but it was amazing. It showed us that there was a vast underground complex, at least five or six storeys down. His machine couldn't see all the way to the bottom, but it saw a lot.

"I convinced Mark that Duffy could help us in the Caribbean. So, I went to Florida to tell him about our project, and he knew exactly what we needed to do. The day I got there I discovered he was living on top of a diner he owned. His business had taken a bit of a hit, and he ran the diner to keep a roof over his head and food on the table. I didn't like seeing him in such a difficult spot, so it was good I was bringing him that business.

"Once we finished our project in the Caribbean, Duffy confided in me that his wife had left him, and that he was thinking of closing the restaurant and moving somewhere else. Mark believed he had use for a man with Duffy's talents, and to date we've used him for a few things.

"So when Duffy told me he wanted to move, I of course asked him where. He didn't know, but the only criteria would be it needed a port so he could set up his business. I suggested

Montreal, and he liked that idea, seeing as the rest of us are here too.

"He told me, 'I have to keep my boat in Florida though, Andrews. That's where the jobs are for marine exploration, and if I'm not local, I'll lose out on opportunities.' I agreed with him. So his boat is still moored in the Florida Keys, while his office is up here with the rest of the technology he has."

"How is he settling into Montreal?" asked Gwen.

"Well that's the thing, he's not," I answered. "He's hiding in the office and that's not good for anyone. I have an idea, though, that I wanted to talk to you about."

"Okay. Could you grab me another drink please?"

"Do you want a full glass of milk or a half-glass?" I asked.

"Full please, I'm thirsty," answered Gwen.

I got us both a beverage and returned to the sofa. "So, I was thinking…" I started.

"Yes…"

"Well, this condo isn't really a great place for kids. There is no yard, its decor is hard, and there are no families in the building."

"Okay…"

"How would you feel about moving?"

"Where?"

"Close to Mark and Falon."

"Do you mean buy a house?"

"Yes. With a back yard where we can have a swing set, and grass for our little one to run through."

"Our little one will not be running anywhere for a year or so!"

"I know, but…"

"You want a house for him/her to grow up in," said Gwen.

"Yes, I do. If we're going to be parents and have a family, I want to do it right."

"There are all kinds of 'rights,' and they don't all have to have a single-family home."

"I know, but I think it will be nice. We'd be close to Mark, Falon, Lora, and Rick. Close to our people, and our children will have a place to play outside that is safe."

"You kind of have your mind set on this, don't you?" asked Gwen.

"I think I do. But if you're not interested, we can wait. All the points you made are correct. I don't believe the building association will care if we have one child."

"That's a thing?"

"It could be. This is an adult-only building. I'm not sure how strict they are about that."

"What would you do with the condo if we move out?"

"I would keep it. In fact, we could rent it out or turn it into a vacation rental."

"Hmmm, that's an interesting idea. Providing income. This is a beautiful spot, and could be a great investment like that. You've sold me on that idea."

"Really?" I asked. "That seemed too easy."

"Making money on this property will offset the cost of purchasing a new property. So that's a win-win. So let's go house shopping!"

"There's another part to this," I said. "I would let Duffy live here. He could sign a lease with us. This is close to the port, only about a fifteen-minute walk, and it's close to Mark's office and mine."

"Have you asked him yet?"

"Yes, I did. Full disclosure: I kinda suggested it to him as a solution."

"Hmmm. I agree, Duffy is a good fit here. A bachelor, but it would be a good place for him to land. And we know him—well, you do, so that's better than leasing to a stranger."

"You agree?"

"Yes. Now let's go look for a house. I want to move well before we have this child, and that leaves us only a few months!

15—Negotiations

Abeo

After that first hook-up with Margaret, I had never intended on keeping in touch with her. I went on with my life. But I couldn't forget her. No matter what, her face haunted me. The shape of her chin, the curve of her shoulder, the smell of the indentation between her breasts, everything haunted me. Traveling around the world, I would see faces in the crowd that looked like her and my heart would stop, my breath would catch, and I would sweat. I lost all kinds of sleep dreaming about her. Our lovemaking had been intense and so satisfying. It replayed in my dreams every night, leaving me hard and sweating every morning. My shower and I were becoming very intimate.

I called my captain, who had remained a friend all these centuries, and told her about Margaret.

"Oh my, you've got it bad!" she said. "What are you going to do about it?"

"I don't honestly know," I answered. "I haven't felt like this since Aran."

"Well, you have to do something, because if you keep going like this, you'll mess up badly. And we can't afford you to mess up."

"Agreed," I said. "Perhaps I'll look for her again and see if the feelings are still there. Who knows, maybe this is just a trick of my mind. After all, I've not laid with a woman for a very long time before her."

"Yes, and I told you that was unhealthy. You need to release that inner animal and have conjugal activities—carefully, but you still have to have them."

"I know, but it's just not the same without love."

"You're a romantic, as the humans say. You want the happily-ever-after and all that goes with it."

"I almost had it with Aran."

"Yeah, but we couldn't let you change her. It would have been too difficult on her."

"I'll let you know how my second encounter goes."

"You do that. And for God's sake, wear protection!"

"Yes, ma'am."

It was a few years after that, before I had an opportunity to return to Halifax for the bank. I researched the company she worked for, and discovered they would be having the same event in Halifax soon. I could coordinate my schedule to be there at the same time and run into her "accidentally."

The moment I saw her again, all the feelings flooded back into my body and just about knocked me off my feet. *Well, there's my answer. I'm hopelessly in love with this woman. My body knows she's my mate.*

We spent six weeks together. The lovemaking had been glorious. That first night, I forgot to wear a condom, and prayed my mistake would not have consequences. She told me she had contraception, so perhaps we would skip that excitement. After six weeks, I needed to deal with another issue in another country. I had to leave. It broke both our hearts, but that was the reality of keeping a thousand-year-old business alive. I had to admit, I had a very difficult time leaving her side. Her face haunted me, and my body craved her like no other.

Not long after I left, I received a message that there was a call to the Zurich bank for me and a message was left. I knew it was Margaret without even checking. She was the only person who had that phone number. It was a bogus card in case I needed one. I had given it to her just in case she would call me.

Her call to the bank in Zurich was a bit of a surprise, and I had to find out why. I had hoped that it wasn't an emergency, but just in case it was, I needed to go to her and discover the reason for her reaching out to me. She had left me her address when we were last together, telling me that she lived in Montreal.

I waited a couple of weeks after the message before flying to Montreal. Once I heard her voice on the phone, it was like a match going off, lighting up my libido. Suddenly, I needed to be with her again. I needed to own her, body and soul. This was confirmation that my soul wanted to be mated to her and only her.

Not since the very first human I laid with—Aran, all those millennia ago—had a woman captivated me so. Aran bore me twenty children, all in pairs or triplets. It was then we discovered how aggressive our sperm could be. It made it essential to be very careful when copulating. Before contraception, every human woman I laid with was at risk of becoming pregnant. So I made a decision to not be with anyone.

Now, my captain didn't have that problem. Human males rarely impregnated our females. There were only a few females in our original group that I could have sex with, and both became pregnant by someone else, but only one child at a time. There was something about humans that was different.

When I arrived at Margaret's apartment, my heart was thumping in my chest. Anticipation of seeing her again had me excited. When she opened her door and her face was in front of me again, I gulped quietly and felt the muscles in my body contract with tension. My balls got swollen, and my cock grew. Everything became excited and responded to her presence.

I tried to be casually pleasant and go slowly, but I caught a whiff of her arousal too, so I pounced on her immediately. Having her again was a delight. It made my soul fly high and sing. This was the one woman for me, she was my mate. Now, I had to let her know and I had to find out if she felt the same.

When I detected the tiny life forms swelling her belly, I almost cried with joy. She had smelled different when I finally got close to her. Her skin was sweeter, she tasted more … something. But when she took my hand and placed it on her belly and smiled at me, the surge of joy I felt was incomparable to anything I have felt before.

"Mine?" I asked.

"Yes," was her answer, and then she told me she had been with no other since we first laid together. *Oh my!*

I listened to them, their tiny hearts in synchronization with each other. They were fraternal twins. I had fertilized two eggs. I knew I would need to be careful making love to her now so that I didn't dislodge them from their perch inside her womb.

"No other man will do it for me now, I'm afraid. You've spoiled me for the whole human race," she had said.

Did she know I wasn't human? That was impossible. I had been very careful.

I chose to make a joke of it by asking if there was another species she was considering. We laughed, and that was a relief.

She was surprised I could tell there were twins, but I told her I could hear two heartbeats.

Loving her again was sweet magic. I couldn't stop myself from biting her again. I needed to be there for her, for these children. I needed to strengthen her. Delivery of twins in this day and age was not a big deal unless there were complications. But these babies would be larger than most human twins.

The best way to strengthen her was to give her venom. It would slowly change her DNA, and eventually make her close to invulnerable. If she felt the same way, I wanted to give her the option of becoming immortal with me. That way, the babies would be born invulnerable and would only need a final dose at puberty to be fully immortal.

Every time we had sex, I would make sure she got a dose of venom. But first I needed to find out if she felt the same way.

With my decision made, as soon as she woke up I would tell her that I will help her with the babies—whatever she needed would be provided. If I couldn't be there physically all the time, the least I could do was to make sure she and they wanted for nothing.

Her beautiful eyes opened a crack, and a smile split her face like sunshine coming over the horizon.

"Margaret, my love, you're back. How do you feel?"

"Mmmm, deliciously relaxed and content," she answered. "My love? Is this a new moniker or do you mean that?"

"I mean that. My absence from you has taught me that my heart, body, and soul have fallen hopelessly in love with you. I am entirely yours. I cannot live without you. And I need to know if you feel the same way."

"Abeo, my beautiful man, I've felt that way since the first hook-up we had. When you left, my world shattered and I was lost. I wasn't interested in any other man. You had filled my soul with love."

"I want to be their father, in every way. I want you to be my mate, forever."

"Forever?" she asked. "That's a long time. Not till death do us part?" She was grinning widely now.

"Even past death, my love. I will find you," I said.

"Well then, I could really use the help," she said practically. "After all, twins will not be a simple way to learn how to be a parent. Twins run in your family, eh? You could have warned me!"

"I'm sorry, I didn't think you would become pregnant so easily."

"Neither did I! Oh well, it's done now, and I'm happy with my decision to keep the babies. But I'm even more happy that you want to be a parent with me."

"I will take care of you. Anything, and I mean anything, you need, you just ask," I said. "I'm a man of means, so I don't want you lacking anything. I cannot be here all the time, so I will do what I can financially."

I saw her slump in disappointment."I want you here with me," she said.

"I know, and I will be here as often as I can. But my business takes me all over the world and I cannot escape that. However, I can spend longer periods of time here than elsewhere."

"That's very generous of you, Abeo," she started. "I don't need your money, but your children will need their father. I would rather your body be here than your money." She gently blushed with that statement, so there was definitely a double meaning to what she just said.

"I would rather my body be here too, if not only for them, but for you too," I said. I could see the disappointment deepening. "But! There is a but. I can make this city my home base so that I always come home here between trips, rather than Zurich."

Her face lit up. The sheer happiness shining through her eyes almost overwhelmed me with love. Yes, love. I recognized this feeling now. I loved her. Even after learning my lesson with Aran, I loved her. How painful it had been watching Aran grow old and sick and die. I never wanted to live through that again. Hence, I would change Margaret.

Looking back at her face, the hope shining there, I leaned over and kissed those delicious lips.

"Does that mean you'll move to Montreal?"

"Yes, I'll move to Montreal."

"Will you move in with me?" she asked hopefully.

"How about we share a house? I can buy us a house large enough for a family of four or more, and we can all live there."

"That sounds perfect, actually."

Margaret didn't seem happy with my suggestion. Do I need to do more? Does she want more?

"Do you have any preferences on neighborhoods?" I asked.

"As long as there is a yard for them to play in, and large enough to take us all, nope," she said. "Um, what shall I refer to you as? Not my boyfriend, so what?"

Ah, she's looking to label me so she can explain everything to the people in her life. Hmmm, what shall I tell her?

"You can use 'boyfriend' if that works for you. I kind of like that."

"Really?" she squealed, and then she jumped on me, plying me with kisses all over, and that of course revved up my libido and it was no time at all before my cock was once again looking forward to connecting with her.

"I see you would like to play some more," she said demurely. "May I?" At that, she slid down my body and took hold of my cock with her hands and started to stroke it. That just about undid me, because I rarely had ladies willing to take me on. By most human standards, I was a tank, too large for most to take all of me.

"You know, I've never really seen you clearly," she said to my cock. "My, you are a big boy, and so full. I love the way you fill me up. But for now, let me give you some pleasure."

She delicately licked my cock, which made it jump in delight. Like an ice cream cone, she delicately licked it all around the tip and used her lips like she was drawing some cream off the end. It was an astounding feeling. As she got into the licking, her strokes got longer and her lips moved farther down my head, until she was able to completely envelop the head in her mouth. There was no way she would be able to take much more. I felt her hands start to stroke my shaft, and the amount of squeeze was just right to give me shudders, as her other hand gently cupped my balls and squeezed them too. Somehow she stimulated my whole genital area, and the result was an orgasm coming on quickly.

"Ah, ah, ah Margaret, you are bringing me … ah … to a climax," I sputtered out. "Margaret, I'm going to cum in your mouth, stop!"

"Mmmm hmmm," she answered without removing her mouth. The sound vibrated down my shaft and zinged me, making the climax acute and imminent.

"Ah … ah … oh … fuck … geez … oh God … Margaret—oh fuck, I'm coming."

My balls squeezed and my shaft elongated and the seed spewed forth down her throat. By the time it had finished, she was almost choking on my cock, but not quite. She very proudly pulled off me and licked her lips.

"I didn't have any worries, did you?" she asked.

"I didn't know you could do that."

"Well, you've never given me the chance before. You're very salty, but I like it. How is it you're still hard?"

"Um, it takes a lot to finish me."

"Oh, that sounds like a challenge. I'm game. I've got stamina."

I grinned at her and knew that was true, but she didn't understand what finished meant for me. It meant to give her everything I had, and that would turn her into an immortal. I could not do that. Not without her knowledge or consent. That was one of the rules of our kind. No consent, no change.

"Well, my new boyfriend, let's say we go house hunting?"

"I think that's a fine idea," I said. "Thank you for that. It was amazing."

"My pleasure. By the way, thank you for agreeing to move to Montreal. I figured that I would have an upward battle convincing you to be part of the twins' lives. I didn't want to raise two kids alone, not really. I wanted you to want to be here, but I wasn't sure how to convince you. So I just want to acknowledge just how remarkable your attitude is, and how grateful that this 'negotiation' didn't have to happen. I didn't want to play the typical female cards. I didn't want to tell you how I felt because I wanted you to want us. And you do, so it's all good."

"As you said, my pleasure," I responded. Because it was. I was looking forward to being a mate to this woman and raising my kids. I would show her my world, and invite her to join me. Then we will truly have forever together.

16—A New house

Margaret

Abeo made good on his promise to make sure I lacked for nothing. Parcels and deliveries started arriving the following week. I had to store the boxes behind the sofa or there would be no place to sit down.

"Abeo, we need to talk," I said to him one day after receiving three packages from the baby store.

"Is there a problem?" he asked me.

"No, but I'm running out of space in my apartment. I need a bigger space."

"You're right. Let's go shop for a house," he said, looking at all the boxed new furniture he had started buying for the twins. "We can't stay here."

"There is a new area being built now, with lovely homes. I think I'd like to build there," I said.

"Let's look at the models and the neighborhood online." Abeo opened a site where they had lovely photos of a planned community with schools and parks and a variety of housing, from semi-detached and low-rise apartments to single-family homes. Most of the houses didn't have grass yet, but they were all very pretty, and the right size for us.

"This house is pretty." I pointed to a two-storey building. "It has four bedrooms and a finished basement."

"That could be useful. Shall we go visit them?" asked Abeo.

"Lead the way."

He drove us out to the West Island to visit new developments. Some of the builders had model homes in different neighborhoods, so we drove quite a bit. The neighborhood in general was barely a year old. Not all the artist's illustrations were available as model homes, which was disappointing.

We stopped by another sales office and were looking through their models when an agent came and spoke to us. "We have some of these homes available as models if you would like to walk through them," he said.

"That would be good. Where do we go?" asked Abeo.

"This one here is a five-bedroom, with an option for a sixth bedroom, and a six-bedroom model is just over on the next street. You can walk through that one. It hasn't been decorated yet."

We navigated the streets over to the new model. They were muddy, and large equipment was all over the place.

"Look, this house has neighbors across the street," I said.

Abeo parked on the gravel driveway and we got out and stood in front of it.

"I like the front, Abeo. It's quite pretty. What do you think?"

"If you like it, I like it." He took my elbow and helped me cross the rocks to the front porch. It had a wide wraparound porch. When we opened the front door, I gasped at how spacious it was inside. We were met with a double high entryway and a beautiful circular staircase.

"Oh, this is quite beautiful!" I exclaimed.

"I like it too," he said. "But the floors are not finished. We would need them to do that."

"Let's walk around." We discovered large rooms for a living room and dining room, and a wonderfully modern kitchen with space for large appliances. There were large floor-to-ceiling windows across the back of the house, for a large space with a fireplace. We found the laundry and a guest bathroom on the floor too. Upstairs there were six bedrooms, all of pretty good size—two had ensuites. This house was designed for a multi-generational family.

"Abeo, I really love this house. Can we afford it?"

"Without a doubt, my love." Let's go back to the office and put an offer on it. That will make sure it will be ready well in time for us to be settled before the twins arrive."

Walking back inside the office, the same agent approached us. "Hello, folks, how did you like the model?"

"We loved the house," said Abeo. "I'd like to put an offer on it today."

"Let's sit down and write up the paperwork, then," said the agent. "By the way, do you have financing?"

"Yes, that's not a problem. I can likely pay cash. Can I get a discount for cash?" asked Abeo.

"Cash?" The agent choked a little. "Um, cash, yes, we can do cash. But the laws in Canada need us to break that down into several payments."

"No problem. I can have a cashier's check by the end of day for the down payment."

"Wonderful," said the agent. He was suddenly very attentive. "Let's go over all the details now, shall we? Once that is done, I'll have an offer to purchase for you to sign."

We spent the next four hours filling out contracts and deciding on flooring and paint colors. It was exciting to see it all come together.

"Now a couple of details: can this be completed by December 6th?" asked Abeo.

"That shouldn't be a problem, sir," said the agent.

"Good, I will pay overtime to ensure we get into the house by then. As you can see, we are pregnant, and I would like our children to come home to the new house."

The agent looked at my very distended belly and his eyebrows flew up. "Oh! Of course. I will put a note on the offer that there is incentive for a rush."

"Thank you."

Once the offer to purchase was signed, Abeo called the bank and had a cashier's check for the total down payment delivered to the agent's office. The new house would be finished in time to move in before I delivered.

Later that month, we had another doctor's visit. The ultrasound showed the twins as well developed and one of each. The doctor had to keep checking his notes, because he thought they were further along by their size. I just kept getting larger and larger. My belly resembled that of an elephant by now.

"Your due date is December 6th?" he asked.

"No, it's December 20th."

"Okay, then we need to make sure you're booked at a hospital for this delivery."

17—False Labor

Margaret

I had been warned. The doctors warned me, friends warned me, my mom warned me, but I honestly believed I would have nine months to prepare for being a mother.

Nope. I went into false labor late in my eighth month. That scared the shit out of me.

Apparently, this was common for twins. But I wasn't going to let that happen. Those babies needed nine months to incubate. They were going to get nine months to incubate.

I quit my job and resigned myself to bedrest for the remainder of my pregnancy in order to give them the most time possible. The doctors told me that was best. Thankfully, the hospital bed was at home and I had a full-time nurse waiting on me. Talk about the lap of luxury!

When it happened, I was shopping. I was thankful that my water didn't break, I just started to have pains. I had learned my lesson, and I kept Abeo's phone number on me at all times. So I sat down in the store and called him immediately.

"Is everything all right?" he asked me.

"I think I've started labor pains."

"Go home immediately, I'll meet you there."

"Where are you?"

"Not far." *What does that mean?*

"I think I should go to the hospital."

"Okay, then go there, and I'll meet you there. Which one?"

"Lakeshore."

"See you soon."

Instead of driving, I ordered an Uber and got to the hospital within thirty minutes. I left the car at the store. I figure Abeo could pick it up.

I walked into the emergency wing and immediately got attention, because I was huge—I mean elephant huge.

"How far apart are the contractions?" asked a nurse.

"I've just had two in the past thirty minutes. But I don't want to take chances."

"How far along are you?" asked the nurse.

"Almost finished my eighth month." The nurse took a stethoscope and put it up to my belly.

"Oh, it's twins, that explains a lot. Okay, let's get you up to obstetrics and into a bed. You may not be in labor, but with twins we need to make sure. We want them to cook as long as possible."

On the way upstairs the nurse asked, "Do you want me to call the father?"

"I did before coming here. He's on his way. His name is Abeo, Abeo Musa."

"Right, I will make a note of that on your file."

An hour after my first pain, I was comfortable in a bed on the fifth floor of the hospital, and my clothes were hanging in a locker. I called my mom to let her know, and she said she would come and see me. I was currently waiting for Abeo to arrive. That happened ten minutes later.

"Sorry it took me a while. Traffic from the airport was crazy."

"I'm just glad you're here." He leaned down and gave me a wonderful kiss that made my toes curl. The nurse had come into the room and cleared her throat.

"Oh, hello. I'm Abeo, the father."

"Pleased to meet you. Your wife is fine, it was a false alarm, perhaps because she was on her feet shopping," said the nurse reproachfully. "She will need to stay off her feet for the remainder of her term."

"That is not a problem. Does she have to stay here?"

"We can arrange for nurses to check in on her at home, but it's best if she was monitored 24/7."

"Money isn't an object when it comes to Margaret. I shall set up a hospital bed and all the equipment she needs at home. Can you recommend a home nurse you trust?"

Astounded by his generosity, the nurse hesitated. "I can make a list for you of the equipment and where to get it. I'll also put a list together of nurses who would be interested."

"Thank you, nurse … Chapel," said Abeo, looking at her nametag.

"Do you get teased?" I asked the nurse.

"Over my name? Yes, all the time. People are forever asking me if I've seen the captain. It gets old."

"I'm sure it does."

"Sweetheart," said Abeo. "I will go make the arrangements and be back to you shortly. Do you need anything?"

"I'm hungry."

"I'll bring you some food."

"Oh that won't be necessary, dinner will be served shortly," said Nurse Chapel.

"No offense, but I've seen hospital food. I'll bring her some food."

"Fine."

"Rest for now, and try to sleep." Abeo placed his hand on my belly, which was uncovered at the moment, and leaned down to place his ear on it too. He murmured something to his kids very softly so I didn't overhear. He stayed that way a minute or two before kissing my belly and saying out loud, "Don't you push your mommy. You stay there for a while longer. Don't be in such a rush to come out here. We will be here waiting for you. We so want to meet you, my children. We love you."

The nurse wiped a tear from her eye and left the room, embarrassed at witnessing such an intimate moment. I, on the other hand, had a tear, because I was so touched by Abeo's love for his twins. He'd been consistent over the past four months, being there with whatever I needed. Never once reneging on his promise.

"I'm off." He kissed my forehead and left the room, leaving me to feel his children romping around inside of me. I could swear they were fighting already.

Sleep took me as I lay there, sending me to dreamland, where my children were grown up and I was a very old woman and they were still in their twenties, which, mathematically, wasn't possible. In the dream, I kept getting older while they did not, nor did Abeo. Suddenly, Abeo was carrying me across water, laying me down, and biting me with fangs. *Like a vampire!* But after he did that, I started growing younger again, until I was a twenty-year-old again. Our children, a boy and a girl, joined us on the water and we skimmed across the surface lightning-fast until we landed on a grassy knoll. There, we lay down and watched the clouds and called out shapes.

I watched other people walk by us. They would age with every step and then turn to dust. Each person was like that. They started out as a child, and the farther they walked the older they got, until they floated away on the breeze. I was getting upset about the disappearing people, and I was trying to sit up to warn them, but my son was holding me down. Struggling in my dream suddenly woke me up to the sound of my name being repeated over and over again.

"Margaret! Margaret! Margaret! Wake up, Margaret!"

I opened my eyes and Nurse Chapel was over me, shaking me awake.

"Ah, there you are. You were dreaming and it didn't look like a good dream."

"No, it was not. It was weird though."

"Do you want to tell me about it?"

"I'm losing it. Abeo and I were there, and my kids were both grown up. Abeo looked the same but I was really old."

"Uh huh."

"Then we went to a park or something. People were walking by us and with each step they got older until they became dust and blew away."

"Oh!"

"There was something else, some other detail that was strange … it's on the tip of my memory …"

"Who was it about?"

"Abeo. He carried me across water or something."

"Anything else?"

"He kissed me on the neck, but it hurt. Did he bite me?"

"My!"

"Yes, he bit me. He was a vampire in my dream! Then I became young again."

"Wow. You're right, that is a weird dream. What do you think it means?"

"Haven't a clue!"

The nurse handed me a piece of paper with a list of equipment and names. I noticed her name was first on the list.

"Nurse Chapel, do you want to be my nurse?"

"I would like to, yes. I've got about three months of leave owed to me, so I can take the time off to care for you."

"You're hired, then. I'll tell Abeo." I sent Abeo a photo of the list of equipment and told him that Nurse Chapel wanted the job. By the end of the day, he had everything arranged and set up in the house. The nurse wanted to delay my departure from the hospital until she checked out all the equipment to make sure it was all working as it should. The following morning, she came dressed in street clothes.

"Margaret, everything checks out. Your husband has quite the eye for detail. Everything is brand new! We can transfer you to home today. I've ordered an ambulance to do this. He will meet us there."

"Us?"

"I'll accompany you in the transport."

"Oh, that's lovely, thank you."

"Not at all, I'm on the clock right now. Your husband told me to start tracking my hours yesterday."

"You know, he's not my husband. He's just my boyfriend."

"No, he is not a boyfriend. A boyfriend would not go to such lengths. He is your husband in every way but the ring. And that is a cheap thing, the ring. Everything else is important."

"Thank you. May I have your first name? It feels odd always calling you by your title."

"Yes, Nyota. My first name is Nyota."

"Is that another name from Star Trek?"

"Yes, unfortunately. My parents were big fans, and they named me after Uhura."

I smiled. "It suits you though. They're heroes in my book."

"Thank you, Margaret."

The transfer from the hospital to home went okay. The new hospital bed was set up in the new living room that was empty. All we needed to move were boxes stacked out of the way. The bed was much more comfortable than the one I had at Lakeshore.

Abeo had set up a TV with Internet, Netflix, Prime, and Disney. So I was going to have lots to watch. Nyota was directed to use my bedroom upstairs for her use, and she spent the rest of the afternoon moving in her clothes and necessities.

It was understood that while Abeo was here, she only needed to be available, while other times she would be on duty. That would leave us privacy as well. Since we were still having sex, I was grateful. Abeo assured me that it would not hurt the kids, and judging by their reactions, he was right. We just had to be creative on positions. Currently, being taken from the back was my favorite.

Nyota bid us good evening and went to her room after dinner. Abeo looked at me and his eyes suddenly hooded and started swirling.

"You're looking at me like you want to eat me," I said.

"I do."

"Well, then, let's not waste any time. I don't want you to be hungry."

He picked us up—because I was three—and placed us very carefully on a prepared blanket on the floor of my temporary room. I no longer wore any undergarments, because they just didn't fit. My boobs were huge, and my belly—well, I was the girth of a whisky barrel.

Abeo quickly pulled up the gown I was in, exposing my belly and my center.

"I'm so big, I'm an elephant."

"You are beautiful, you are pregnant, and your body is perfect," he said as he took lotion and started rubbing it all over my big belly. It was soothing and sensual at the same time. Every time his hand got close to the apex of my legs, my coil tightened and I got a little wetter. His hands were large and warm and the lotion slippery and he spread it all over my belly. I could feel the twins move around as his hand moved across my skin. They had a connection already. I could feel them push out with their hands as if reaching for their father, and his hand brushing over their tiny fists.

All the while, he murmured in what I presumed was his native language. I realized that some time ago I didn't recognize the language, and my efforts to find out what it was failed. His voice was musical and hypnotic. I didn't understood the words, yet their meaning was clear. He reserved his language for the children, and I didn't mind in the slightest.

Abeo looked at me and wrapped his arms around my belly and stayed there a minute or two.

"Is that your native tongue?" I asked him.

"Yes."

"What is it?"

"It's an African language," he said. "Now I want to love you too, because you are the vessel that carries them. You must not be neglected." He removed his clothes and knelt by me, then helped me out of the gown entirely. He gently took one of my swollen breasts in his hands and that made me gasp. He gently kissed the nipple one at a time, holding it reverently. He knew it would be very sensitive.

One of his hands slid down and over my belly until it found my mound, spreading the folds with his fingers. He explored the sensitive bundle of nerves and rubbed and pressed down on it until I was panting with desire.

"Abeo, give me more, I need more."

He moved down and knelt between my legs and spread them wide as he buried his face in my slit. His nose was rubbing the area between my vagina and my nub, inhaling the smell of me. When his lips closed around the nub, I screamed out as I nearly climaxed, but his steady sucking instead tightened the coil that was ready to spring open. One of his fingers slipped inside me, rubbing that very sensitive spot, causing my hips to jerk on him. Then another finger joined the first, and he slowly started to finger fuck me. Each time he pushed inside, he sucked on my nub. The gentle pressure of his teeth nearly sent me over the edge again as I sucked in my breath.

He added another finger to my vagina, and the finger fuck became more urgent, thrusting as deep as he could go and sucking on me at the same time. By the time his fourth finger joined in the fun I was about to pop. That did it. As a mighty orgasm exploded out of me, I released myself all over his hand. That had never happened before.

"Ah, my beautiful woman, you came for me, how delicious." He was lapping up the juice like it was wine. "You taste amazing. Now you are wet for me."

"Oh my, am I ever!" I sort of felt delirious, and there was still the feeling of being penetrated in my vagina. When he rolled me over on my side, I didn't know what he would do.

He picked up my top leg and opened me up. I could feel his cock, hot and wet, right at my opening. He was so ready to take me. I could feel him position himself carefully, and push in until his head was inside. A sigh escaped my lips as the feeling of him sliding home took over me. As he pushed in, he got closer. I didn't realize he was on his knees. As his cock reached the end of me, he stilled to let my channel feel him, adapt, and hold him. It was the single most amazing feeling, to be completely full. He was touching the very end of my channel, and my womb was very sensitive. As the two touched, an electrical charge zinged me making me climax again. This time it was a small one, but the waves from it skittered through my body as I shuddered. He tapped me again, and another wave hit me. I could feel the twins move around too. As if they knew their father was closer somehow. I suddenly felt pressure pushing down toward his cock from inside me.

Abeo gently pulled out and thrust back in hitting the end again. Abeo gradually got faster, and as he did, his cock increased in hardness and elongated a bit. My body was all over the place. Arousal and lust were making me very hungry for him.

"Abeo!" I shouted. "Ah. Ah. Harder, deeper!"

He pulled out and thrust all he could in this position. It didn't have the same force. "We need to change positions. Can you get on your hands and knees?"

"Yes," I said, as he helped me to that position. My belly was so big, it nearly brushed the floor. It was like lying on a Pilates ball!

He took hold of my hips and hammered into me, holding nothing back. As he plunged over and over, the heat began to rise again as my body started to crest that wave. My boobs were banging together and banging on my belly, which was now resting on the floor, and my boobs next to it. Still he hammered me; his cock felt like steel as he abused my vagina, and still I wanted more. I couldn't get enough—I started to push against him to add to his force.

And all of a sudden we were there. The orgasm took me. I screamed his name, and the tears of release poured down my face as my body let go. His last thrust had him explode inside me, and I could feel his seed pouring into me. His arms wrapped around my body sitting me up on his cock. His arm was between my boobs and my belly and his face was by my head. He was murmuring to me, even though the words were unintelligible. I felt him lick my neck, and then a sharp pain followed by a floating sensation, as if my blood had just been flooded with a drug.

He held me close as his cock still poured seed into me. My breasts were leaking and dribbling down my belly. I couldn't move, I had no spine, no legs, nothing. My head was drifting high above me, and when I looked down I saw the two of us, me sitting on his lap, impaled with his cock, and his head was on my shoulder, his mouth was wrapped around the muscle in my neck. Then I saw him lift his head and I saw them: fangs, like a vampire's but he wasn't sucking blood out of me. I saw him lick the place where they had impaled me, and the wounds disappeared. Then all I saw was black.

The clock on the wall said 11:03. I blinked. *Wait! I've lost three hours.* It was just after eight when we finished dinner and started to make love. What happened? I checked myself out. I was still lying on the floor. Abeo was spooning me from behind, and his cock was warm and reassuring between my legs. The babies were tripping inside me. I could swear one was doing somersaults. I pressed a hand into my belly and said "Shhhhh, be quiet in there."

He or she stopped for a moment and started some other activity. I reached back and touched Abeo. "Hey, are you awake?"

"Mmm."

"Mmm is not an answer, Abeo."

"Mmm."

"Hey, I need to pee!"

"Oh! Sorry!" He jumped up and helped me upright. It was then I felt all the semen pour out of me like Niagara Falls.

"Oh, you gave me a lot of semen!"

"Wait a minute, let me get something to clean you." He returned a minute later with some hot water, cloths, and towels.

He took great care in cleaning me, inside and out. He even carefully cleaned between my folds.

"Let me help you to the washroom." By the time I was finished, he had the evidence of our heavy sex cleared away. He helped me up into the bed and tucked the blankets around me, kissing my hand.

"I hope it wasn't too rough tonight," he said.

"No, I somehow needed that. My body craved that. It was just right. I think the twins enjoyed it too. They were doing somersaults when I woke up."

"I lost control, and I hadn't meant to."

"Don't blame yourself. I kept asking you to go further, asking for more, so it was both of us. I needed that, and apparently so did you. It was amazing. I don't know how, but sex just keeps betting better. I mean, where do we go from here?"

18—Moving Day

Margaret

While the pregnancy was going well, our new house was having delays. First, the color of the tile we chose was no longer available and we were called in to pick another. Then, they short ordered the hardwood flooring, so they had to get more—and there was a delay due to shortage of that. So we had to change the flooring so they could do it all over again. At least they weren't charging us for this mistake of theirs. So it was touch and go with the house.

The sales agent called to warn us that not everything would be done before we moved in.At least the move date hadn't changed. We would have two weeks in the house before my delivery date.

Abeo had hired a moving company to pack us up a few days before the move. They had been here for the past four days and there were boxes everywhere. They were trying to keep the containers in each room to make it easier to offload at the new house.

"Uh, excuse me, those need to be packed really carefully, please!" I called over to one of the men handling my mother's china. "Those are very special and very fragile!"

"Yes, Mrs. Musa, we're going to pack this carefully."

Making sure the boxes were labeled properly was essential for moving into the new place smoothly. Abeo was going to be away next week. He couldn't avoid it. So it was just me.

Moving day arrived. The old apartment was packed up and transferred to a truck in storage. We got to move into the new house two days later. The landlord wanted me out of the apartment two days before the end of the month so they could clean and paint.

That meant I'd be in a hotel for two nights. When I arrived at the hotel, I thought the man at the front desk was going to have a heart attack when he saw how pregnant I was.

"Mrs. Musa, are you sure you'll be okay alone in the room?" he asked.

"Yes, I'll be fine. My mother is coming to help," I said. I got upstairs, me waddling behind the bellhop who was pushing my luggage. Some kids running down the hall thought it was so funny that I waddled like a penguin. *Just wait, you little brats, until you're so pregnant you cannot walk properly.* When I got upstairs, I ordered food for mom and I. When the food arrived, I yelled to the waiter to come in. He brought in a trolley and I handed him a tip. I wasn't that hungry. I settled myself on the sofa and put my feet up. I wasn't going to move. My mom knocked on the door about an hour later.

"Come in please!" I called out.

"Cavalry to the rescue!" my mom said as she came in. "How are you doing?" she asked me.

"I'm tired, but okay. Abeo will be in tonight. He's bringing the keys to the new house."

"You need sleep," she said. "Here, let me help you into bed." She helped me out of my clothes and into bed, then left and closed the door to my room, and that is the last thing I remember until Abeo woke me up.

My dream was very arousing. I felt two very large hands rubbing my body in all the right spots. I felt them caressing my belly, easing the tension on my skin. I felt them cup my breasts and hold their weight while fingering my nipples. I felt them trace lines up the inside of my legs to the fire between my legs. I was moaning and moving as I felt myself getting hot and wet. I reached for the hands that were heating me up and brought them to my mouth and bit their fingertips. My fangs had popped out and they poked small holes in the fingers, but the wounds disappeared and the owner of the hands groaned in pleasure.

When I felt the happy drug coursing through me, I sighed in pleasure as those very large fingers slipped between the folds of my mound. I opened my legs to invite whoever was doing that to do more. My own hand slid down my body and slipped between the folds, rubbing myself, and our fingers entwined. The heat was almost unbearable and I needed release. The fingers were replaced by his hard shaft and I groaned with delight at the pressure and the feeling of connection. His cock was hot and hard as it pushed life into me and filled me up. I felt my hips being lifted off the ground and I was floating as his cock plunged into me again and again, building up my climax. His hand went back to the bundle of nerves and rubbed it back and forth in rhythm with the dance his cock was doing. My climax was epic as the wave broke over me, sending ripples all across my skin.

"Margaret!" I snapped my eyes open to realize that I was not alone, and Abeo was standing over me.

"Was the dream true?"

"My love, I can make it true again." He was undressed and had been rubbing oils and lotions all over my belly and inside my legs.

"Oh, I need you to take me!"

He helped me to my knees, and sat behind me, with his torso up against mine. His cock was between my legs as he slid his hands in front of me and between my legs.

As he explored my body, I heard a quiet groan from him in my ear. I lifted up and felt him slip his cock inside. It felt like making a familiar connection. Our bodies were linked once more, and that felt right.

A doggystyle position gave him all the control and he used it to fuck me gently and thoroughly, bringing me an orgasm that left me like a massive puddle of jelly and very happy.

"Is that better?" he crooned, after he caught his breath.

"Mmmm hmmm," I murmured. "I really needed that after today."

"Happy to oblige." Abeo curled around my body and we fell asleep like that.

Something woke me up suddenly. When I opened my eyes, I was alone in bed, and the covers were over top of me. So I have no idea what it was.

Did I imagine Abeo coming in last night?

Getting up, I waddled to the outer room to find my mom watching TV and eating breakfast.

"Good morning, sunshine," said my mom. "It's moving day! Coffee is made over there, some breakfast food is on the table, and Abeo went to the house to supervise the movers."

"Coffee … I need coffee." I stretched my back when I stood, but the twins were moving around a lot. "Did you kids have fun last night?" I asked them, as I ran my hands across the stretched skin. I felt them move around like they were playing soccer or something.

"Mom, did Abeo come in last night?"

"I heard him come in very late, then leave again before sunrise," she answered. "So did you two have fun last night?"

"Mom!"

"Just saying."

"I remember having a dream. I thought it was all a dream."

"No, there were some very real parts," she said.

I left my mother smirking to go have my shower. My mother had a healthy dirty mind. She was still sexually active, even though contemplating that was a little nauseating for me. *No one wants to think about their parents having sex. Ewww!* She was not a prude either, willing to speak on just about anything.

My phone rang and I reached out of the shower to get it.

"Hi, love," said Abeo. "Oh, I can hear a shower. Are you all wet and naked?"

"Yes, I am," I said. "Can everyone hear you?"

"No, I'm in the car by myself. The truck is on the way to the house."

"Yeah! I'll meet you there."

"Got it."

I felt awake once I was dressed after my shower. I had on a spring-green knit mini dress that hugged my curves. I had never bothered with undergarments. Frankly, they were uncomfortable when you were this pregnant. Naked was so much better. People showed off their baby bumps now, so who was I to be shy about it? Of course, I didn't have a "bump." I had a Pilates ball.

When I got to the house, I parked my car down the street past the only other house on the street. I heard Abeo inside, directing traffic. I stood there watching for a few minutes. The moving guys whistled at me as they carried the stuff inside.

Abeo came out and I could see my dress had just the right effect on him. "Margaret, oh my God you are sexy today," he said as he stood behind me. "Your body is so curvy and sexy. I just want to slip my hand under your dress and bury my fingers in your pussy," he whispered into my ear when he was close enough so that our bodies were leaning against each other.

I purred at him, turning my head just enough that he could see my neck stretch. "Bite me."

Abeo growled low and shifted his pants. "Oh, you get me so hard."

"You get me so wet," I countered. "I cannot wait until we can christen the new house. I wore this especially for the occasion."

"I can smell your arousal, love," he said, pressing into me. His hand slipped under the bottom edge of my dress and snaked its way to my hot, wet, center. When it got there, a deep groan whispered from his lips: "Oh, you are so wet." He removed his fingers and licked them, all while looking me in the eye with those swirling irises.

"Abeo stop!" I whispered, even as I pressed myself against his hand. "You'll get me, but wait until we're alone!"

He licked his lips. "Waiting, knowing what's underneath. I'll be scenting your arousal all day, and it will drive me mad." Abeo growled with anticipation as he turned his face away from me.

"I can wait." I answered, and then pulled away. My own body was ready to jump him right there. Holding hands, we both turned and looked toward the house.

19—New Neighbors

Falon

I was watering the plants in my front window when I spotted moving trucks on the street.

"Mark! The new people are moving into the house across the street. This is exciting! We'll have new neighbors."

"Nice, perhaps we'll get to meet them later today."

"I'll watch for a while." I finished my plant watering and sat in my reading chair by the window with a book, looking forward to watching them move in. Perhaps I would get a glimpse of the people who bought the model home. It had to be a family, because the house was huge, with at least five bedrooms. But so far there were only the movers taking things out of the truck and into the house.

A few delivery trucks also arrived, and that was an interesting dance. Clearly, they had purchased new furniture and had it delivered. There wasn't enough room for the delivery trucks though with the moving truck in the way, so there was this truck ballet that happened each time.

Mid morning, a very handsome man in a very expensive car parked down the street. He reminded me of a celebrity because he walked with such grace. After he went inside, another car showed up five minutes later and parked in front of our house. A very pregnant woman struggled to get out of the vehicle, and stood on the muddy street, adjusting her very form-fitting dress first and grabbing a heavy sweater from inside the car. The dress was a lovely shade of green and it certainly complemented her complexion and auburn hair. But, oh my God, she looked like she was carrying a litter! I continued watching as the man came out to meet her. He guided her up onto the grass and out of the snow- and mud-covered street. At least she was wearing low boots. There wasn't much snow on our front lawn.

It must have been her husband, because they became quite intimate standing there in front of my house. His hand slid down to her leg and then around to the front of her. It stayed there a moment caressing her as they were engaged in visual conversation. You know, the kind that a couple speaks with their eyes? Thoughts whipped back and forth between them, then he slipped his hand under her hemline between her legs. Her reaction was priceless: a big grin as her lips opened and her tongue flicked out.

His reaction was even more interesting. He nuzzled her neck and then turned his face away. Fangs had elongated out of his mouth, and his eyes were glowing. She said something to him, and he removed his hand. They parted a little and his control on his fangs and eyes returned; they blinked out of existence before turning back to look at her face.

"Oh my!" I murmured quietly to myself.

"What was that? Did you say something to me?" asked Mark.

"Umm, the new neighbors just put on quite the show. I think they thought they were alone."

"What kind of a show?"

"Sexual."

"In broad daylight?"

"Yup. That's not all. Mark, he has fangs."

"Did you say *fangs*?"

"Yup. They were all hot and heavy like, deeply looking into each other's eyes, when he slid his hand under her dress." Mark had joined me, standing behind the curtain at the window.

"Wow! She's really pregnant," he said.

"No kidding. He clearly touched her sensitive spot, because both of them reacted. His fangs elongated, and to cover that up, he hugged her and turned his head away from her—toward our house. So I had a clear view of them and his glowing eyes. She may not know."

"And she's pregnant with his kids," he answered. "Do you think he's one of us?"

"I'll find out. She must be a human."

"He's not part of my family."

"Let me go out and introduce myself."

"Why don't you go over and offer help from us?" asked Mark. I'm sure with all those deliveries, they're going to have some assembling to do. She won't be able to help while pregnant."

"Oh, that's a great idea."

Grabbing a coat because it was December, I picked my way across the road, which was covered with snow and mud from construction vehicles. While it wasn't a cold December, it was still chilly enough to need a light coat. I got across the street, but they didn't have a lawn or a driveway to walk on. More importantly, the truck occupied the only semi-dry part of the property right now.

"Hello there! I'm Falon Robertson—we're your neighbors across the street. Welcome to the neighborhood!"

The couple turned around, startled for a moment, before they found their voices.

"Oh, hello. We figured everyone was at work and we were alone," said the woman. "Hi, my name is Margaret Thistle, and this is my husband, Abeo Musa."

"Pleased to meet you both. My husband and I work from home, so we're always here. Say, would you like to come to our place and have some coffee? You can watch the movers from there while staying warm."

"Oh, that's awfully generous of you, but I'd better go and manage where they are putting everything," said Abeo. "But my wife could use a seat."

"It's okay, Abeo," said Margaret.

"Go and relax, I'll manage this and call you when the men have left. That way we can walk through the house in peace."

"If you insist," she said, turning to me. "I'm all yours.".

"Come on, I'll introduce you to my husband," I said. "When are you due?"

"In about a week."

"Had you meant to call it this close? Moving and giving birth—wow, talk about being busy!" I said.

"I know, eh?" said Margaret. "No, the house was supposed to have been ready two months ago." I opened the front door for her and she stepped inside.

"Oh, your house is lovely!" she said.

"Thank you. We didn't need a big place, and this is perfect for us to have a home office each. Come in by the fire. I'll get some coffee."

Mark walked out of the kitchen at that moment, carrying a tray with mugs of coffee, cream, sugar, and cookies.

"Margaret, this is my husband, Mark Chisholm. Thanks, hun, for bringing coffee service."

"My pleasure. Hello, Margaret, nice to meet you."

"Pleased to meet you too, Mark."

We all sat down and silently sipped our coffee for a few minutes. The fire was roaring as much as a gas fireplace could, but it was a nice radiant heat.

"So, Margaret, you're due in a week. Any idea what you're having?" I asked.

"Yes, twins. One of each. That's why I look like a Pilates ball."

Laughing, I said, "Not quite, but close. It must be heavy carrying around two full-term babies."

"Oh yes, I've been exhausted for the past three months. Mostly bedridden. We had a scare at eight months and I had to quit work."

"No kidding. I don't think I could have done that."

Margaret's phone rang, and I could hear her husband telling her the movers were done and gone. "I'll be waddling away now," she said as she got off the phone. "As soon as we're set up, I'll have you over for dinner."

"That didn't take long. It was a pleasure to meet you two. And welcome to our street!"

I watched her waddle up to the garage door and go inside. *She's right about the waddling, she looks like a penguin!* I thought. I picked up my book again and sat back down to read by the window. Several hours later, the doorbell rang. I saw that it was Margaret.

"Hello again. Do you need help?"

"Maybe. The movers have gone and we're going to the hotel. I thought I'd let you know we'll be back tomorrow morning."

"Have you got everything moved in?"

"Yes, everything is in, but I could really use some help unpacking after all. There are some more deliveries to come as well. And Abeo has to leave for a business trip, so it's just me. Bending over is just not in the cards."

"No problem," I said, chuckling. "I will get my husband to come and help. He's useful for putting things away high up." Mark popped into the room at that moment.

"Did I hear that someone needed some help?"

"Oh! You've got good hearing!" said Margaret.

"One of his many special attributes," I said.

"How about we start tomorrow morning. I'm rather bagged and I have a hotel room for tonight."

"We'll grab some tools, garbage bags, and other things we know we need from experience, and come over for say 10:00?"

"That's perfect. Thank you so much."

The following morning was a Saturday, so we weren't working. I made a big breakfast for Mark and me, and we fueled up before meeting Margaret. As soon as we saw her car drive up, we walked over.

"Good morning!" I said, when she opened the door. Going inside, I said, "Oh, this is a lovely layout. It has a nice flow to it."

"We preferred the squarer layout rather than a front-to-back split," said Margaret.

"I can see what you mean. Feels like more space."

"Come, we'll start in the kitchen."

"Oh yes, the kitchen is the first place to unpack. Always!"

"So can we be nosy about each other?" asked Margaret.

"Go ahead, we're an open book!"

"What do you two do to be able to work from home?"

"Mark is an investment banker. They invest in different businesses, help get new ideas off the ground, that sort of thing. I manage a charity called the Tiny House Project. How about you guys?"

"I was just an admin, working for a big conglomerate. I've quit my job so that when the twins are born I can be a full-time mom. I get mat-leave for the first six months, so that is something. Abeo is also a banker—international. His bank does foreign investment too, so he's traveling all over the world wherever the money needs to go."

"That sounds fascinating. How did you two meet? How long have you been together?"

"You'll love this! In a bar about four years ago! Who meets anyone meaningful in a bar these days? It's such an old cliché."

"Oh my, that is funny. We met in a bar too!"

The three of us laughed at the coincidence of it all.

"Abeo and I were just a hook-up at first. Then we met again three years later and spent six glorious weeks together. O-M-G, the sex was outstanding, like the best sex I have ever had in my life!" Margaret gushed. Mark and I looked at each other.

"I know what you mean. Something very similar happened to us too," I said. "Right down to the instant attraction and ground-shaking sex."

"Perhaps I should go to another room and start on larger items, ladies?" asked Mark. I glanced at him and he was just a tiny bit pink. "I mean, if you're going to talk about our prowess, I shouldn't be here."

Margaret and I looked at each other and burst out laughing again. Girls talked openly, while guys did not.

"Perhaps that is best, then we can dish," I said. Margaret smiled wide. I had the feeling we could be good friends. I didn't know if she had a friend with whom she could dish these kinds of things to. I had Lora, and it was important and fun to be able to share things like that.

"Mark, there are beds to put together upstairs. Would you mind?" asked Margaret.

"Not at all. Beds are my specialty," he said with a wolfish grin on his face. I groaned and did a facepalm. That was a little too close to the truth. *Sigh.*

Margaret caught a different meaning for the joke and went bright pink as Mark left the kitchen.

"When did you know?" she asked me.

"Know what?"

"Know that he was the one you wanted to spend the rest of your life with?"

"Oh, almost immediately. The moment I saw him, there was a pull between us, something inevitable about it, that drew me to him like a moth to a flame. I really couldn't stop myself. I must admit I was smitten at first sight."

"You too?" she asked. "I didn't think that happened in real life, yet it happened to me, and I've been questioning it ever since. I had that exact same feeling when I saw Abeo."

"What happened?"

Margaret went on to tell me about their first night, in lovely detail. I was shocked at how closely it aligned with my own story. Not the sex, because we didn't have sex immediately, at least not with Zisis. With Mark, it wasn't until he came to visit me. Then we couldn't keep our hands off each other. The other part of her story that rang all kinds of bells was the fact that he disappeared, and had a job that would keep him away for long periods at a time. My immortal sense was tingling. Could we have found another immortal?

Margaret was describing her negotiations with Abeo and how he wanted to be part of their lives, so he had purchased this house for them all to live together. I hoped for her sake that he meant that and would not be away more than he was present. Twins were challenging, especially at first.

"What about you?" she asked.

"Well, Mark and I met in New York, while I was stranded there because of the weather. He saw me, I saw him, and it was an instant connection. He came and had dinner with me, we danced, and I so wanted him to jump me, but he was a gentleman that first night. He dropped me off at my room and gave me a kiss goodnight but wouldn't come in. The following morning we met at the elevator, I gave him my number—*hint, hint*—and I was gone."

"Then three months later he came to Montreal for a business trip. I met him at his hotel room and we couldn't keep our hands off each other. And yes, oh my God, the sex was mind blowing. He actually tipped me."

"Tipped you?" asked Margaret.

"Yeah, his term for being able to fill me completely and hit the end of my channel and touch my womb."

"I've heard that term from Abeo. How could that be?"

"Huh! I don't know. Maybe there is a club for extra-large guys where they share the secrets of tipping women?" I asked sarcastically.

"Maybe!" said Margaret. "Abeo does that to me. I've never had a man fill me completely before. It's such an amazing feeling."

"Oh my, yes, and once you've got that, there isn't anything else."

"Tell me about it. I joked to Abeo that he had spoiled me for the rest of the human race. He asked me if there was another species I was considering."

I laughed, but I understood his question, I think. "Did you give him suggestions?"

"No, but horses came to mind," she said, laughing hilariously.

I joined in with her. Our immortal men might be able to compete with a horse. I was convinced now, it was just a question of proof. I need to get Lora in on this.

"You've got to meet my best friend, Lora. I think we'll all get along smashingly. She lives close by too. We should get together for a girls' night. I haven't had one of those in ages!"

"Oh, that would be so nice. I haven't had many girl friends, and it would be nice to have two. But let's leave that till after these twins are born."

"No! You won't have a life after that—not for a year at least. Now is the better time. We'll take care of you, don't worry. Lora is a mom of three."

"Okay, but it will have to be soon. I'm about ready to drop these children off at a bus station!"

20—House Christening

Margaret

Two days later, we finally were alone and had the house to ourselves. There were boxes everywhere but it didn't matter. I found the box with the linens and brought down two large blankets that Abeo spread out in front of the fireplace. I hung a sheet on the front window to give us some privacy in the living room.

He turned to me and drank in my shape.

"Oh God, woman, those curves are driving me wild. I must have you. Let's christen the house, shall we?"

I nodded. He picked us up—because I contained two—and placed us very carefully on a prepared blanket on the floor in our new living room. My boobs were huge, and my belly—well, I was still the girth of a whisky barrel.

Abeo gazed at me lovingly, as he quickly pulled up my dress over my head, exposing my body. I always wore knit dresses these days. They were easy to put on and take off, and they were comfortable.

"I'm so big, I'm an elephant," I said.

"You are not an elephant. You're beautiful, you are pregnant, and your body is perfect," he said as he took lotion and started rubbing it all over my big belly. It was soothing and sensual at the same time. He covered every inch of me, paying particular attention to my very sensitive nipples and the overstretched skin on my belly.

He loved me, making me feel like a goddess, and oh so special. We lay side by side by the crackling fire and drifted off on a pillow of warmth and happiness. He had his arm wrapped around my belly, his palm flat against the tight skin, feeling for his children to kick. My head was lying on his outstretched arm, while his warm breath tickled my neck. I fell asleep by his side.

I awoke after the sun had set. It was dark in the house except for the firelight. Abeo had left my side and replaced his arm with a pillow and covered me with a blanket. He walked back in the room and smiled at me. Then he joined me on the floor again and let me sit between his legs and lean against him while he leaned against the wall.

"For two days," he murmured, "I have been watching you and your beautiful curves in that green dress. I'm glad we got to christen the house."

"Me too. I don't know how, but sex just keeps getting better. I mean, where do we go from here?"

"Did you feel any different?"

"What do you mean different? Like you were much deeper?"

"I was tipping you. But the force I was using didn't hurt you?"

"No ... did you bite me?"

"Yes, I did. It's a sexual response I tend to suppress, but this time I was too far gone, my mind wasn't here, just the animal. Sorry about that."

"You didn't leave a mark, did you?" I asked. "Some guys get off on biting and leaving marks, that's not cool."

"No, I didn't leave a mark."

"You know, if I wasn't already pregnant, I'm absolutely positive this night I would have. You have a potent cock. I just love it too."

We sat in silence for a minute listening to each other breathe.

"Abeo, we haven't decided names for our twins," I started. "I still like Joseph and Stephanie."

"I would like to honor African heritage. My grandfather was called Abimbola—it means 'born to be wealthy' and is meant to be a good omen. My great-grandmother was named Keyshia. It means 'favorite of everyone,' and means she will be well loved."

"I like those names too. Can we add my names too, so they have a choice what to use in school?"

"Do you think those names would bring ridicule in North America? What are you thinking?"

"No, just to give them names from my family as well. Joseph would be after my grandfather, and Stephanie after my mother."

"I like that very much. Abimbola Joseph Musa and Keyshia Stephanie Thistle."

"Why give them different last names?"

"It is tradition among my people to name the boys after their father's line and the girls after their mother's line."

"It's different, but I like that too," I said. "Okay, let's do that."

21—New Immortal?

Lora

Rick and I were sitting down to dinner. Anita usually fed the kids first so they could get their homework done.

"Hey, guess what?"

"What?"

"I got a call from Falon today, with some fascinating news: she has a new neighbor and the guy may be an immortal!"

"Really?" asked Rick. "How would she know that?"

"She says their story lines up with ours: instant attraction, best sex ever, deep penetration, guy not around much, you know, the things we all have in common."

"We should get to know them and perhaps bring them into our group."

"You think?"

"Well, if she's right, then being friends with her will be a bonus for her, because she'll have real friends that understand."

"Good point. And if he's not, then being friends with us could prove to be a security risk we cannot afford."

"Right," said Rick.

"I'm meeting them for lunch tomorrow. It should be interesting."

The following day, I was primping and worrying about what to wear, which is ridiculous, really—why should it matter? It never had before. Somehow, I had a feeling this introduction would be different, special somehow.

"Wear your red dress," suggested my daughter.

"I think that is too dressy for lunch at Falon's," I said.

"Just jeans and your green top, then. It sets off your eyes, Mom."

"Good idea, hun. Thanks."

Arriving at Falon's a few minutes later, I stepped out of the car and into mud and snow. "Argh! I should have worn boots! I can't wait until this street is finished!" I heard the front door open, and Falon laughed as I walked up the drive to the porch.

"No time soon, my dear. Don't worry about the mud, you can take your shoes off and run around barefooted."

"My kind of party!" I said with a smile. "Will the boys be joining us too?"

"Unfortunately, not this time, it's a girls-only party. Gwen is on her way."

"Perfect," I said as I took off my shoes. "We get to have dirty conversations about our boys when they're not around."

Just then we heard a car horn honk. "I wonder who would do that?" asked Falon. "I'll go check."

In the meantime, I walked back to the kitchen and poured myself a cup of coffee and went and sat in the family room. A few minutes later, Falon came rushing back inside and yelled, "Gwen's gone into labor! I called 911 and the ambulance is taking her to Lakeshore. I'm on my way over to keep her company."

"Oh my God. What can I do?" I asked.

"Can you wait for Margaret?"

"Yes, then I'll follow you to the hospital."

"Thank you! Oh, I've called Andrews."

"Well, that's a development," I said to myself out loud. "I guess I'll wait for Margaret to arrive then go home." It wasn't long before the doorbell rang. I set my cup down and answered the door. My jaw dropped.

I knew the woman instantly. We had gone to school together as girls. We hadn't really been friends but we chummed around a little. Margaret had been an awkward girl. Not that I was a member of the A crowd, but we didn't move in similar circles.

"Lora!" squealed Margaret. "As I live and breathe, it's Lora O'Reilly! Oh my God, it's been so long!"

"Maggie! Maggie Thistle—how is this you?" I screamed. We were both jumping up and down squealing in delight—well, I was jumping, Maggie not so much.

"Wow, you are the last person I expected to show up here," I said. "Come in and let's chat. There is a development I need to let you know."

"What's that?" asked Margaret.

"We were going to introduce you to three of us—we're all friends and we all live nearby, sort of a welcome-to-the-neighborhood party."

"That's awfully nice of you. Thanks. But where is Falon?"

"That's the development. Falon is on the way to the hospital to be with the other girl, Gwen, who just went into labor."

"Oh, she's pregnant too? How interesting."

"Yes. It's a neat coincidence. Anyway, we'll have to postpone this party for a few days, I guess."

"That's alright," said Margaret, as her face started to turn red.

"Are you okay?" I asked.

"I don't know, I just got the most awful twinge in my back."

"Twinge as in pain?"

"Yes, kind of a rolling pain."

"That's a contraction," I said. "Oh! You're starting your labor too! Do you need help?"

"No thanks, I'll call Abeo. I will go back home and wait for him."

"Are you sure? Maybe I should walk you back."

"It's okaaaay," she said as another pain happened.

"It's not okay. Let me call 911 for you."

"Alright, but Abeo needs to be told."

"Give me his number and I'll let him know for you."

"Thankssssssssss," she hissed while enduring another contraction. "You better hurry up with that ambulance. I think these kids want out now."

"On it."

22—Surprise!

Gwen

My due date was in a couple of weeks. I was huge, heavy, and feeling crappy. Wintertime is not a nice time to give birth. It's miserable, cold, and hard to get around—you need to put on boots! Still, it had been a long time to be this big and heavy. I was lucky, the pregnancy had gone well. Nothing had happened that had been a surprise, which was good. You didn't want surprises during a pregnancy. Andrews had been the perfect daddy-to-be, getting me everything I needed— massages when my back hurt, rubbing my feet at night, and bone-removing sex when I was tense.

We moved into our new house two months ago—a new house that was finished not too far from Mark and Falon. Andrews was correct, it was nice to have a house with a yard. It wasn't a large house, four bedrooms, but it would give us space to grow. We managed to just get the nursery set up and finished last night. There was still some painting to do in some of the rooms, but all in all the house was just what we wanted.

We didn't have to move much, because we left the condo furnished for Duffy. We decided to go shopping for new furniture for the new house. It was fun looking at decor together and getting things we both loved. It turned out, we both liked a homey feel and natural colors. Everything, including all the new baby stuff, was delivered directly to the new house, saving us a bundle in mover's fees. All we needed to move were clothes and small items.

Andrews had been a wonderful mate. The baby had been very active, a boy, and I could swear he was playing football inside me. The doctor said all that was normal. He was a big baby, and that was why I was so big. I felt like a house now. Andrews had to help me up off my ass when I needed to stand up from a chair. Getting in and out of bed was a challenge too. Once I was lying down, it was fine, but getting back up again? I felt like a beached whale. I spent a lot of time lying down. These last few weeks of my pregnancy, Andrews had stayed home to help me.

A month ago, not long after we moved in, I got the strangest call from Falon.

I was sitting in the family room reading when I heard my phone ring. *Damn! I left my phone in the kitchen.* I struggled to get up, and by the time I got to the phone, it had stopped ringing. Looking at the display, I saw that it was Falon, so I sat back down on a chair and called her back.

"Falon speaking."

"It's Gwen. You rang?"

"Yes! How are you doing?"

"I'm doing okay. Sorry I missed your call, but I didn't have my phone with me. It takes so long for me to get up. I can't wait until I deliver this baby!"

"Sorry to have disturbed you. But I have some exciting news! We have met a new immortal!" cried Falon.

"What do you mean?"

"New people moved in across the street yesterday. The man is immortal. I saw his fangs."

"The woman isn't?"

"I don't know. Possibly. She's very pregnant—with twins!"

"Oh my God, I feel huge with one baby, I can't imagine two!"

"Lora and I are going to visit her before her due date and get the scoop," said Falon. "Would you like to join us?"

"I would love to. When and where?"

"We've planned a lunch at my place tomorrow. Lora is coming too. That way she can meet three new ladies that live close by at once."

"Sounds like a plan. See you tomorrow!" I said.

Except that didn't happen.

The next morning, the day of the luncheon, while I was on my way over to Falon's house, I went into labor. The first contraction took me by surprise of course. Gasping with the pain, I pulled over to the side of the road and took a deep breath, waiting for the pain to subside. I timed when the next one started—it was only twenty minutes, so I figured I had time. Andrews was downtown working so I called him first. Since I was almost at Falon's, I continued to her house.

I parked my car in Falon's driveway and opened the car door. As I tried to stand up, another contraction gripped me, making me scream out. Holding on to the steering wheel, I sat there gasping for breath. I inadvertently touched the horn, and startled myself when the car let out a blast. Laughing at myself because it was like the car had a contraction, I sat back down in my seat as another contraction happened. They were speeding up. I saw Falon come running out of the house and stopped when she realized what was happening.

"Gwen, I'm calling 911 immediately."

"No, I think I'll go home."

"Gwen, isn't this early?" cried Falon. "You cannot do this by yourself."

"No, not really, but I'll be happy to have him out. Can you get a hold of Andrews for me?"

I heard sirens approaching from a distance and took another deep breath as a contraction doubled me up. The flashing lights of the ambulance stopped and suddenly there were two people helping me out of the car and onto a stretcher.

I overheard Falon speaking to one of the EMTs. "Of course."

They bundled me into the back of the ambo, and just before the door shut I heard, "Excuse me, which hospital are you taking her to?" asked Falon.

"Lakeshore."

"I will follow."

All I saw was the back of the ambo as the EMT got in beside me. I felt the vehicle starting to roll. Looked out the back windows, I saw intersections and lights zipping by.

"It's going to be okay," said the EMT. "We'll get you to the hospital in five minutes. How far apart are your contractions?"

"I don't know. They were twenty minutes but they sped up."

"Okay, when is your due date?"

"Sometime around now," I said.

"That is not a problem. Just try to relax and work with your body's contractions, okay?"

"Okay."

"Your friend will meet you at the hospital. Can your husband be there too?"

"Falon is going to call him for me. He's downtown."

"Who is your doctor?"

"Koby, Ryan Koby."

"He will be notified as soon as you get checked in," said the EMT. "And there we are, we're here. It will be just a minute and we'll have you out of the truck and into Emerg."

"Wow, that was fast!"

My gurney was wheeled right into the hospital. Three nurses met the EMTs and leaped into action. All the same questions were asked and answered, and they whisked me off to the obstetrics ward. I was "checked in," and onto a bed in about twenty minutes, with all kinds of monitors working. A doctor came in to check on me who was not my doctor.

"Hi there, I'm Dr. Mason. Dr. Koby is not available right now, although he does have privileges at this hospital. I'll take your case until he can get here, okay?"

"Okay."

"So Gwen, is it? You're about one week short of your due date?"

"Yes. I had a sonogram about two weeks ago. The baby was healthy and ahead of schedule in terms of development. He is also a big boy."

"Usually that means we got the date of conception wrong when that happens," he said, with a condescending smile.

"I'm pretty sure we didn't get that date wrong."

"I'm pretty sure you did," he mansplained. "Anyway, let's do another now, and see what's happening, shall we?"

Falon came running in the room at that moment.

"Gwen, I'm here!"

"I'm sorry, miss, only immediate family."

"I am immediate family. She's my sister," said Falon. "I'm here until her husband gets here."

"Very well, please be quiet and sit over in the corner," said Dr. Asshole. Falon gave me a scrunched-up face to show her displeasure at the rude doctor. I couldn't help myself, I broke up laughing.

After the sonogram, he seemed even more puffed up and "right."

"Well, your baby is fully developed and is coming today. There doesn't seem to be anything wrong, so we'll let nature take its course, shall we?"

"I guess. How long do you think?"

"This is your first? It will probably will be sometime before we get to the good part. So relax, and I'll have a nurse check in on you periodically. If your contractions change in any way, alert the nurses."

"Very good, Doctor," I said, and watched him leave the room. Falon came and jumped on the bed beside me.

"Lora was at the house when you arrived, so she is waiting for Margaret, and they'll come to visit together," said Falon.

"So tell me about this Margaret!"

Falon dropped her voice to almost a whisper, which we could hear of course, but no one else could.

"Well, they were moving into the house across the street from us. It's been under construction for four or five months now, so I think there were delays. Anyway, a woman got out of a car and she was standing on our side of the street watching the activity of the movers when her husband came out of the house to join her. I saw him get hooded eyes and slip his hand under her dress—which was very form fitting and sexy—and I could tell by the look on her face that he was touching her there on the street in front of our house. They exchanged words, heated but not angry, then he hugged her ferociously and turned his face away from her and toward our house. Then I saw his eyes swirling and his fangs elongate. They continued to hug and she was lifting her leg and grinding into him, until he got control of his fangs, and he kissed her hard. Then they turned to look at the house again together. The whole display was only a few minutes, but it was intense and he had fangs."

"We are intense, that's for sure," I said.

"No kidding. Anyway, I went out to introduce myself and welcome them to the neighborhood. She is so pregnant she makes you look like four months."

"Really?"

"She's having twins," she said. "And she is about to drop them. Her due date is next week too."

Just then, a big commotion happened outside in the hallway as a gurney and a group of medical staff wheeled an extremely pregnant woman on her way to a delivery room.

"That looked like Margaret!" said Falon. "Let me go check."

Now wouldn't that be a coincidence for both of us to have our babies on the same day?

Falon came back a few minutes later all excited. "Yes, it was Margaret. You're having your babies on the same day!"

"Wow! Oh, oh … ah … oh God that hurts!" I yelled as another contraction took me. Then another, as I felt my body forcibly trying to move my baby down to the doorway. "Andrews, you and your big huge wonderful dick did this to me!" I muttered under my breath. "Well, if you can fit going in, this should fit coming out! Oh God!"

I screamed as another contraction—it felt like about seven on the Richter scale—took me again. They were getting stronger and closer together. I grabbed Falon's hand and squeezed her thumb. *It's a good thing she's immortal now too. Otherwise, I would have broken her hand.* Lora walked in as well and threw down her bags and came and helped me.

Together, the three of us weathered the contractions, and Lora had me breathing, because strangely, my instinct was to hold my breath during the pain. *Is that why they teach you how to breathe?*

My contractions were about three minutes apart now, and very heavy and long. I could feel the baby being pushed into my channel. It felt like I really needed to poop. My legs instinctively opened to let him out.

Andrews arrived too. He took the front position, taking over from Falon. She went and told the nurses that my contractions were about three minutes apart.

The nurse came in and lifted up my sheet and checked my body.

"Okay, you're dilated about eight cm now. That's very good. That didn't take long at all. We'll prep you for delivery, which may happen in the next hour or so."

"I want to see. May I?" asked Andrews once the nurse had left.

"Of course, my love. You put him in there. It's your purview to see what is happening," I said sarcastically.

He looked anyway. "I don't see anything."

"I believe you have to wait until my cervix is entirely open at ten cm before you will see anything," I said. "I was doing research."

Dr. Asshole came in just then and looked at all the people in my room.

"Okay, you can stay," he said, pointing at Andrews. "The rest of you wait in the room at the end of the hall."

Lora and Falon gave him the evil eye and walked out with their stuff, leaving Andrews sitting by my side.

"Okay, let's take a look, shall we?"

He did his thing, and said, "Wow, that is a quick baby. You'll be at full dilation shortly. So we will get you prepped and ready for delivery. Sir, are you going to want to be there?"

"Yes, of course," said Andrews.

"Well, you need to come with the scrub nurse and they'll get you ready too."

"Bye, honey, I'll see you soon," he said, leaving with the doctor.

Nurses came in and did stuff to me. I'm not sure what. One of them was to give me the epidural. That wouldn't last long for me, so I'd just have to bear it. No pun intended. I think they shaved me too, and washed me. That felt nice. Then I was being pushed into an OR and draped with all kinds of sheets.

My contractions were almost nonstop at this point. Every time my body wanted to push, I joined in and helped. So it actually didn't take long before the baby was in the doctor's hands and they were checking him out and washing him off.

When they came and put him on my chest, I nearly cried. He was so beautiful, just like his father. The milk chocolate color of his skin glowed against mine. There were tears in Andrews's eyes, too, as he gazed at the two of us. He kissed me, then our son before he was escorted out of the OR.

"Ms. Mitchell, they're going to take your son, weigh him, do the measurements, and get him dressed. They 'll bring him to you for his first feeding in your room shortly. Okay?"

"Yes." I couldn't really speak. I didn't have any thoughts going through my head other than *That's my son! I have a son!*

A little later, Falon and Lora were allowed back in my room. All four of us were there chatting when they brought in my baby.

"Here you go, here's your son, and he's hungry!" said the nurse.

They placed him on my chest and he immediately started searching around for a breast.

"Huh! Just like his dad, always looking for a breast!" I joked. I opened up the hospital gown and brought my breast to his mouth. He latched on with a good strong bite. "Ow! You little bugger! That hurt!"

Andrews laughed that time. "I guess he doesn't have my touch yet."

"Not at all!" I smiled. It took a few minutes before the milk started flowing, but he didn't give up. He was like a little vacuum cleaner. Once he was finished, the nurse came in and took him away.

"We're going to set him up in his bassinet and bring him back to stay for the day. He'll spend the night in the nursery, but we'll bring him back for feeding. We suggest you get some sleep," said the nurse. "That means you guys should leave and let her sleep."

"Aye-aye, captain," said Lora. "Actually, you'll want to sleep. We'll come back tomorrow, okay?"

"Bye! Thanks for being here," I said as they filed out of the room. I suddenly felt overwhelmingly tired. How strange. I closed my eyes and everything went black.

23—Bundles of Joy

Lora

We left Gwen to sleep. Andrews, Falon and I walked partway out of the ward.

"Wait, Falon, should we check on Margaret while we're here?" I asked.

"Won't hurt. Let's go to the baby nursery."

The three of us turned around and walked back down the hall and past Gwen's room to the nursery with the big windows. There were at least twenty babies in there, all color coded in pink or blue. The last names of the babies were written on cards on the ends of the clear bassinets. I spotted Andrews's baby, right next to the window first. He was adorable in his little blue cap.

"There is your baby, Andrews," I said, pointing him out. "Do you have a name for him yet?"

"No, we haven't discussed names, strange. He is beautiful, isn't he?" said Andrews.

"He is indeed," said Falon. "Oh look, there, on the other side, I see Musa."

We all moved to the other side; there were two bassinets marked with Thistle. A pink and a blue. "Oh, they are beautiful too. Look at them, so tiny," I said.

"I'm not sure they are tiny. Andrews's baby is big," I said "He was ten pounds! They look about seven or eight pounds, which is big for twins. That's like having a fourteen-pound baby in your belly!"

"At least they delivered okay. We'll stop in and see them both tomorrow," said Falon. "Andrews, are you staying?"

"I'm going to go and get some food for Gwen and come back to the hospital," said Andrews.

"We'll see you tomorrow, then," I said. "Falon, shall we go find Margaret?"

"Yes!"

We walked down the hall toward the nurses' station to ask where Margaret's room would be.

"She's in the other wing, room 2434," said the nurse on duty.

"Thanks," I said. "On the way over there, let me give you some background."

"Oh?" asked Falon.

"I knew Margaret in school. She was kind of a loner and didn't have a lot of friends. I would hang out with her sometimes because I liked her, but she didn't fit in with my friends at all."

"Why not?" asked Falon.

"She was a little too 'goody two-shoes' for them," I explained. "She always had her homework done, never missed a class. She didn't drink or smoke. She was a model student. She was smart, very smart, and that didn't sit well with a lot of people. She always had the answer. I didn't mind. I thought it was cool to have someone that was so smart as a friend. But it rubbed most people the wrong way."

"Hmm, I can appreciate that. I was like that in school too. Unpopular. I was definitely part of the 'D' crowd."

"Well, she didn't seem to be part of any crowd," I said. "During the summer, she and I got pretty close because there weren't school friends around. She was always interested in subjects like the paranormal, aliens, and magic. We would talk for hours about it. She loved archaeology and believed the scientific community was dead wrong about the civilization of people She believed that there were much earlier civilizations and there was evidence to support it. She would spend hours poring over books and watching documentaries. We also clicked on volcanoes. I loved everything about volcanoes, and we would watch both fiction and non-fiction volcano movies. We had a bucket list item for taking a volcano tour one day."

"So what happened?" asked Falon. "How did you lose contact?"

"I'm not really sure, it just happened. School ended, we didn't see each other anymore. She went to college, I didn't, new crowd, new friends. No real single reason, really."

"It'll be nice to reconnect for you," said Falon. I detected a bit of something in her voice.

"Don't worry, she won't take your place. You're my person, Falon."

"I appreciate you saying that," she said. "Look, we're here."

24—Connecting

Margaret

"Don't worry, it's going to be fine," said the EMT to me as I lay on the stretcher in the back of the ambulance.

We made it to the hospital in ten minutes flat, I don't know how. I think he ran some lights and stop signs. The EMT's took me in and I was sent up to delivery immediately.

Once they had me upstairs, I called Falon and got her voicemail, so I left a message.

"Falon, it's Margaret. Thanks for having Lora at your house to wait for me. As it turns out, my water broke today also. I'm at Lakeshore Hospital, also having babies."

Only an hour later, a set of twins graced my life. The girl came out first, followed very closely by her brother. When I gave their names to the nurse, she was a little confused, but they eventually got the spelling.

I called Abeo, and left a message with him too, giving him the surprise that they wanted out early. The nurse brought them in and showed me how to feed them for the first time. I was surprised how strongly they latched on, and in no time at all it felt like they had drained me of milk. Of course, the nurse told me that doesn't actually happen, the flow reduces, but the breast is never empty like a bottle. It takes only about twenty minutes for the flow to resume and an hour for the breast to be full again. They are really perfect feeding machines!

"How often do I feed them?" I asked.

"As often as they really want, usually every two to three hours. The frequency and the volume they take will change as they get older. I would try to get them on the same schedule, but it doesn't always work," said the nurse. "Also, get yourself a twin nursing pillow. It will make it more comfortable for you."

"Thank you for the lessons," I said.

"It's my job," said the nurse with a smile. "Now get some sleep, you're going to need it. We'll bring them back in when they get hungry."

I dropped off quickly, but woke up when I heard voices in the room. It turned out it was just the nurse checking on things. Sometime between the third and fourth feeding, I was wide awake, and decided to get up and try walking around. I made my way to the nursery to watch my twins. There was another woman standing at the window making baby noises through the glass.

"Hello. New mother?" I asked.

"Yes, I gave birth yesterday."

"Oh, me too! Hi! I'm Margaret."

"I'm Gwen. There is my son there." She pointed to her baby in the first row."

"He's adorable. I have to find mine."

"What's the name?"

"Thistle or Musa, it should be two."

"Oh, you had twins?" asked Gwen.

"Yes. Oh! There they are on the other end."

We walked down the hall to look at my two babies. "Oh, they are beautiful. What lovely names. What nationality?"

"My husband's. I think it may be Nigerian. But we also gave them Canadian names so they would have a choice in school."

"That's a good idea. Kids can be cruel, and unusual names encourage cruelty, unfortunately."

"Exactly," I said, nodding. "Does your son have a name yet?"

"I'm afraid not. We've been behind on that score. I'll have to push Andrews to work with me and decide."

"Well, I hope to see you again," I said. "I'm going back to my room."

"I'll walk with you."

The two of us went back down the hallway, and I left her at her room and continued on to mine. *I must ask her for her number so our kids can play together. They're the same age. How cool!*

I still hadn't heard from Abeo, which wasn't unusual, just disappointing. My mom picked me up from the hospital five days later, with both my bundles. I was not looking forward to unpacking the boxes. Opening the front door, I got a very pleasant surprise: My mom had unpacked everything on the main floor and the kitchen. It was all set up.

"In fact, I've done seventy-five percent of the boxes already!" said Mom.

"Wow, Mom, that's amazing! Thank you. That is so helpful," I gushed.

"Well, things may not be in the right place as you would put them, but at least they're out of boxes. I've flattened the boxes and left them in the garage."

"Mom, I just don't know how I can repay you."

"Let me see my grandbabies!"

"Come here, they're asleep, so I'm going to go and put them to bed."

"I'll help," said my mom. As we climbed the stairs, I saw that my bedroom was all set up and my boxes of clothes were put away. I cried and hugged my mom in gratitude. In the room next to mine, the bassinets were set up too. Mom had received all the new baby furniture, and it was all put together.

"How did you do this on your own?"

"I didn't. Mark from across the street came over and helped me put together the cribs, and Abeo hired someone to come place furniture and assemble as needed. They also helped me finish the unpacking."

"This is amazing. I also went out and got you all kinds of supplies. You have enough diapers, onesies, and socks for a month, or at least until you decide if you're going the disposable route or reusable."

"What would you do?"

"I'd use a diaper service and go with something reusable," said my mom.

"Let's do that. Do you have a service in mind?"

"As a matter of fact I do. I already called them and have numbers for you." She pulled a slip of paper out of her pocket and handed it to me.

"Huh, a full-service weekly price is only fifty dollars. Is that for twins?"

"It's based on the number of diapers you use. So it will probably go up with twins."

"I think it's worth it. Let's sign up."

I looked around the twin's room and sighed in relief because my husband had hired someone to come in and decorate, paint the room, and put up beautiful draperies. It was a beautiful room. Mom had brought some sweet touches into the room too, organizing their toys, adding lights, and getting a baby monitor all set up.

We kissed the kids and walked out quietly and went downstairs.

"Let me make you a cup of tea, and you put your feet up. It's going to get tiring quickly, so learn to rest when they do."

"Thanks, Mom."

The doorbell rang, and I went to get it. Falon and Lora were on the porch.

"Welcome home!" they cheered together.

"Thank you both."

"We won't stay long, but here are some necessities," Lora said, handing me a basket of baby things. "We'll come back and visit in a few days."

"Thank you. I look forward to it."

It was around 10:00 p.m. and I was relaxing with a cup of tea in front of the TV. I heard the front door open quietly.

"Abeo, is that you?" I called out, because I didn't have the strength to get up again.

"Yes, love, it's me." He came into the living room and knelt down beside my chair and hugged me gently and placed a chaste kiss on my forehead. "You look tired, but beautiful."

"I am tired. It has been nonstop with the twins. They're eating frequently. When they're not eating, they're pooping or peeing."

"Has your mother been here to help?"

"Yes, she's been an angel. She retired to bed already. I was just waiting for you."

"I'm happy you did. Let me take you upstairs and you can show me our beautiful children."

He turned off the TV and scooped me up in his arms and carried me up the stairs. Outside the twin's room, he set me down gently, and we opened their door quietly.

At the side of their bassinets, he wept openly with joy at the babies resting inside. Touching each of their faces, he whispered their name, and placed a kiss on their forehead. He spoke some words over them, and was about to leave when his daughter opened her eyes.

She cooed and looked her daddy in the face and her eyes twinkled. She recognized him! Perhaps it was all that talking to my belly, she knew his voice.

"Sleep, my little princess. Daddy's home. I love you," he said in English.

I took Abeo's hand and led him to our room, where I gave him a proper welcome. The heat rose in my body as well as his almost instantly.

Breaking from the kiss, he held me and looked into my eyes. "Let me shower, and then I'll make my acquaintance with my wife again, properly," he said.

My body danced with delight as I turned down the bed and sat on it suggestively.

"You do that, husband. I'll be here." I think I fell asleep on him.

25—Introductions

Margaret

The next morning, was chaos. My mother, while I was feeding one, would take the other to bathe. Abeo learned how to change diapers. Feeding and changing fell on all of us for a few days until we got the twins on a schedule and I developed a routine.

When the weekend came around we were prepared, albeit tired from lack of sleep, to have friends over. Everyone was excited to meet the twins and Abeo. The first visitors arrived just after lunch. Lora and Rick arrived with their kids and housekeeper.

"Lora, it's so good to see you again. Come in, I'll introduce you to my guy and the babies."

Abeo was waiting just inside to take everyone's coat as they came in.

"Abeo, this is Lora Robertson. We were high school chums," I said.

"Lora, it is a pleasure to meet you, please come in," said Abeo.

"I love your voice!" said Lora, taking Abeo by the shoulders and hugging him. "Welcome to the neighborhood! This is Rick Benal, my husband, my children Minni, Pascal, and Trent, and our family keeper Anita."

"Each one of you, welcome, and come in. We have coffee and croissants in the kitchen," said Abeo.

I took Lora and Anita upstairs to see the babies, while everyone else went to the kitchen with Abeo.

"Oh, they are beautiful, Margaret," Lora said. "Anita, imagine having a baby again!"

"Si, Lora, I do. Perhaps it's in the future for you and Ricardo too," said Anita. "Your children are beautiful, Margaret. If you ever need a sitter, just let me know. I'm very well versed on babies."

"Thank you, Anita, for your offer. I will take you up on that! Of course, you'll have to beat out my mom, because she's their self-appointed official babysitter," I said, laughing.

They each took turns holding and cooing the twins before we returned downstairs.

"I see you're all unpacked and moved in well," said Rick.

"Yes, I hired some people to come and make sure everything was set up, painted and such," answered Abeo. "I also understand Mark and Falon came over and helped too." The doorbell rang and Abeo excused himself and walked to the front door while I took Lora and Anita to the kitchen for coffee. I could hear him answer the door.

"Hello there, I'm Abeo. Come in, please. Everyone is getting coffee in the kitchen."

"Hello, Abeo, I've met your wife when we helped with the furniture. We're across the street," said Mark.

"Oh yes, of course. Sorry, so many new people. I owe you two a great debt of thanks for helping Margaret too."

"Hello, Abeo, nice seeing you again," said Falon.

"Come, come, follow me," said Abeo.

As they made their way back to the kitchen, I stopped and looked up from the conversation I was having with Lora.

"Falon! We're in the kitchen" I called to her.

"Margaret, it's nice to see you again," said Falon as she got close.

"It is. The twins are asleep, hopefully for another hour, upstairs. Would you like to go see them?"

"Not just yet," said Falon. And the doorbell rang again.

"I'll get it!" said Margaret. "Excuse me, ladies. If you want, grab some seats by the fireplace and I'll come find you."

"Will do!" said Lora. I went to get the door. When I opened it, the woman I had met at the hospital was there with her bundle too.

"Oh! Gwen, nice to see you again," I said. "This is Falon and Lora, neighbors of mine."

"Hi Falon, Lora," said Gwen. "We're all good friends, actually, some are family. This is my mate, Robert Andrews."

"Come on in. Make yourselves at home!" I motioned them past me. "You're a tall, cool, drink, Andrews. Gwen, we have similar taste in men."

"Is that so?" asked Gwen with a little edge in her voice.

"Let me introduce you to my Abeo," who had arrived behind me at that moment and I felt a hand placed at the small of my back.

"Who is this, Margaret?" he asked.

"This is Gwen, the woman who I spoke about, and her 'mate,' Robert?" I asked. "'Mate' is an unusual title. This is Abeo Musa, my…"

"Call me Andrews, everyone does. Think of us as married," interrupted Andrews. "Good to meet you, Abeo."

"I'm her mate as well," said Abeo, smiling at me, understanding that "boyfriend" didn't seem important enough to me.

"Come into the kitchen," I said. "Gwen, the girls are sitting by the fireplace if you want to join us. Would you like to put your baby upstairs while he's asleep?"

"Andrews, what do you think?" asked Gwen.

"I'll do that, and I can take a peek at these awesome twins I've heard so much about."

"I'll show you," said Abeo.

I took Gwen into the family room and we found Lora and Falon there, as well as their men. All had taken seats either on a chair or on the floor. The kids were at the kitchen counter with Anita.

I sat down beside Lora, and Gwen sat beside Falon.

"This is a very tight-knit group, I see," I said.

"We're like family, really," said Falon. "We look out for each other. Now that you're here, you can join our circle and we'll look out for you too."

"That's nice of you to say. It will be handy to have so many aunts and uncles!" I said.

We had visitors all day on Saturday. My mom stopped in, and my cousins that were in town, which was strange because I don't have a relationship with them. Friends from work stopped by too with well-wishes. Eventually, everyone went home, and Abeo and I slumped on the sofa, exhausted.

"What a day!" I said.

"I didn't know you knew that many people," said Abeo. "I think they'll have lots of built-in aunts and uncles!"

"Yes, and from people I don't really know yet," I said.

"I think Lora's group will be people we will come to know well, I suspect," said Abeo.

"Why do you think that?"

"Because I sense some kind of kindred spirit in them. I can't put my finger on it, but that group felt like family to me."

By the time the twins were two months old, Lora had arranged a party for all the babies— Gwen's and ours—to celebrate their birth.

The men passed cigars all around and went out to the backyard and smoked them together. There was a natural comradery with them that was nice to see. I watched Abeo with the men out of the corner of my eye. He was right, there was some sort of kinship between them. They all had a few things in common: They were all very tall men. They all were very beautiful men. They were all powerfully built, even though they were not over-muscled. And they all carried themselves the same, a confidence in them that was undeniable. I thought about it for a few moments and it hit me. They were like predators. They had the grace and confidence of apex predators. I'm not sure if that was a happy thought or not. Not one of them seemed mean spirited. In fact, they were gentlemen, in the truest sense of the word.

While the guys were outside, us five girls, because I'd brought my mom with me, were inside talking about babies, children, teens, pregnancy, and motherhood in general. They had showered me and Gwen with more baby gifts, to the point it was almost embarrassing. These three children were going to be very spoiled. Certainly, I would never be short of babysitters. Now that was unexpected!

The three babies were all happily lying on a blanket together cooing and grabbing each other's fingers and toes. It was fascinating watching them all. It was as if they spoke a language only they knew and that they understood each other perfectly.

After all the gifts were opened, we all sat back and had cocktails. My mom decided to leave at that point to go home and get some work done. That left the four of us on our own.

"It's nice to be able to have a grown-up drink again," I said.

"Are you breastfeeding?" asked Lora.

"Yes, I am," I said.

"Then you can't drink yet," she said. "My advice is to pump your breasts before you have a cocktail, then you can drink. Do you need a pump? I have one you can use if you like."

"Ah ha! Secrets. I need to know these secrets. It's been almost a year since I could behave like an adult! Please, if you don't mind. I'll go get my own, but tonight would be useful."

"No sex for a year?" asked Gwen.

"Ah, no, we were having sex right up till the night my husband had to leave for business a few days before twins were born," I said. "In fact, I think the sex helped the labor. My man is a very lusty man, shall we say?"

"Oh, good. That had me worried."

"Why?" asked Lora.

"I didn't do without sex because I was pregnant," said Gwen. "I was afraid that was wrong, but my man is very lusty too."

"I think all of them are," said Falon. "It goes with the libido and the fangs."

"Fangs?" I asked. "What are you talking about?"

"Oh, ummm, I think you should talk to Abeo about that," said Falon.

"No, I think I need to know," I said. "That was a strange thing to say, and I need to know why."

"Don't get upset, it meant nothing," said Lora, looking at Falon. She got up and left the room.

"No, it did mean something," I said. "You know, I saw something I questioned Abeo about and he just waved it off like I'd seen something fictional. Then the day we moved, I thought I saw the same thing, but didn't mention it. I was waiting for the right moment so I could corner him."

"What did you see, Margaret?" asked Gwen.

"Fangs, like you said," I said, expecting them all to laugh at me. "I saw fangs extend down out of my husband's mouth."

Falon and Gwen looked at each other. They knew what I meant! They were not shocked or surprised.

"Okay, ladies, give it up. What is going on?" I asked.

"Gwen, do you want to handle this question?" asked Lora, returning with a bag in her hand. "Here's the pump, Margaret. Use it while we talk and then you can have a drink. You may need it in a few minutes."

Silence fell over the small group for a minute. The three of them kept glancing at each other and silently speaking with their eyes. It was growing uncomfortable. I was about to speak up myself, when Gwen broke the silence.

"Sure, I'll take the plunge," said Gwen. Then addressing me directly, she continued, "First off, Margaret, we aren't human. We suspect your husband is one of us. An immortal. I was born immortal, so was Mark and Rick. Andrews and these two ladies transitioned."

When she stopped talking, silence came back. It was like their talkative little mouths were sealed shut. I looked from one to the other, reflecting on what she said. The only thing I think I heard was...

"Not human. Not human?" I said. "What do you mean, not human? What else could you be?"

"We are a race of beings who are immortal," answered Gwen. "Our ancestors came from a different planet. We live thousands of years."

"I think you're pulling my leg. I don't know what's happening, but I'll get to the bottom of it."

26—Becoming Immortal

Andrews

Rick brought the four guys outside to smoke cigars in celebration of two of us becoming fathers. It was noticeable how we all instantly got along. There was a connection between us like we had been lifelong friends.

Our conversation stayed with the small talk, questions about work, how we met our girls, etc. But none of us dared to broach the subject I knew was on our minds: immortality. Abeo was clearly an ancient soul, because he resonated that way. Having met several immortal people, I could now tell when I was in the presence of one.

Gwen had an old resonance about her, older than Mark. But Abeo was something altogether different. Mark glanced through the windows to where the women were gathered around the fireplace.

"Perhaps we should rejoin the ladies," he suggested.

"What do you suppose they're talking about?" I asked.

"Sex," said Rick. And we all laughed outrageously.

"No kidding," said Abeo. "My woman is a lusty girl."

"You too, eh?" asked Mark. "It's always about sex when there are no men around. They get quite raunchy by themselves."

"Margaret is quite raunchy when it's just us," said Abeo. "Sometimes I'm surprised how well she keeps up with me."

Rick gave him a sidelong glance.

"I've witnessed this phenomenon," said Rick. "So why don't we go back now that the cigars are finished." As we walked into the living room, the girls fell silent and started giggling.

"See, I told you. They're talking about sex," said Rick, with a grin. He walked over to Lora and sat behind her on the chair. She then got up and sat on his lap.

I pulled up a chair beside Gwen, and Mark sat beside Falon. Abeo went around and stood behind Margaret.

"Gentlemen, we were just telling Margaret about your prowess, that's all," said Gwen. They all giggled.

"Yes, and they told me about a particular characteristic you guys all seem to share," said Margaret.

"Oh, what's that?" asked Abeo.

"Fangs," said Margaret.

"Really?" asked Abeo, looking at each of the group sitting in the room carefully. "Is that right?"

"If we've jumped the gun, we're sorry," said Gwen. "We hope we haven't ruined the surprise for Margaret. But your story was so much the same as ours, we all drew conclusions. It kind of slipped out."

Abeo's face changed slightly, to look like he was suppressing a spike of anger. It was clear he didn't want to address this particular issue in public. I glanced at Gwen to see if she realized what was happening. Her eyes told me that she did, so I had to trust that she had seen something we hadn't.

"I see," said Abeo, as resolve changed his features. He sighed and said, "Well, since the secret has been set free, we might as well continue."

"Margaret," said Gwen, "we'd like to welcome you into our world. Abeo, you *are* among friends here," said Gwen, turning to look at him meaningfully.

Abeo stood there silently for a moment or two, then nodded. "I'll get myself a seat, for I expect this is a long story."

"Now, what's this about fangs?" asked Margaret.

"Abeo, do you want to answer that question?" I asked.

"I can do that. Where do you want me to start?"

"At the beginning?"

"Margaret, myself, and it seems some of our new friends were born to a different species of people," started Abeo. "We are descendants of a species that came to this planet before the end of the last ice age. Ours is an aggressive species, and we have predatory characteristics like any other apex predator on this planet, such as heightened senses, superior strength and speed, as well as a defensive weapon in fangs and venom."

"Ah, ha! I saw that!" said Margaret. "I saw that quality in all four of you somehow."

"Our fangs have other uses than just defense," Abeo continued. "They are also used during coitus to enhance the sensations and experience. Both sexes have fangs, and both can deliver this substance to their partners."

"Yup, some of us were born that way, and others were turned," I said.

"Turned?" asked Margaret. "Like in vampires?"

"No, not vampires," said Abeo. "Although the vampire legend came about because some of our kind were careless and stupid. They ended up scaring whole villages of humans until they believed we were demons. What Andrews is referring to is the transition from human into our species."

"Why would you do that?" asked Margaret.

"The only reason it should be done is for true love. However, it has been done for other reasons in the past. Our species was forbidden to form permanent relationships with humans because of the problems that occurred when that happened. However, over the millennia, some of our kind have found a human true love match, and in order to not be separated, the human was converted."

"Andrews, do you want to tell your story?" asked Gwen.

"My story," I said, "Started with my decision to be with Gwen. I needed to accept her invitation to become one of them. Both Gwen and Mark suspected I may already be an immortal descendant, but I was never 'finished,' as he put it. Until the transformation is finished, the person is not immortal. From what I understand, this ceremony would have been done when I hit puberty, but I would be changing as an adult. The stakes were bigger."

"How so?" asked Margaret.

"For one, it could kill me. Turning or transmogrification was a serious thing. The human mortal body had to die and the DNA remade. So there were risks. The older the person, the higher the risk."

"So you had to die?" asked Margaret.

"I was facing death, yes. That's why I was nervous. Not that I hadn't faced death before, I was well versed in death, having watched many of my platoon members get blown to bits overseas. While I didn't like death, I had an uneasy truce with it. I had narrowly escaped on a number of occasions. In fact, I still wasn't sure how I made it through the last one.

"That was the one that ended my military career. It almost ended me. As it was, they had to sew my arm back on and basically rebuild one leg. Those army doctors did a remarkable job. But the years of rehab were painful and frustrating. Many times, I wanted to give up. I tried to kill myself once, and failed. It was a man called Duffy that saved my ass.

"Duffy found me with my wrists slashed and glued them back together before taking me to the hospital. After a year of psych, they let me go. PTSD was the all-in-one diagnosis for vets. It covered a multitude of problems and gave the doctors an easy answer. Except there wasn't an easy treatment.

"Back on my own, I barely had the use of my arm, and my leg pained me every day, all day long. Again, it was Duffy that saved me. He told me to come work for him. Gradually, my hand ability came back to what it is now, almost one hundred percent. At least it was good enough to service a lady properly, and I could do some fine motor skill work, just not for a long period of time.

"But death and me—yeah, we had a truce. I wasn't about to let death win now after fighting nearly five years to regain my life. But here I was, about to do battle with death again, only this time there were no guarantees.

"I was proud of what a specimen I was. The scars on my body were irrelevant now because I had worked very hard to rebuild my body. The scar that wrapped around my left shoulder was scary looking. It looked a little like caulking, because it was raised. The large gash down my thigh was also dangerous looking. You could tell it must have opened up my leg to the bone just from the shape of it. But those scars no longer said weakness. There isn't an ounce of weakness anywhere in my body. Gwen can attest to that."

"So why were you so scared?" asked Margaret.

"Gwen explained the procedure. I would need to get aggressive with Mark so that he fought me and used their natural defensive weapon, the venom, on me. In a battle, enough of that same venom was designed to kill their enemy. A measured dose, delivered just so, would change a mortal man into an immortal man. I knew that Mark was much stronger than me, so that in itself wasn't a worry. I was told that the venom, along with an injection they would give me, would 'remake' my DNA. My mortal body would die and I would be restored as an immortal. I had been told that it was very likely that all the old scars would eventually disappear. Falon said her scars had disappeared within six months."

"I have to interrupt at this point," said Abeo. "This ceremony describes a very ancient rite. It is a rite that is no longer necessary, and no longer practiced by most immortals. Please continue, Andrews."

"I believe that was the reason for my hesitancy. I earned those scars. They were badges of honor. They were a living testament to what I'd survived. They were proof that I lived through death. They were proof I had cheated death. So, really, my decision was between keeping my own ego intact and being with Gwen. Luckily for me, it really wasn't a difficult decision. Gwen is my life.

"So there I was, going to a ritual that would see me transform. Falon had made the arrangements in her office. Apparently, they had converted their conference room into a chamber like the one she had been taken to for her transformation. Transmogrification—that's the word they used.

"I had been told that I would need to spar with Mark. But that was a laugh, really. His strength easily overcame me, and he had me pinned quickly. Once the venom was delivered, I went into a coma. My body shut down, and for a few days I was basically like a cocoon while my DNA was being rewritten.

"I woke up tired but stronger. A simple test showed an ability to heal fast, proving I'd become immortal. Virtually so, because we can still be killed."

"How long were you unconscious?" asked Margaret.

"About two and a half days," I answered.

"Two and a half days? Is that normal?"

"No. But it's probably because I was over forty," I said. "Within a few weeks I started noticing other changes. They were happening faster than the others had. Again, Gwen had a theory that I may have been born with immortal DNA and just not been activated."

"That was an intense story, Andrews," said Margaret. "But what is an immortal? Actually?"

"That, my dear, is my job to explain," said Abeo. "Let's go home, shall we?"

27—An Overdue Explanation

Abeo

Even though it was a short drive home from Lora's, the twins woke up because of the cold air. So the first thing to do was to feed them. On Lora's suggestion, Margaret used the new breast pump from Lora and Rick, earlier that evening, and it turned out to be a very good one.

In the meantime, I was heating up the milk in the bottles and Margaret was sitting in the twins' rocking chair waiting. As soon as I gave them each a bottle, they grabbed them with their tiny fists and started drinking with gusto.

"I didn't think they would be able to do that at such a young age," said Margaret.

"Children of our species are a little more advanced and develop quicker than humans."

"But they are not your species, are they?"

"Yes, they are. They were created with my sperm and venom, and I've given you small doses of venom twice during your pregnancy to ensure they were born with immortal genes. They just need one final dose."

"Oh, was that what the biting was about? Giving me venom? I feel like I should be feeling angry or something, but I'm not."

"Not entirely," I said. "I was going to explain all this to you, but your friends just beat me to it."

"Well, since we're talking about the elephant in the room, why don't you give me your explanation?" Margaret laid the twins back in their respective bassinets and sat on the loveseat in their room. We had included that in the twins' room so that we could both sit and be with the children.

"Thank you, I will. Like they said, we are not human. I am from a species who originally came from another planet. Our planet was dying, and one of the seven ark ships that left to find a new place to colonize, came here. We landed about 33,000 years ago, long before humanity had any civilizations. We created a home using our ship down on the island you call Antarctica. We lived under the ice to stay hidden from the indigenous people. We foraged all over the planet for food, and eventually ran into humans.

"At the time, they were very primitive hunter-gatherers. We watched their development for centuries, millennia. Isolated in our ship, we could no longer reproduce with just our own kind. All of the people were related to someone on the ship. So we needed new blood. By that point, the humans were similar enough that we could mate and produce offspring. We just didn't know what kind of offspring they would be. At first, and for a long time, the offspring wasn't viable. We wouldn't let our males have sex with humans. Instead, we brought humans to have sex with our females.

"We took millennia to experiment on and off again as we met different cultures. Eventually, humanity evolved enough that we could have babies with them. Babies started being born to us as humans, but we could transform them once they were fully grown. Eventually, one of our males mated with a human female. It was an experiment to see if we could impregnate them, and it was more successful than we dared. It caused quite a problem, because all the females of that particular group of humans now wanted to be impregnated by us. They believed multiple births were favored by the gods. We left those children human, but some of them developed special skills like magic.

"Magic? You mean that exists too?" Margaret asked.

"Yes, there is a magical world out there hidden to most humans. Fast forward to the present day. Our kind has been living on Earth in plain sight, yet hidden from the human world. We live among humans, and guard the secret of who and what we are. In order to remain hidden, we have to maintain the facade that we are human. Nothing extraordinary can happen to draw attention.

"For a very long time, the different groups from the original expedition kept in touch. However, for the last thousand years or so, the groups have become isolated, and communication has stopped altogether. We don't know where each other is anymore. I have no idea if the others held to the rules we laid out or not. I know that after my first human relationship, I stopped having sex with humans."

"Can you show me your fangs?" she asked. So I thought of her with me, and they descended. As well, my eyes glowed in arousal.

"When aroused, our fangs elongate. You can also see my eyes change. Some say they swirl, as well. Our sense of smell is heightened too. This is the natural way we detect aroused females, by their scent. Coitus is rough between our males and females. More of a wrestling match for dominance than a leisurely act of tenderness. Naturally, we use our fangs to subdue the female, drug her to ecstasy to make her very ready, so that we can impregnate her. It's not dissimilar to cats, actually."

"Why was it necessary to subdue your females?"

"Because they are aggressive, and want to be dominated before they copulate. It's part of their sexual desire ritual. It adds to their pleasure. And ours. Dominating a woman is in our blood, and when the woman likes it, it sets our animal free. Great sex is rough. I also believe that we as males are endowed much larger than the females. Thus to make it work, the female must already be having an orgasm so that she is ready to take us inside."

"And human females? Have you had trouble penetrating them?"

"No, their bodies are quite soft and easy. But as I said, I have stayed away from sex with humans for a long time."

"Why?"

"Because I discovered I can impregnate them easily."

"Oh, yes. I see. So you have little Abeos running around everywhere?"

"No, and for that reason, I abstained. I had a family with one woman. When she died, I was broken. It took years for me to heal, and by then my abstinence didn't bother me. I occasionally sought out other immortals for recreational sex, but when I lost touch with them, that stopped too."

"What changed?"

"You. You changed me. From the first moment I saw you, I knew you were my mate."

"Why do you call me a mate?"

"We believe that there is one, possibly two if you're lucky, a match for everyone. One true-love match, that mates two individuals forever. We don't 'marry,' but we form permanent bonds. We become mates."

"Why do you call yourselves immortal? Are you literally immortal?"

"No, we can die. We live extremely long lives. For example, I was born here on Earth, to two Zydeans, many millennia after we landed here. I was about twenty years old when I met my first human, Aran. She was the woman I copulated with. That was seventeen thousand years ago."

"Seven…?" I swallowed. "…seven … seventeen thousand? Is that a normal lifespan?"

"Our planet's system was much larger than this one. Our 'year' was much longer than yours. Time was measured completely differently in our home world. So I don't know how to relate that. Perhaps here we are more invincible, so we will live longer than we used to. I don't know."

"So if you can die, how?"

"It requires a catastrophic injury, like losing my head. We don't get sick either. Human diseases don't affect us. We heal from most injuries, and yes, we can get injured. It's not like we have impenetrable skin or something. Our bones break, our skin cuts. But they heal very fast. If I lost a limb, it would eventually grow back. It would be excruciatingly painful, but it would return."

"What if someone put a stake in your chest?"

"It would hurt like hell but not kill me. I'm not a vampire. They don't exist."

"Good to know. So at the party they said that the legends of vampires started with you guys?"

"Yes. It's quite silly, really. From what I understand, a small group of our people went up into the Caspian Mountains to live their lives in peace and away from humanity. This was thousands of years ago. However, human villages sprung up around their mountain home and they started noticing things they couldn't explain."

"Like what?"

"Like a man wrestling a bear, biting him in the neck to kill him, then dragging him back into the woods or a deep dark cave."

"Ah yes, the ol' 'bite to kill' story. How did they arrive at vampires?"

"Believing in witchcraft and such, the villagers called them demons. Then along came Vlad the Conqueror. The rest is history."

"Can I go back to Aran? Who was she?"

"She was the first love of my life. But I was inexperienced in love, as I was so young. My captain wanted to see if we could copulate with humans and produce children. I was one of the men selected to participate. Aran was the leader of her tribe and the women selected the fathers of their children. In their society, the women were the landowners and in charge. She chose me out of a few men to copulate with. Our first time was ceremonial, in public, in front of all the village. It was strange.

"When Aran missed her first cycle, she announced she was pregnant with my child. The village celebrated. When they realized it was twins, they elevated her to goddess level. I fell in love with her and decided to stay with the village. Every time we made love, if she was not already pregnant, she became pregnant with twins or triplets. She got pregnant eleven times, bearing me more than twenty children. She was a hero to her people, and lived like a goddess."

Margaret gasped hearing that part of the story. "Twenty children?"

"Twenty, more than twenty. I lost count. When she died of old age, which was about fifty in those days, I was devastated, and broken. I had to leave the village because every woman of childbearing years was trying to get my seed. It was uncomfortable because as soon as a girl started her menses, she was old enough to contribute to the village population.

"I ended up staying away from humans for a very long time. I spent years looking for my old group, and in due course I got back in touch with my captain. The captain, one of the pilots, and myself lived together watching human history unfold. With the invention of contraceptives, I thought I could enjoy the pleasure of a woman again without the worry that they will get pregnant. At least I thought so, until you."

"Clearly I was very fertile in spite of the IUD," said Margaret.

"My sperm are aggressive, and an IUD didn't slow them down. They wanted to procreate with you. In fact, from that first time I was driven to procreate with you, my body craved you. I couldn't stop thinking about you. And six weeks of sex with you, well the inevitable happened. I bit you."

"I remember. I asked if you had bitten me. You had said yes, but there were no marks, and I was so high I thought my brain just made it up," said Margaret. "I fantasized about that, though, over and over again. The idea that you bit me and sent me into oblivion was so erotic, it got me wet no matter where I was or what I was doing. I had to start wearing leak proof underwear because I would end up gushing at the thought of you. I had a bad case of horniness for you."

"When you called and left a message, I was already at the point that I had to contact you again or go insane without you. I was very glad to get that message, but I had to pretend I hadn't."

"Did you know I was pregnant?"

"Not until I saw you. As soon as I saw you, I could smell the pregnancy and hear the tiny heart beats."

"Smell the pregnancy?"

"It's another of the predator senses we have. We were predators on our home world. Our senses of smell, sight, and hearing are heightened beyond human ability. Like animal predators here, we can smell emotions like fear, excitement, contentment, and we can detect much more subtle scents too."

"That's handy."

"It is. It lets me, as a male, know when I'm actually pleasing a woman."

"So that's your secret!"

"One of them," I said, grinning.

"What language were you using when you spoke to my belly?"

"My native language."

"Will you teach me?"

"I can, yes."

"Will our kids grow up like you?"

"They will have some of my abilities, yes. However, to become fully like me, they'll need a final infusion of venom when they have gone through puberty."

"Will that make them fully immortal?" she asked.

"Yes. I was going to test the kids to see where their development was."

"Development?"

"Yes, I gave you several doses of venom during your pregnancy, which would have been absorbed by the twins in utero. This will give them strength, and the ability to heal, and the ability to become immortal."

"Do you want to test the kids? To see if they were immortal?" she asked.

"It's an easy test. Now that they've finished eating, it will take but a moment."

"Go ahead. What do you have to do?"

"Make a small incision on their palm."

"Go on, before I lose my nerve."

I went and retrieved a sharp knife from the kitchen and made small cuts on each of their hands, waiting to see the result. Sure enough, blood welled up at first, but then the wound started to close, and vanished as if they were never made. It took about five minutes, but it was gone. Not even the ridges on the palms of their hands were marked.

"Wow, that is something to witness. Are you the same?" she asked.

"Perfect! They have immortal genes. Yes, but my body reacts faster because I am fully immortal. Do you want to see?"

"Yes, please."

I took the knife and cut deeply into my hand. She watched as the wound bled profusely for a moment, and then the skin knitted itself back together in seconds. There was no evidence left that I had been cut except for a tiny dot of blood.

Margaret licked her lips as she was watching. "Would that work on me?" she asked tentatively.

"Not yet. Once you were turned, yes. But an adult human needs more than one dose of venom to turn."

"Haven't you given me several doses already?"

"Tiny ones, just for the twins. You would require a large dose. You've had one of those too," I explained.

"How many large doses?" she asked. Margaret looked at me. I could see her mind working on what I had just told her. She was considering the consequences and ramifications of what I said.

"Probably two more."

"Have you always had the name Abeo Musa?"

"That is a question out of the blue. No, my original name was Wendell."

"I was suddenly curious. No family name?"

"No, that isn't our tradition. Only one name."

"Let's name our next son Wendell, then. I'd like to keep that name alive."

"Next son?"

"Clearly, we need more children. I have a goal to reach. What did you say, twenty?"

"You're kidding, aren't you?"

"Maybe a little … but I always wanted a large family. And we can have that rough sex you were describing. That sounds like fun."

"Why don't we put ourselves to bed, then?" I stood up, holding out my hand, and waited for her. I wasn't sure if there was anything else we needed to say. So I waited.

Eventually Margaret stood and took my hand and led me to our room.

"Just a minute while I slip out of my clothes and into something more naughty," said Margaret. She returned a few minutes later wearing a black negligée, and sat on the bed beside me.

"Now where were we?" she asked as she watched my fangs elongate at the sight of her. "Mmm, Mr. Musa, are you happy to see me?" She reached up and touched my fangs, and that sent shivers through me. She had never really seen them before.

"Those fangs are kind of sexy," she said. "I can't explain it." Then she reached for my cock, lighting up all the nerves and making me very horny again. Before her eyes, my fangs fully lengthened and started dripping venom. Her reaction wasn't what I expected though.

She leaned over and kissed me, licking up the venom and rubbing her tongue on my fangs. "Uh huh, definitely sexy … oh, and they pack a punch! Oh my!" She swooned a bit as the venom she licked up hit her bloodstream.

"Oh God," I groaned, and leaned back. "Ah, Margaret, you have no idea what that does to my libido."

"What does it do?"

"My fangs are very sensitive. They are what you would call an erogenous zone. They seem to be connected directly to my libido. When you touch them, it lights up my body."

She looked down at my pants, smiled, and pressed her hand against my hard shaft. "I can see that." Then she leaned over and kissed me again, hard this time, demanding entry into my mouth, something I normally didn't allow. But I couldn't deny this woman. I opened my mouth, accepting her tongue, and she explored my mouth, and caressed my fangs with her tongue, sending even more zings to my cock.

I was groaning and a growl escaped my throat as she smashed her lips against mine. I could smell the arousal strongly on her as she slid across the sofa and sat in my lap. Wrapping her arms around my neck, she continued to assault my mouth. My fangs were at their longest now, when she purposely pricked her tongue on the tips and pulled away.

"You're playing with fire right now," I gasped.

Immediately, her body went into an orgasm. I felt her shudder as it took her. She leaned her head on my shoulder and made mewling sounds of contentment.

"I'm preparing myself as you had described," she said a few minutes later. "I had wondered how I could orgasm so many times in a row. Now I know."

"Yup, it's a strong aphrodisiac." My cock was so swollen and hard right now my pants were straining, and it was painful. "Love, give me a sec, I need to adjust something or risk cutting the blood off."

"Oh! Here, let me." She reached down and pulled off my belt and undid my jeans and slipped her hands inside, taking out my engorged cock. The relief was palpable on my face. After helping me remove my pants, she straddled me and trapped my cock. Her body weight provided comfortable pressure.

"What if someone comes over?" I asked.

"We won't answer the door," she said. She was very wet, and as she moved her body along the length of me, my need for her ramped up.

She leaned down and I bit her neck lightly, with just enough venom to spice things up. I felt her shiver with pleasure. Lifting her body slightly, I could feel the head of my cock cupped in the soft skin of her vagina, teasing me, tantalizing me.

Watching me closely, she slid him home slowly. A sigh escaped both our lips as we reconnected. I felt like I was home.

"I am not wearing protection," I murmured into her ear.

"That's okay," she whispered. "I don't want to break this connection. Oh my God, it feels so good to feel you inside me like this. I would stay like this forever if I could."

Giving birth had somehow made her channel not as tight. So the sense of being squeezed wasn't there. Slowly, she started moving her hips in a back-and-forth motion which made contact on all sides. She gasped as each sensitive spot was rubbed, but she didn't go faster, she kept up a slow, steady rhythm. I could feel the orgasm building in both of us.

"Ah. Ah … ah. My God. Oh. Margaret! Oh my God. I'm not going to last!"

"Touch me, deeper, touch me! Ah. Ah. Ah. That's it. Touch me!"

As I tipped her with my cock, another orgasm shattered her, and that caused me to release. My cock emptied itself like a firehose as the pressure exploded out of me. Margaret kept moving, eking out every shiver, every drop, every sensation as we both relaxed.

"Now bite me, please," she said. She leaned her head exposing her neck so I had a clear place to bite. I kissed and licked the spot. With a hiss, my fangs bit into the flesh of her neck and my venom pumped into her blood. I felt her shudder in pleasure and moan as the drug took hold and she orgasmed again and again.

"Oh, that was so good. Thank you," she said as she was coming down.

I was watching her face when she smiled and said that. I couldn't love her more than I did at that moment. My Margaret, how did I get so lucky to find her after so many years of loneliness? A tear slid down my face as the deep well of emotion overcame me and suddenly I was holding her tightly with the thought I never wanted to let go. I knew right then that I needed to make her immortal with me, because I would never survive her death. *Not again.*

"What's wrong?" she asked. "Why are you crying? Am I pregnant again?" she asked me right out. Having absorbed the information I gave her, she correctly understood what I could and could not do.

I inhaled her scent deeply. There was no trace of conception yet. But I hadn't given her a full blast of me this time. That needed a much more violent form of sex than what we just did.

"No, you're not."

"What will it take?" She asked.

"To get pregnant?"

"Yes, that and to make me immortal like my children and you?"

"To get pregnant, requires rough sex, consensual rough sex. To become immortal, it requires that several times, with massive doses of venom. The venom is what turns you."

Again, Margaret sat there, with me still inside her, thinking, her channel clenching and unclenching, squeezing me and stimulating me. Her hips gently moved as she stimulated both herself and me.

Several minutes later: "So, the really 'energetic' sex we had was what impregnated me." It was a statement, not a question. "You had said you lost control, is that what you mean?"

"My clever Margaret. Yes, that was when I impregnated you. I was so far gone that there was no way I could rein in the animal, the sex was that intense for me. It's like a switch in my head I can resist only up to a point. When the sex is that good, I cannot resist."

"Abeo, I know I'm in love with you. I have been since that first night. I hope saying this doesn't make you feel trapped. But I want to be like my children. Like you. I don't want to leave this world and them still in it. I want to have a long life with them. And with you, if you'll have me. I'm just a plain human, with no particular skills, but I love you with all my being."

"Oh, Margaret, no other words would have made me happier. I'm in love with you too and have been since the first time I saw you. I believe we could be soulmates. Among my people, we believe that there is a being who we are meant to be with, a soulmate, a true love. They are hard to find, but when you do, you know it instantly. I believe that is what you are to me. No other explanation fits."

She wiped a tear that was rolling down my face.

"I'm crying because you've just made me the happiest man on this and any other planet." I kissed her deeply, letting her tongue enter me as I entered her, sharing fluids and sensations. But when she stroked my fangs again with her tongue, a growl leaped out of my throat and my cock hardened inside of her.

"I want you again," I growled.

"Me too. I cannot seem to get enough of you."

"This time it is not going to be gentle lovemaking," I warned her.

"Yum. I love it when you take me, you animal. Will you give me more venom, enough to change me?"

"Is that what you want?"

"Yes, I do."

"Then come here, my love," I said. "I can do this with a bite or with an injection."

"The bite is much more fun," she said.

I held her tenderly, and bit her deeply, giving her a large dose of venom. She instantly had an orgasm and flew into oblivion. I would wait until she came down this time before making love and giving her another dose.

An hour later, Margaret opened her eyes and took me in. I was lying next to her, watching her.

"Oh, that was good, my mate. Now fuck me hard and give me another dose. I don't want to be separated from you by eternity."

I would take her as rough as she wanted, and we would make some more babies tonight. I wanted to own this woman.

She wanted to own me too. Our lovemaking was brutal and dominance driven. She dominated me and then I dominated her. We rode each other like horses and screamed with abandon at climax. When I bit her this time, she exposed her neck to me, asking for savagery. The bite drained me completely, leaving me feeling weak. She fell unconscious quickly. And I watched over her.

Strangely, our babies did not wake up during our escapades. They slept for the rest of the night. I was ready for them in the morning though, with bottles from the pumped milk freshly warmed up. Once they were changed, burped, and dressed in fresh onesies, I laid them together in their playpen and went to check on my mate.

Margaret was waking up. Her eyes fluttering was the first sign, and a smile was the second. When she spoke, it was heavenly to hear her voice.

"Abeo, have I started changing yet?" she asked.

"Yes, the process will have started. You may need more venom later. I will watch you."

"How are the twins?"

"Fed, changed, re-dressed, and happily playing with each other," I said. "Margaret, you make beautiful babies. I think they are the most beautiful children I have ever seen. I do want to make some more with you."

She gazed into my eyes for a moment.

"It's not a question of money. You know that, right?" I said. "I can afford to hire a nanny to help you if necessary. You don't have to shoulder the entire job."

"I know, you do so much for us already," she said. "I'm not used to being a 'kept' woman. I'm used to being independent. You're keeping me comfortable, and we never want for anything. Thank you for paying the mortgage and utilities too. But without a job I feel guilty that you're shouldering the whole financial burden."

"Do you want to work?" I asked. "A career is good for the mind and soul, something to give you purpose. But it's not necessary. I'm a man of means, and this is a small expense for me. I'm happy to provide you and our children with a house large enough for a big family."

"A big family sounds nice. Don't you think we should wait until they're at least past the diaper stage to have more? By the way, I appreciate that you have been able to stay home. It's been so nice having you here for the kids."

"That was what I promised, and it was important to me. Unfortunately, me being here all the time will come to an end soon. My bank is starting to ask me when I can travel again. I will continue to put them off for as long as I can."

"We'll manage, Mom and me. If I need more help, I'll hire someone."

"That's good."

28—Innogen

Andrews

Back in the present, I glanced at my watch and saw that it was close to the time our guests would be arriving. We were hosting a pre-long weekend barbeque. At least our yard now had grass instead of mud, so people could sit outside and the babies could lie on a blanket in the grass. I finished up getting the patio ready.

"Are the steaks ready for grilling?" I asked Gwen.

"Yup, they've been marinating all morning. The potatoes are cleaned, wrapped, and ready for the fire, and the salad is made and sitting in the fridge."

The doorbell rang, and Gwen went to answer. Soon I heard Falon's voice at the door as she came inside.

"Mark is emptying the car and bringing in what we brought," said Falon.

"Oh, what's that?"

"Some wine we tried that is really good, some new cigars for the men, and a dessert I made."

"Wow, thank you!"

I came into the kitchen to greet her.

"Andrews, nice to see you—it's been a while," said Falon.

"Hello, Falon," I said, walking over and giving her a hug. "Thanks for coming. There are seats outside on the patio, some under shade, some in the sun."

The front door opened and Mark came in with a box of goodies.

"Mark, you can leave that all in the kitchen on the island. I'll put it away," said Gwen. "Do you want to open a bottle of your wine before dinner?"

"Yes, one of them is a nice aperitif," said Mark. "I will bring it out to the patio."

A moment later, the doorbell rang again, and while I brought Falon and Mark outside Gwen went to answer. A few minutes later, Gwen had Lora and Margaret with her and was bringing them through the patio doors. All three women were laughing and chatting together. Once they were outside with Falon, Gwen went back in the house and returned to the patio with more glasses.

"Hon, I left the front door open so our friends can just come on through," said Gwen. "I will leave the patio doors open, too, so we can hear people."

Just then, we all heard Rick's voice inside the house. "Hey! Where is everyone?"

"Out back," I yelled. "Come on through!"

Rick and Abeo appeared at the patio door also carrying boxes of goodies.

"More presents?" I asked.

"Just some wine, a new scotch, nachos, and homemade salsa," said Rick.

"I come bearing baby stuff," said Abeo. "Sorry, should we have brought something to eat?"

"No! Not at all! Just yourselves. Where are the twins?"

"Still asleep in the car. I'll bring them back once I unload this box here."

Unloading the boxes, Gwen put the bottles in the fridge and the food on the counter while I went to check on the steaks, I flipped them over in the marinade. Then I went outside to be with our guests.

It was nice to have a patio large enough for four families to comfortably sit. I had the firepit built in the middle of the seating area so everyone could enjoy it. Looking around at our friends, there was still enough room for when all the kids would be here. Right now, Abeo took the twins upstairs to sleep in our son's room.

Dinner was a hit. The food all turned out delicious, and Falon's dessert was to die for. Rick even wanted the recipe. I lit the fire and everyone took a seat and a blanket to snuggle in, because it was May, and it still got a little cool at night. After dinner, we snuggled around the firepit and sipped spiked hot chocolate.

"My, we have gone through so much this year already!" I started.

"Tell me about it. Moving, birthing—phew it's nice to be able to relax," said Gwen.

"I hear you!" said Margaret. "This is very nice, being able to sit around with grownups and just talk. We need a campfire story!"

"That's a good idea," said Gwen. "What story do you want to hear?"

"I'd like to hear the story of how you brought all the witches here," said Margaret.

"I think I can do that," said Falon.

"It started for me when Lora called and asked me to get everyone to meet her at the occult store.

Now, the occult store is actually not a store, but another dimension. That means, it doesn't exist here in our world and needed a magical incantation to get there. Only people who were members of the supernatural world could enter. I didn't have an address to it, but I could show us where it was, so we all went together.

"We drove to a really sketchy part of town and went to the back of an even sketchier looking building. Even the shadows seemed sinister. I was standing in front of a battered-in door with graffiti all over it. I pressed my palm on a pentagram and the door started to waver like a mirage on a hot summer day. The next thing we knew, we were all inside a dark room filled to the ceiling with cabinets and displays.

"The door slammed behind me," said Falon, as she stomped her foot hard and was rewarded by a few jumping. Then she continued.

"Lora was there. As soon as we were all inside she started speaking to the air. I mean, there was no one there. She looked a little crazy!" I said, making a hand signal to show crazy to get another reaction. *"But suddenly there was this ball of light floating in front of her. A spooky voice answered her too, and told us to follow the light."*

"The spooky voice was Esperanza, a witch that had been trapped in the occult store as a caretaker of sorts.

"We all started following the ball of light, Lora was leading, and it brought us to a room with a large mirror. I asked her what we were doing and her answer was 'We're going to jump through that mirror!'

"Jump through a mirror? Now I really thought Lora had lost it.

"But it turned out to be exactly what we did. Lora spoke to the mirror and it shimmered like ... like ... oh, the Stargate! Remember? And then the silver surface settled, looking like water or mercury. Lora told us to all hold hands, and then she stepped into the mirror.

"We ended up in this place that had a large gothic looking building and vast gardens outside its walls. Lora explained that it was a convent of sorts where her great-great-grandmother was. Just then, an older woman dressed in loose flowing robes walked out from behind a hedge.

"Lora introduced us all to Innogen, her grandmother, and Innogen explained to us that she needed all six of us to help her escape the dimension we were in. That's right, dimension. It turned out we were in a pocket dimension separate from our reality. Innogen had been trapped there.

"Innogen wanted us to stand around her in a circle, holding hands, and to focus on our love for our mates. She did the rest. I heard her mutter things under her breath and repeated the words over and over, getting louder each time. It didn't take long before there was a reaction. I saw swirling light around each pair of hands, and the more she chanted the bigger those swirls of light got until they encompassed all of us. It looked like an aurora borealis was surrounding us. When the same sort of light started to envelope Innogen, I realized I was seeing magic energy.

"Innogen's chanting got very loud, and she started drawing the magical energy into her own body. Just as it disappeared, a momentous soundwave whomped, and all the energy got thrown out in a wave like a tsunami passing through all of us and getting larger, faster, and faster.

"Innogen then told us to bring back the mirror and get through it quickly before the dimension dissolved around us. Lora quickly said the words that showed us where the mirror was, and we all tumbled through it as fast as possible. As soon as we were safely in the occult store, the mirror solidified again.

"And that is how we rescued Innogen from the pocket dimension." Falon said.

"That was an amazing story," said Abeo. "To think we have found not only other immortals but magical people too. Thank you for sharing this with us." He paused for a moment then said, "I'd like to say something."

"The floor is yours," said Mark.

"I feel fortunate to have come upon you people," said Abeo. "I was living basically alone with little or no contact with anyone. Too afraid to put down roots, too afraid to love. I had once before, and that could be a story for another fire, but that was so long ago, it doesn't feel like it was me. So thank you. Thank you all for welcoming me and Margaret into your family. Thank you, Falon, for being nosy and introducing yourself. At the time I resented it, but I didn't realize what a bonus it would be.

"Margaret has started her transition, and so she is now a member of the group. She understands the need for secrecy, and that is another reason I'm so grateful for you. We can all be ourselves here among these friends."

"Well, Abeo, our kids don't know about the immortal part yet. We have yet to tell them." said Rick.

"What about the magic?" asked Margaret.

"I'll answer this one," said Lora. "I've always been magical. I was born with magic. My kids have grown up with me practicing and learning how to be a witch. It wasn't until very recently though that I came into my power. Since meeting Innogen, I have learned so much."

"Will you turn your children?" asked Abeo.

"When the time comes, and we explain the immortal thing, they will get the choice," said Rick.

"We could turn them, and then they would understand the need for discretion. That's always the difficulty with children."

"I want to give them the choice first," said Lora.

"That's reasonable. We can still make their transition pretty painless."

"How?" asked Mark.

"Something that wasn't shared openly among my people, was the distillation of the active drugs and catalysts in our venom that change a human into one of our species. We developed an injectable venom that works much better, and quicker," said Abeo.

"Why wasn't it shared openly?" asked Mark.

"Because we didn't want our people to think that they could just turn anyone they wanted. Imagine if you had all kinds of immortals running around without the knowledge of who and what we are. They would jeopardize everyone's existence. So the injection was developed for special cases and only to be used in the event that someone needed to be turned."

"What conditions make it a "need to know" situation?" asked Rick.

"Your situations, when we meet our mate and he or she is human. When there are children," said Abeo.

"So how does the injection work?"

"We inject them with a large dose of distilled venom; about ten ccs. It usually requires three doses to change an adult."

"So no sex, no fighting?" asked Lora.

"No," chuckled Abeo. "Not unless you still want to."

"My family did not have this information," said Mark.

"You do now," said Abeo. "Tell me, are your three children the last of our group?" asked Abeo.

"Only Anita, our housekeeper, would remain," said Rick.

"Anita, because of her age, may require an additional injection. It could be a difficult change too."

"Again, we will give her the option."

"I've got a question," said Margaret. "Will Abeo and I be able to generate magical energy during sex?"

"Not yet, my love. You have to complete your change."

"We can still practice, no?"

"Will you excuse us, folks?" asked Abeo. "I believe I am failing my duties as a husband."

We all laughed, knowing exactly what he meant.

"On that note," said Falon. "Goodnight everyone! Husband?"

29—Pirates!

Rick

It was mid-June and the Fête National long weekend was here. It was our turn to host the barbeque. Mark and Falon were here already when Gwen and Andrews arrived, and soon they were all lying around the pool sipping margaritas. Lora clinked her glass.

"Guys, Margaret and Abeo should be here soon," said Lora.

"I like Margaret," said Falon. "She's a firecracker. I am dying to see those adorable twins again."

The doorbell rang, and Lora jumped up. We could all hear Anita open and greet the couple and their children.

"Oh my God, this is a beautiful house," said Margaret. "I'm so impressed with your decor."

"Gracias," said Anita. "May I take your bags for you and store them?"

"Margaret, Abeo, I believe you met our housekeeper Anita already," said Lora when she reached the front hall. "She is family really. She has been with Rick's family since he was a small boy."

"Pleased to see you again, Anita," said the deep voice of Abeo.

"Oh my, look how they've grown!" said Anita. "How old are they now?"

"They are now six months old. They are advanced for their age."

"Follow me, folks, everyone is outside by the pool."

When Margaret and Abeo walked out the back sliding doors, we all stood to greet them.

"Anita, please bring out two more lemonades when you have a minute," I yelled into the house.

"*Si hijo mio!*" *Yes, my son.*

"Hi guys!" called out Margaret. "Long time no see! Lora, where are your children?" We all chuckled. Since Margaret was let in on our secret, we'd socialized with them a number of times.

"Oh, Minni is at a sleep-over, and the boys are away at their various camps," said Lora. "So it's adults-only this weekend!"

"It's so nice to have you all as family," said Abeo. "I've missed this in my life."

The two of them found chairs and joined in the conversation. It spun around and around, the guys talking business, which always seemed the way it would go. The women were talking babies and decorating. I was busy at the bar making some cocktails, so I had a bird's eye view of everyone.

"Mark, Gwen, Rick, and possibly Andrews, were born," I overheard Lora say. "Falon and I were changed."

"Abeo says I am already starting to change," said Margaret. "He figures one more dose ought to do it."

"The fun way or the clinical way?" asked Gwen.

"Oh, the fun way!" she answered. "I can't get enough of that man."

"I know what you mean," said Falon. "It is a switch. Suddenly I'm full throttle and I just need it so badly that it almost hurts."

"I experienced that too," said Gwen. "I heard that the venom may be addictive. Maybe that's what is happening."

"Huh," said Lora. "I wouldn't be surprised. It is a very powerful drug. Is the venom we have equally as strong?"

"We get venom too?" asked Margaret.

"Oh yes, and we get to bite them too," said Lora.

"Now I really want to hurry up!" said Margaret. "Can I see your fangs?"

Gwen provided the demonstration because she had more control over them than the rest of the ladies.

"Oh gosh, they're cute! Not as big though."

"No, but they work just fine. I prefer to think of them as pleasure spikes," said Gwen.

"Did I hear someone say pleasure?" asked Abeo.

"I did," said Gwen. "Are you interested in receiving?"

"Oh, I had forgotten our females have small fangs. It has been a very, very, very long time since I laid with my own species," said Abeo.

"You're a venom virgin?" asked Gwen.

"Oh man, you're in for a treat!" called Mark across the patio.

"It's an experience you'll never forget, and will wonder how you went without," said Andrews.

"In all your years? You've never had sex with one of your own kind?" asked Margaret.

"Yes, once. But I don't remember her ever biting me."

"How old are you, Abeo?" asked Lora.

"Oh, I'm the second generation of the original settlers that came here," said Abeo.

We all gasped, because we all knew what that meant. "Wait a minute," I said. "That means you're like seventeen thousand years old."

"That's correct."

"Wow!" said Mark. "Since you are as close to pureblood as we know, can you tell me what is different between, say, Gwen and me and yourself?"

"Hmm, I am pureblood," answered Abeo. "Well, first I would say I'm closer to the predator we were than you are. That means my immune system overwhelms a human's. My reproductive system also overwhelms a human's. We live longer, as I prove. And perhaps our senses are sharper than yours. But we'd need to test that theory."

"What do you mean *overwhelm*?" asked Margaret.

"You're pregnant again, and with multiple babies. This will likely be the last multiple birth you will have now that you have started to change."

"Really? How do you know?" asked Margaret.

"I told you, I can smell the change—your body has already produced hormones for the babies."

"I have a question," asked Falon.

"Go ahead."

"What is actually happening to the human body when it changes?"

"The venom delivers a chemical compound that breaks down the DNA and rebuilds it. It's parasitic in nature. The host human dies as a result of the attack, but the body actually survives because the chemicals don't stop the heart. The result is that the body becomes immortal."

"What about if you're pregnant?" asked Gwen.

"The fetuses usually survive the transition as immortals themselves, although not fully formed. Like a child born to two immortal people, they will require that 'booster' shot at puberty."

"So why didn't Falon become pregnant when we had sex while she was human?" asked Mark.

"Perhaps your bloodline has been diluted, and your sperm are not as aggressive as mine."

"How many times have you bitten me, Abeo?" asked Margaret.

"Enough I believe to ensure you change."

"Will I transition during pregnancy?"

"I believe the final process may happen only after you deliver. This point I'm not sure on," said Abeo. "Unfortunately, once immortal, females don't get pregnant nearly as often."

"All immortal children require that booster. The reason is that when a child goes through puberty, their bodies change so much, and their brains expand so much, that in order to develop adult characteristics, they need another massive dose of venom. That used to be delivered through either sex or fighting because that was a natural way, and more pleasurable than just being bitten for nothing. Now, we use an injection—which is more efficient."

"Ah! Now all those protocols make sense," said Gwen. "They didn't before. The reasons got scrambled. But after so many thousands of years, I'm not surprised. I am surprised more didn't get lost."

"So, we didn't have to succumb to ritualistic sexual intercourse in front of a council of elders to ensure my wife became immortal?" asked Mark.

"No, gosh that is creepy!" said Abeo. "You just needed to bite her enough. That's why the venom is addictive."

"I thought I heard it was addictive!" said Gwen.

"Um, yes. It is addictive for both males and females," said Abeo.

"But I don't have fangs yet," said Margaret, pouting cutely.

"Don't worry, you will get them," said Gwen and Falon in unison.

"You will. And it's fun biting your mate…" said Lora.

"Oh ya!" I said as I rejoined the group with a trayful of cocktails. "Here you go, my cocktail for the weekend." I passed out a glass to each person and took my seat beside Lora.

"Clearly, I'm missing out. Abeo, I expect you to bring me up to standard if I'm going to be living among such august people," said Margaret.

"Let's see how it's progressing?" asked Abeo.

"How?"

"To see if you've finished the first transition," said Lora.

"Please give me your hand," said Abeo. She held out her hand and we all watched as he took out a small penknife and made a small incision in the meaty part of her hand. We watched as the wound bled a drop, then slowly closed up and healed.

"Wow! Did you see that? The cut disappeared!" cried Margaret. "I didn't feel it at all!"

We were all grinning from ear to ear, remembering the first time for each of us.

"Welcome to being immortal, Margaret," said Mark.

"Wow. Thanks, everyone. I feel so special."

"Remember," said Mark. "Calling us immortal is a misnomer. We can die. A catastrophic injury to the brain or heart will kill us."

"Yes, Abeo has explained that to me."

"Let's eat!" I said, changing the subject abruptly. Lora was picking up plates, and I started serving the ribs, burgers, and dogs. As each one got a plate they went down the salad table and helped themselves before finding a place at the very large table. Even the babies got to chew on a rib as they sat in the play area.

After our meal, we were all sitting around the pool. Some of us were dangling our toes in the water, others were on deck chairs. Andrews broke the quiet.

"Folks, I have to ask a favor from you all. Gwen and I have not made a decision on our son's name."

"What? He still doesn't have a name after six months?" asked Falon. "What have you been calling him?"

"Son," said Andrews. "So here goes. I need a vote: the two names are Scott Liam or Terrence Douglas."

"How about Terrence Liam?" asked Lora. "Terrence Liam Andrews, kind of has a ring to it."

I looked at Gwen and she was beaming. "Settled!" Andrews cried. "Now we can have his naming day."

"Hey, any chance of getting one of your stories again?" asked Margaret. "I really enjoyed the last one. It makes me feel like I'm catching up on the lifestyle of an immortal family."

"Sure, I'd be happy to," said Andrews. "What story do you want to hear?"

"I think you should tell her the story of the pirates," said Falon.

"Oooo, that's a good story," said Lora.

"Pirates?" asked Abeo. "I'm down with that. You guys were pirates?"

"No, but we had fun with some pirates of the Caribbean," said Mark. "Oh! I've been waiting forever to use that line!" We all laughed out loud.

"Okay, everyone, we need to set the mood," said Andrews. "Let's pull our chairs around the fire and get comfortable, because this one is a long story."

Everyone came around the fire I set in the pit, and brought blankets and pillows too.

"Ricardo, I'm going to retire if you don't mind," said Anita.

"Okay, Mama, we'll see you tomorrow."

"I'll do the dishes in the morning, si?"

"No, I'll get them done tonight. You've done enough today. *Buenos noche.*"

Andrews began: *"This story happened during our expedition to find Group 32, who were a group of immortals that left the ark ship and settled somewhere in the Caribbean.*

"So to set the scene, we had just returned to the yacht after staying with the immortals for three days. As we were getting ready to leave, the immortals informed us there was a pirate boat offshore. We had seen that boat before we landed on the island, but had hoped they had left the area after three days.

"Well, they hadn't. We weren't sure if they knew about the island or not. They could have been tracking our boat, or perhaps they were just trolling around for victims. We didn't know. We made the decision to stay close to shore, and to make our way in the opposite direction from what brought us here. That would mean we would circumnavigate the whole island.

"Now, the immortals had a cool anti-detection device that kept their island invisible. If you didn't know it was there, you couldn't find it except by accident. So we were hoping the pirates didn't know it was there. And we didn't want to suddenly 'appear' out of thin air on radar somewhere. So we hugged the coast as far as we could, all the while watching the pirates on our radar.

"By the time we were around the far side of the island, dawn was just a couple of hours away. We hadn't seen or heard their boat all night, so we thought we were in the clear.

"We had been warned in port there was a problem with pirates in the Caribbean—not the movie—stealing pleasure craft and holding owners for ransom. Sometimes they would dump the

people into the water and just steal the boat entirely. So we suspected that they were after our yacht.

"*Duffy was at the helm of the yacht, guiding it around the shoals and rocks not far from the shore. We didn't know how far out to sea the veil stretched. so Duffy wanted to stay as close to shore as possible. Good thing the catamaran had a very shallow draft. Still, hitting a rock would have damaged the floats to the point of tipping the craft, so that was not something we wanted to happen.*

"*Eventually, we left the shelter of the veil and reached the open sea. There were no other ships, no yachts, on radar, and nothing on the horizon except open water and moonlit swells. It was quite beautiful from the command deck. We had a clear view in all directions. I was up on the bridge with Duffy, and we were all on watch looking for the pirates.*

But that calm and stillness didn't last. My radio squawked. Lora was telling me that she was hearing engine noise on the port stern side.

"*Duffy cut the lights on our catamaran, leaving her a black shadow against the sky and water. You really don't understand the blackness of night until you are at sea without any lights.*

"*There was still nothing on the radar—no other ships or yachts in the vicinity. That meant only one thing, the pirates were very sophisticated and they had some sort of anti-radar system or a stealth vessel.*

"*With their boat in close proximity, we could not make a run. Our boat didn't move that fast unless we had a really good wind. And the night was still. I had an idea though. I let everyone know to come to the bridge to tell them.*

"*I told them I had an idea: we pretend that we were 'unsuspecting' yacht goers having a party. We let them board us, pretend to be frightened, and then take them all down using our immortal skills. Falon was keen on getting to 'vamp out.' I agreed, because there wouldn't be any witnesses.*

"Mark thought it was a good idea, saying he always loved ocean-going parties.

"I turned the music back on really loud, Falon turned on the party lights that outlined the sails, and Gwen lit all kinds of candles to set the mood, and put out food. Meanwhile, the rest of us started to dance and act as though we were drunk and having a party under the canopy. Even though we looked distracted, all six of us were keenly aware of any sound around the yacht.

"The pirates came up alongside the yacht and tied their craft to ours. We didn't flinch, not one of us, we just kept on dancing. Their crew came on board by the diving deck and crept up the deck, taking up positions hidden behind objects. We appeared to intensify our unawareness.

"When they were ready, one of the pirates yelled, 'Everyone stop! Put your hands up and kneel on the deck! You've been boarded!'

"The girls did a wonderful job of screaming and acting silly and stupid, and the guys made a half-hearted attempt to fight them, but we all eventually did as the pirates asked and kneeled on the deck with our hands on our heads. The pirate in charge walked towards us, and touched each of the girls, making lewd comments. The others joined in laughing about how they were going to have fun with them. Three of the pirates separated from the rest and forced the girls to stand and told them to walk below deck.

"Mark told everyone to do as they ask and not be afraid. He played his part really well. He grinned at the girls, knowing they could take care of themselves.

"The biggest pirate then looked at the three of us and started barking orders. I had been looking for an opportunity, but it was Rick who got the first one. The pirate started insulting Rick. I heard Rick say, 'You're calling me chico? Me, a Cuban? Come here and insult me.'

I chuckled when I heard that, because I knew what was coming next. The pirate walked right into his trap. He stepped *right up to him and shoved his face into Rick's. The next thing was priceless. Rick 'vamped' out by displaying glowing red eyes and fangs that popped out as he snarled. The pirate almost pissed himself, scrambling to get away from him.*

"The pirate yelled, 'What the fuck? What the heck are you?'

"Your worst nightmare," Rick answered in a growling voice like he was a demon. Rick lunged at the pirate's neck, but the pirate managed to turn around and run. Rick caught him in one step and had him on the deck and was about to rip his throat out.

"Mark and I were watching, and he whispered, 'Stop! We need them alive.' The pirates didn't hear him speak, but the rest of us did. Rick stopped and looked back at Mark, then stood up holding on to the pirate's collar. The pirate's face was slack as the venom had hit his blood. He was no longer a threat.

"Before we could stand, the pirate leader came on the bridge with another six men behind him and demanded to know what was going on. I couldn't believe Mark's response and had to hold back my laughter.

"He said, 'You see, you've happened upon a group of vampires having a party. Lucky enough for us, you happened by. We were getting hungry and were thinking of getting takeout,' ever so calmly."

Everyone erupted in fits of laughter at that.

"Good line, Mark," said Abeo, wiping tears from his eyes.

"Rick tried to keep himself from laughing too, and I saw him put his hand over his mouth to hide his fangs.

"The pirate was so stupid. He had answered, 'Take out? What, you think Domino's will deliver out here?' Of course, the other pirates broke out into laughter, letting us know all their exact positions.

"Then we heard one of the girls say, 'Ah no, Domino's doesn't deliver what we like to eat.' The pirate leader had spun around with his guns ready to fire, but when he saw Falon standing there, a demure, slender woman in a bikini, he laughed

out loud. She taunted him with a 'come hither look' and motioned with her finger.

"The pirate took one step toward her, and Mark said, 'I wouldn't do that, amigo.' Of course he answered, 'She no scares me...' And that was the last thing he said, as Falon's face suddenly transformed as she leapt on the pirate aiming for his neck, tumbling him to the deck. The bite she delivered only incapacitated him by making him high, but it was good enough.

"The other two girls took out two more pirates, leaving only three more. They closed ranks and trained their guns on Mark and I, who were still on our knees.

"One of the pirates said to the girls, 'Keep back or we kill these two.' However, Rick and the girls didn't listen, and did the slow-walk toward them as if they were in a movie. It was hilarious to watch. All they needed was a wind machine to blow their hair back, and spotlights to emphasize their walk. All four had their fangs out and battle faces on, with red, glowing eyes. It was impressive.

"I glanced sideways at Mark and he nodded. The two of us 'vamped' out as we broke our restraints, jumping up suddenly and attacking two of the three pirates from behind. Gwen got the last pirate down on the deck.

"Mark then said, 'Okay, girls, have fun,' his fangs still out and his eyes still glowing an angry red. In fact, all of the guys were still in offense mode. The pirates screamed and begged for mercy. All that they got was a big dose of venom to make them high.

"Mark decided to interrogate the leader to find out if they knew about the island and who lived there. Mark picked up the mumbling, incoherent, pirate from the deck and sat him in a chair. However, when the pirate looked at Mark, he blubbered even more as tears rolled down his face.

"The pirate begged for his life saying, 'Please, don't eat me!' And Mark, cool as a cucumber, answered, 'I won't if you answer my questions.' He kept his visage like a vampire with full *fangs and red eyes. But it was difficult to hold onto the aggression in the face of such a pathetic man. After spending a few minutes with the pirate, he'd learned their operation parameters and who they normally targeted. They had no idea there was an island there.*

"I asked Mark what we should do with them. I had caught the two men who tried to flee, and dragged them back.

"Rick had the best idea and said we should sink their boat and set them adrift in a dinghy. So that is what we did. We dumped the pirates into their life raft and then opened their seacocks and watched their boat sink quietly beneath the waves. Well, it wasn't so quiet. The vessel gave one last loud burp as the final bubble of air was pushed out and the hull disappeared into the inky black water. It didn't take very long, maybe five minutes, and then the sea was calm again.

"Falon didn't want them to die, so we gave them all a bottle of water and set them adrift.

"I went back to the bridge and started up the engines and turned all the yacht's lights back on. Taking a bearing, I sped her up to turn her a bit and make for port. We passed the dinghy, and the pirates were all chattering about vampires and devils. We knew no one would ever believe them if they made it to shore.

"The last thing we did was report the incident to the authorities when we made port," Andrews said. "They were very appreciative of the fact that more pirates had been stopped."

Everyone applauded the story and laughed at the demise of the pirates.

"That was a marvelous story!" said Margaret. "Thank you."

30—Unsavory Clients

Margaret

It was near the end of July. Abeo was gone on another trip. He left right after the barbeque at Lora's. He had received word from his bank that he had another project to manage. He had been gone about three weeks now—without any contact though, and that was quite unusual. My attempts at contacting him have failed. It wasn't like him to stay out of touch.

So where is he? I was pacing a little. I had just fed the twins and they were down for a while, so I was at odds with myself. I called the Zurich number again and left another message. He told me that he did receive the messages there. I didn't have any other numbers for him other than his cell, and I had filled the voice message box with my calls. So there was no point in calling that number anymore.

I needed help. Lora had told me that Andrews owned a security company. I wondered if he looked for missing people? I decided I might as well ask.

"Hello, Maggie, what's up," said Lora when she picked up the phone.

"How did you know it's me?"

"I programmed your number into my phone, silly."

"Oh, yeah. Why didn't I think of that?"

"What's up? You sound rattled."

"Well, I haven't heard from Abeo and he's been gone for three weeks now. It's not unusual for him to be gone this long, just unusual for him to not call."

"Oh, that is worrisome. You should speak to Andrews."

"That is what I was hoping for. Do you have his number?"

"Sure"

I called Andrews as soon as I was off the phone with Lora.

"Andrews speaking. Nothing is too difficult for us to handle. How may I help today?"

"Hello, Andrews, or do you prefer Andrews? It's Margaret speaking."

"Hello, Margaret. Call me Andrews. What can I do for you?"

"Well, it's about Abeo. He's been gone since he started traveling after the BBQ. Normally, he calls me every day. But I have not heard from him at all."

"That's not good. When was the last time you spoke?"

"Um, the day he left, so the day after the BBQ party. Then I was caught up in life. I lost track of time. I tried calling him to tell him all about his children. He loves getting updates on what they're learning. He didn't call back. That's when I felt something strange."

"What did you feel?"

"I cannot describe it. I was anxious for no reason."

"Okay. May I come by your house and look around? Perhaps there are some clues we can find. Even the smallest thing could make a difference. At the same time, I'll get my team working on tracing his movements."

"Oh, Andrews, thank you. Yes, drop by any time."

"I'll be there in fifteen minutes."

I got off the phone and felt better for having called him. Someone competent would be looking. Could Abeo being immortal be part of the reason he's disappeared? He told me that he had to disappear periodically. Surely he wouldn't leave his children though?

I couldn't tell my mom anything about this. I was glad I now had Falon and Lora to talk to. It was difficult to not be able to share with anyone.

"Falon speaking."

"Falon, sorry to bother you. Are you busy?"

"No, actually. I just finished up my work for the day. What's up?"

"I need to vent, but I can't vent, does that make any sense?"

"More than you know. Can you come over here? Can you bring the babies?"

Twenty minutes later, I had the twins dressed and in their stroller. Andrews hadn't arrived yet, so I left a note on the door and headed out. I brought my breast pump and other gear, because when you have infant twins, you have so much gear to carry around.

Falon met me at the door and brought the stroller inside. Mark picked it up and carried it to the garage, where he separated the carriage from the wheels and put the twins in a quiet room upstairs to keep them sleeping.

Falon sat me down and put a bottle of wine and two glasses down in front of me.

"Oh, I can't drink."

"Then pump. You're going to need a drink."

I got out the pump and set it up.

"I heard from Lora, so I know what this is about. Did you call Andrews?"

"Yes, and that made me feel better he's on his way over—I left a note on my door that I came over here."

"Mark will intercept him. Now, Margaret, we have a wild story to tell you, but when we're done, I hope you feel better."

Confused about where this was going, I shrugged and listened.

"As you know, the six of us are immortals. The year before last, Mark's family went to great lengths to try to keep us apart. They kidnapped him, kidnapped me, sent a thug after me who assaulted me, and we're still not sure they are satisfied that I'll keep our damned secret."

"That seems extreme."

"It was," said Falon. "Now I'm not sure that Abeo is on their radar or not, but it's a possibility. He may have been on his own so long he lost track of the others."

"You guys need a secret handshake or something so you can identify each other," I said.

"You know, that's not a bad idea," said Falon. "Mark, is there a chance that your family could be causing him trouble?"

"I doubt it. He wouldn't be on their radar."

"The vampire hunters perhaps?"

"I'll check on the Order and see."

"Excuse me, are there really vampires? I even asked Abeo if he was one."

"No, there is no such thing as a vampire," said Mark. "However, there is a very old order that goes back five hundred years that has hunted us. They know what we are."

"There seems to be a truce now, though, doesn't there?" asked Falon.

"Perhaps."

"What does this have to do with Abeo?" I asked. The doorbell rang, and Andrews walked in.

"Hello, it seems we have another missing person?" he asked. "Margaret, I'm going to ask you some questions, and please give me as much detail as you can remember."

"Surely."

"Let me say first, because Abeo is an immortal, it will be a little trickier to find him," said Andrews.

"Why?"

"Because immortals can change their appearance, at least the old ones can. Show her, Mark."

Before my eyes, Mark's face changed subtly and became someone else. Not very different, but enough that it was not the same person.

"Wow, that's useful."

"Yes, and it prevents us from using facial recognition to find him," said Andrews. "But we'll try that first. If he's hiding from someone, or trying to avoid discovery, that will be his toolkit."

"What were his plans, Margaret?" asked Falon.

"He had a business trip, unspecified length. It would keep him away, and he was sad about that, but he promised he would be home as soon as possible."

"Do you know the bank he works for?"

"Not really. I have his business card, but it only has his phone number on it and nothing else. I know it's in Zurich. I don't understand the woman who answers the phone, so I couldn't tell you the name."

"Gwen can help with that. She speaks German."

"But it's in Switzerland."

"Yes, and German is one of the four languages spoken there," said Andrews. "We'll start there. Now how much clothing did he take?"

"Hardly any. He rarely takes clothes, perhaps a few shirts. It's like wherever he goes, he's got a ready supply of clothes there."

"That could be the case. That would make sense if he was a single guy and traveled to the same places often. It would make it simple to be on a plane quickly."

"Has he ever told you what other cities he visits frequently?"

"I'll have to think about that." *Did he mention other cities?* "He has told me he usually stays in hotels that have efficiency rooms. His tastes are high, so they would need to be suites. He's also a pilot, and he flies himself around."

"Excellent, Margaret! Those are great details. Anything else?"

What else did I learn? "He said he is usually in a place for up to a month at a time. So he still may not be missing, just out of reach. That's it for now."

"That is very good, Margaret. That gives us a number of leads to work up. I'll be back in touch with you tomorrow on the progress. But, if you ever want an update, don't hesitate to call me, okay?"

"Thank you, Andrews."

I had another doctor's appointment after meeting Andrews. The day Abeo left, he let me know that we were pregnant again. So I made an appointment to check on the new pregnancy. When I got home, I needed to tell the kids. They needed to know they were going to get a brother or sister.

I woke them up from their long nap at Falon's, grateful that they slept soundly while we were all discussing Abeo's absence.

"Wake up, my little monsters."

Bimbo made baby noises as he opened his eyes. Keyshia smiled at her mother.

"I want to talk to you guys," I started. "I know you're very young, but I think you may understand me."

They looked at each other and nodded at me.

"Momma is going to have more babies," I said.

The twins smiled at me.

"That means you will be getting a new brother and sister because your papa specializes in one of each," I said, thinking of Abeo.

"So we need to go and design your bedrooms to make room for your siblings. Let's see what color you like. It's hard to believe you're only six months old."

When Abeo explained to me why the kids were developing so fast, he had said, "Our children develop faster. They will be the equivalent of eight or nine intellectually by the time they are three."

We need homeschooling, I thought. They'll never be able to sit in public school. Come to think of it, so will Gwen's child. With all these immortal children we will need our own school. Maybe that is something I can do!

31—Business Partners

Abeo

This business trip wasn't supposed to be so long. I had told Margaret I would only be here for two weeks. I had yet to explain my business to Margaret and the other immortals. As far as they were concerned, I worked for a human bank.

Our original group left the ship and settled in the Cascade Mountains near what is now Washington State. They stayed on the east side of the range because of the weather, which was sunnier. When some of that group broke away to explore the West Coast, my old captain Tuata, one of our pilots Lucas, and I decided to leave the group and go out on our own.

The three of us found each other a few centuries after Aran had died and I left the humans. We kept in touch with each other, but kept our distance too. They had expressed concern about me being in the same place for so long. They were concerned that I was risking being discovered and, therefore, their existence was in jeopardy of being discovered too.I kept assuring them that this was not the case, that my identity was watertight, and there was no connection to them whatsoever.

The three of us hadn't planned on becoming wealthy, but we had to do something with our time. So we became merchants, buying and selling goods in different parts of the world. We traded with each other, and brought exotic products across the seas. Sometime during the first century we realized that we had to store the riches we had accumulated.

At the time, Romans used temples to store their wealth. The priests kept track of deposits for rich citizens. We did not want to use their temples, so we built our own and stored our gold and jewels there. Eventually, we built underground vaults and hid our capital inside. As humans developed ways of tracking money, we adapted and eventually created a bank on the site of our vault. As money became notes and coins instead of gold and jewels, we started exchanging one for the other. We kept the money fluid and changeable.

We've been on this planet so long now that we have amassed more wealth than a god. As a result, we had to devise a way to secretly and carefully distribute it to charities around the world to keep it from accumulating any more. We realized that we needed our own bank.

Our bank never looked big, or small. We specifically made sure our building wasn't ostentatious, that our clientele was not ultra rich. We practiced "a medium sized" reputation. We established a ceiling on the amount of assets in the bank, and when we reached that, we had to start giving away some of it or else it would draw a lot of attention to us. We were all of the opinion that if it got out just how much was in our collective bank, every highly paid thief in the world would be taking shots at it. So, we had maintained a studied look of averageness.

In the world of banks today, that is very difficult, because all banks strive to be the biggest, with the most holdings. We had to curb that greed. Shareholders were carefully screened to be average people, not blue-chip collectors, to make sure no one expected huge profits. We kept the salaries of the top executive well below the levels of banks with similar wealth in them. And most importantly, we kept the knowledge of just how much money was stored by the bank a closely guarded secret. Only my former crew members knew.

We were constantly shifting the money around from one form to another—gold bullion to stock, stock to cash, cash back to gold bullion. Always changing, and always making sure there was a little loss each time. It did nothing to devalue the hoard we had. Lose a million, we still have trillions left. We could have bought and paid for our own country a few times.

Hence the charities. Lucas came up with the idea that we could regularly donate to charities that actually do some good. Like the ones that built schools or put in water treatment plants. Tuata found a charity called the Tiny House Project and thought that would be a good investment too. We could help the fledgling charity expand into more countries and do good work there. This was the reason I came to Canada in the first place. I was supposed to make contact with the group who ran that charity. But before I could make that connection, I met Margaret.

And the rest, as they say, is history.

When my association to Margaret actually got me closer to the people involved with the Tiny House charity, I couldn't believe my luck. My first business trip back to our headquarters was to inform Tuata and Lucas that I have made contact with the chair of the charity.

My two partners worked in different parts of the world. Tuata was responsible for the Middle East, Africa, and India. Lucas worked in Europe, Russia, China, and Malaysia. I was in charge of North and South America, the Caribbean, and all the island nations.

This business trip was necessary because one of my partners was worried that something about our bank had leaked out—that there had been a group of people poking around our little bank in Switzerland and might be close to discovering its secret. When I arrived, nothing seemed out of the ordinary until two gentlemen came in to ask some questions. They wanted to know when the bank was built. They wanted to know who the owners were, how long, how many employees, etcetera.

Over the years, we'd been very careful to "go out of business" several times, "get purchased" several times, and made sure there was a paper trail of false documents anyone could follow. For a brief spell, we even tore down the bank and built an apartment building on the site. Being the landlords, we collected their rents and reinvested it back into the building. Eventually, that too had to end and become something else. The property went back to being a bank.

The reason we stayed apart was so we could be each others' buyers and no one would recognize us. The paper trail of ownership of the property stretched back unbroken for two hundred years. Before that, there was a fire at City Hall and the town's records were all destroyed.

Things like that happen more often than you can imagine.

It might be time for another fire, perhaps at the bank. Since I was the current owner of the bank, I was the only one seen going there. Tuata and Lucas were not allowed anywhere near the facility, and I decided that the bank should go up for sale again. I notified Tuata, who would come in and provide the buyer's story. If this didn't throw whoever was snooping off the trail, *then* we would need to burn the building, or perhaps tear it down in favor of a different new modern building. But that might have problems too.

I needed to think about this. I called Tuata late at night.

"What is the problem, Wendell?" she asked.

"There are people sniffing around and I'm not sure what their purpose is. They may just be interested in purchasing the building."

"We cannot allow that to happen."

"No, of course not. I have to find out who they are and why they are asking questions."

"Get back to me when you find out. If I have to come and buy the bank, I can be there within twenty-four hours."

"Good to know."

My investigation led me to discover that a surveillance team was operating in the village just outside of the city. They were casing and mapping one of the oldest villas in the area. The villa was owned by a cult, and the people inside were certifiable. It was a story in the village that they thought they were vampire hunters. Why the surveillance company was looking at my bank became clear when I started going over the accounts. It turns out the cult kept their money in our bank.

Damn it! This could bring unwanted eyeballs our way.

When I examined their customer records, I discovered that they had been with our bank since before the last fire, so for over two hundred years. I looked into the details of that account and discovered they had bullion, jewels, as well as cash in our vault. There was a small fortune in their account, enough that a small bank like ours shouldn't have it, because we didn't have the security to keep that much money safe. But maybe they were playing the same game—being average. If their money was in an average bank, authorities would not notice how wealthy they were.

Frankly, I didn't want their money in our bank. We had lots of little accounts, but not businesses. They appeared to be the only business account. How did they open a business account? The signature was not a name I recognized. But then I had only been the owner for fifty or so years—since the Second World War. That was a dicey time. I was "my father" during that time. We were afraid our little bank would be exposed by the Nazis. They would have loved to have found the stash in our basement.

I decided to reach out to someone I had met only a few times: Andrews Andrews, who ran a security company. Maybe they could help.

"AGP Security."

"Hello, is Robert Andrews there?"

"May I ask who's speaking?"

"Tell him it's Abeo."

I could hear the telephone equipment clicking through, but it was taking a few more clicks than expected.

"Abeo! My man, we've been looking for you?"

"Really, why?"

"Because Margaret was worried and said that you've been gone a long time without calling her regularly."

Oh damn, yes, I haven't called in a while. Something like this could blow my cover! I can't have security companies and people looking into my business, it will uncover who we are. I'm lucky that it's people I know so far, but I have to stop this.

"Well, you found me. Everything is fine. I've just had something to deal with. As a matter of fact, it's the reason I'm calling you."

"Oh, okay. Well, what seems to be the problem? And may I let Margaret know I heard from you?"

"Yes! Please! I will call her when I get off with you. We've had some suspicious inquiries at our bank in the past few months."

"What sort of inquiries?"

"The kind a surveillance company would do. I'm not sure why."

"Do you have any names? Like a contact that went to your bank?"

"Yes, the man left a card. It says Grisham on it."

Andrews started laughing out loud with big belly laughs. When he finally caught his breath, he said, "Oh my, it's a small world. That's my guy. You're in Switzerland?"

"Yes. Why are you investigating my bank?" I was a little annoyed.

"We are not. We're investigating a group in the area called the Order. Something must have led the investigator to your bank. I will tell him to leave you guys alone. By any chance, do they have their money with you?"

"I looked them up, and yes they do. They're quite old. They have been with us for two hundred years."

"How interesting. We should work together. That way I can maintain your secrecy and still operate on them."

"Do we need to have a change of ownership or a fire? "I asked. "That's how we usually deal with someone sniffing around too closely."

"No! And those methods don't work in the modern era anyway. They'll just bring more notice to you. Are you coming home soon? I can let Margaret know."

"Working on it!" I said. After I got off the phone, I decided to collect all the documents that pertained to this customer and copy them. I'd take them back to Montreal and hand them over to Andrews for their investigation.

Next task, call Margaret!

I was relieved that it was not someone digging into us. I would also update Tuata. She'd be grateful as well. *Wait 'til she hears about our new friends, and immortals to boot.*

32—Future Plans

Andrews

Abeo returned to Montreal about a week later, bringing me copies of his bank's records detailing the activity of the Order. This was incredibly helpful in filling out our files and our knowledge on them.

"Abeo, can we share this information with the group?" I asked him.

"Why?"

"A few reasons. First, I think your strategy is very good for hiding wealth. Especially old wealth. I think Mark could benefit from knowing this. Two, you indicated you wanted to invest in Falon's charity. They'll need you to disclose where the money is coming from. And three, you will end up with some new customers."

He considered my explanation for a few minutes, pacing back and forth in my office. When he at last turned toward me, his phone was in his hand.

"I need to speak to my partners first. May I do that in private somewhere?"

"Of course, we have a soundproof phone room, for just this sort of thing. Right this way." I led him out of my office and down the hall a few feet to basically a closet that we have soundproofed and made impervious to listening devices. It had no windows, so we painted it a bright colour and made sure the lighting was bright. Otherwise, it felt like a tomb in there.

Abeo returned to my office ten minutes later with a smile on his face. "My partners agree, this opportunity is worth 'keeping in the family' so-to-speak. So please, go ahead and share the information with Mark and the others."

It was the last long weekend of the summer, and the soft launch of Rick and Justin's new restaurant was around the corner. Rick wanted to have one last party to test all the dishes they were going to serve. Justin had given Anita all the recipes for the new dishes the restaurant was going to have on their first menu, and she had made them all for us.

In addition to the four couples and children, Duffy was invited too. Mark hiring Duffy was a key step in his ultimate plan—most of which I didn't know.

Mark took advantage of the get-together to speak to everyone about business.

"Friends, now that everyone is here, I'd like to have a meeting with the nine of us briefly," said Mark. "Rick, where can we go so that we will have privacy?"

"We can use my office. I can lock the door," said Rick. We all followed Rick to his office.

"Friends, I've got some very interesting news to share with everyone," said Mark. "First off, you know that Duffy here was read in before the Caribbean trip. I've engaged him and his company in a project I call Island Paradise."

"What is that about?" I asked.

"It's about finding a private island that perhaps we can all live on," said Mark. "I'm looking at how to future-proof our lives."

"He started searching for and mapping remote islands, on which we may someday build our own private sanctuary."

"Wow, that is interesting," said Rick.

"Second, Abeo here has a business that we can incorporate into our plans, if he wants to, that will help make that possible," said Mark. "As immortals, we need to be cognizant of the future, and plan for it. We may not be able to remain invisible forever. His business is a bank. He owns this bank with two other immortals.

"Third, Abeo has offered to invest heavily into the Tiny House charity. This is a strategy that he and his partners have come up with to disguise the amount of wealth they've accumulated. They give their money away to charities to help humanity."

"Abeo approached me a few weeks ago with a very generous offer. He and his bank will become one of our largest donors, but they want to remain silent donors. So thank you so much Abeo!" gushed Falon.

"I have to admit, Abeo, I was impressed with your strategy for keeping small," said Mark. "As a businessman, you've been dealing with hiding wealth for a long time. In this day and age of everything being digital, it's difficult to stay hidden. I admire your group for their ingenuity.

"I have one more thing to say. I think the principal players here—those of us with large bank accounts—need to have a meeting, perhaps once the restaurant has launched, and start to formulate some real plans."

There was a chorus of agreement from everyone.

"I would also like to make an announcement," said Rick. "As Justin is not here, I would like to let you know that we can reveal the name for the new restaurant. We wanted to give her a personality of her own. So please welcome into the world, L'Escalade!" Rick pulled a sheet off a large rectangular sign that would hang on the building soon. We all applauded.

"Justin had said that the location spoke to him of old-world charm. So we styled the name in 17th century lettering. He visited old France and brought back decor ideas that would capture that charm. The restaurant is going to be truly beautiful inside, elegant and opulent, and we wanted her name to reflect that. You really feel like you are stepping back in time when you walk in."

"I love the name," I said.

"Me too," said Falon and Gwen.

"Any other business?" asked Mark.

Heads were shaking, indicating no. So we all left Rick's office and returned to the pool deck.

We were all happily tasting the delicious menu while all the kids were eating their own meals. After dinner, the older kids were having a blast in the pool while the adults all were in the hot tub—except for Anita, who was taking care of the babies. Anita brought her cousin Carlos up from Georgia to help with serving and barkeeping. He hadn't been read in yet, but I expected if he stayed that would be a condition. His dream was to start his own catering business. Anita was going to help him get started.

I was watching the youngest children, who were now nine months old, all of them walking and starting to talk. Amazing, really. Margaret was right, they were all developing quickly. We would need to homeschool them. They just won't fit into a "normal" school. So how did we do that? Who would do that?

Our future was not obvious, and it would be increasingly difficult to blend in with humanity. Mark might have the right idea, looking for an island for us. But the next generation of our people was already here. Soon, Falon and Lora would have kids too. Margaret had two more on the way. Lora's older kids would become immortal eventually. There was a whole community here.

Listen to yourself, worrying about things that haven't happened yet, I chastised myself. I couldn't help it. Ever since becoming immortal, and a father, these thoughts had invaded my mind and dreams. I thought we would need to do something. It was a question of what and when.

As a security guy, it was my job to see all the dangers, the leaks, the potential issues. It was also my job to come up with solutions, and I didn't see many of them. I wasn't used to not having solutions. Technology might not be the friend we thought it was either.

33—More Babies!

Margaret

I was ready this time, not like the last time when we were moving house during the same week.

My first set of twins were not even a year old yet. *What am I thinking?* I was seduced by my husband and his desire for lots of kids. Me, the mother of twins already.

Like the last time, I was as big as a whale. These two were active as well, a testament to the fact they were immortal. But now, this time, so was I. So healing afterward wouldn't be as bad.

I was only the second immortal woman to have babies in our group. Gwen had one on the same day as my first set of twins. They got her out of the hospital fast, to cover up her speedy healing. Abeo was suggesting that we deliver these twins at home, for the same reason. I wasn't going to disguise the healing so easily.

It was scaring the crap out of me, though. Home delivery? No drugs? *What if something goes wrong?* Granted, Gwen told me that they had a doctor who could come in to help if I wanted. She warned me that he was a very old dude.

I had been researching home births on the internet, and one of the warnings was that multiple babies should not be home birthed. *Well, that's me.* I could see why: more complicated, more opportunities for things to go wrong. But I kind of liked the idea.

Some people used a birthing pool. I even saw one woman who gave birth in the ocean. It seemed home births were a personal choice, and only one that a healthy woman with healthy babies could make. Well, I was very healthy, and so were the twins. *So let's give it a try.*

Abeo purchased a birthing pool. It was a small, aboveground, saltwater swimming pool, so that would work. One thing I learned was that babies breathe liquid until they come out. So it was important to let the birth happen completely before bringing the baby's head out of water. In other words, don't rush to get the face above water.

It was recommended to have a doula or midwife present, but I didn't know one that could keep a secret. Would she need to keep the secret? Perhaps she could just come and help with the birth then leave. The first woman I called was a recent immigrant to Montreal from Nigeria. She was practiced in traditional birthings and was familiar with water births. She explained she used the time-tested traditions of her people to ease babies into the world. I liked the sound of that.

In the end, I chose that doula from Nigeria, to come help with our birth. She told me to call her when my water broke. Today was my due date, and the babies were very active. They were playing a soccer game inside there. I could barely stand because my belly was so heavy it knocked me off balance, so I was lounging on a chair in the TV room. Abeo was the perfect father today, keeping our first twins occupied with activities, eating, and napping. Perhaps I would call Anita to help when I went into labor. *In fact, maybe I should call her now just in case.*

"Hello, Anita."

"*Ola*, Margaret, what can I do for you?"

"I was wondering if I could pay you to babysit the twins when I go into labor."

"Of course, Margaret. I would be happy to babysit, but you don't have to pay me."

"That's very generous of you. We are doing this today."

"Do you need me there now?" asked Anita.

"Please?"

"On my way."

My water broke before she arrived. Luckily, Abeo had the twins down for a nap. He called the doula and we knew it would be half an hour before she arrived. Based on my first experience, the babies might be here by then. The last birth was very quick.

At the end of October, it was not nice outside, so we couldn't use the pool outside. Instead, Abeo set it up in the basement. It was actually a small inflatable swimming pool but it was deep enough to cover my chest when I was sitting on the bottom. When I expressed my concern that it would slosh water all over the floors, or worse yet, collapse when I leaned on the side, he purchased a portable hot tub instead. It too was inflatable, but the sides were much more stiff and less likely to collapse. And it heated the water—bonus.

He set up the hot tub in the basement and had it running. The water was heated to about 37C. He had also placed cedar decking tiles all around the tub so we wouldn't have to walk on concrete.

"I like having this inside," he said to me. "It will be nice to use it during the winter when we cannot go outside."

"It is a luxury to have a hot tub in the house," I answered. I was trying to get up the stairs to step over the side, but I couldn't see where I was going.

"Margaret, wait, let me help you," said Abeo. "Why do you insist on doing everything on your own?"

"It's just me," I said. "I don't feel like I should be asking people for help doing this shit."

"But you have to."

Abeo actually got into the tub and helped me step down and sit on the shelf inside. Oh my, the water was perfect, and it came up to my neck. I could feel myself starting to relax a bit, when a contraction started.

"Ow!" I screamed. "Geez, that hurt!" The first one was only a poke really, considering what was going to be happening. It woke me up, though.

Abeo was out of the tub and kneeling on the floor outside of the tub. I heard the doorbell ring and Anita answered it, and then footsteps coming toward us and down the stairs.

"Hello, Margaret, how are you doing?" asked the doula.

"Okay. I guess. Just had my first contraction," I said.

"So lots of time."

"No, not necessarily. The last time, it was only an hour."

"Okay, then let me get set up quickly." The doula set her things up beside the hot tub, while I went into another contraction.

"Breathe, my love," said Abeo, mimicking the breathing routine we had been taught. "Breathe."

"That contraction was long and hard."

"I'm ready," announced the doula. "I'm getting in there with you, okay?" I looked up and saw she was wearing a garment sort of like a wet suit.

"What are you wearing?"

"This is a wet suit, because I will get chilled standing in the water."

"It's a hot tub, and the water is heated," I said.

"You'll be working hard, I won't," she said with a grin.

Another contraction took me, and we yelled together, and breathed together, as she helped me push down. She massaged my belly and my shoulders, and kept the warm water over my shoulders to keep me comfortable. When the next contraction came, I instinctively opened my legs and curled around my body as it pushed hard. She reached between my legs and touched me gently.

"Your baby's head is crowning. Push again, Margaret."

So I pushed again. Out popped our little girl into the water. The doula waited until her feet were clear of my body before clamping the cord and raising her face to the surface. She instinctively opened her mouth as soon as she touched the air, how remarkable. A loud, healthy wail erupted from her mouth at the cruel interruption of her warm cocoon. The doula washed her gently and then got out of the tub and swaddled her tightly and left her in a bassinet. She just made it back into the tub in time for my second child. Like before, the second followed the first quickly. It seemed he just about swam out on his own.

Again, the doula kept him under the surface until he was clear and she had clamped the cord. The instinct to breathe instantly took over as soon as his face was above water. Once he was swaddled, she came back to help me with the after birth. Abeo was already working on emptying the water so he could clean out the tub.

He had brought down warm clothes to wear after the birth so I could climb into those and wrap myself up in blankets with my new twins.

"They are both healthy and perfect. Do you have names for them?" asked the doula.

"Yes, we do," I said. Then I had another contraction. A powerful one. "Um, there is something wrong. I am having another contraction."

Abeo came and took the twins from me. The doula got out her stethoscope and listened to my belly. She looked at me in a mix of horror and wonder.

"There is another child still," she said with awe in her voice. "How did you carry three such large babies?" She quickly helped me out of the warm blankets and pants, and got me back into the tub, although no water was left.

As soon as I sat down, another wave of contractions took my body, leaving me breathless.

"Breathe! You must breathe!" she said.

Abeo was beside me, holding on to my hands as I pushed with everything I had.

Another baby popped out, another girl. She was smaller than the other two, but still a good-sized baby. Five minutes later, the last afterbirth came out. This time the doula double-checked my belly to make sure there were no more surprises. After washing off the little girl, she too was weighed and measured, and swaddled.

The doula gave me the last child, while Abeo held the boy, and the doula held the girl.

"Wow, I've never been present at a triplets birthing, especially a natural one."

"Grace. The third one should be called Grace. Grace Naomi Musa."

"I love that, Margaret," said Abeo. "The other girl is Téonie Thistle Musa, and the boy will be Wendell Thistle Musa."

"What a beautiful family we have," I said, tears flowing down my face. The feeling in my chest was like my heart was about to explode in happiness. The pressure made my breathing hitch as I gazed at my beautiful daughter Grace. What a gift.

34—Reflections

Mark

Why does the end of the year always make me reflect back on what has happened? It was not quite the end of the year, but I was thinking that this time last year babies were coming into our world, and new friends were on the horizon. We had a new home along with Rick and Lora.

Falon and I had had a successful year in business. Her charity was running smoothly, and Lora continued to work with her. My businesses were doing well and I'd found interesting projects to employ Duffy and his crew as well. In general, our group had expanded, and succeeded. All except Falon not getting pregnant. I had hoped that would happen to us.

Sitting in my home office, staring out at the snow falling gently down, my mind roamed freely. I focused momentarily on a snowflake, perfect in its formation, swaying side to side as it fell silently to the ground. I watched it as it lay down on the other flakes that fell before it, as it bonded to them, creating a whole, and I realized that this group I'd become part of, this group had done much the same thing. We have fallen into each other and bonded to become a whole.

It was only five years ago that I had faced a life without Falon, that I was being sent away to recreate myself, to become someone else. My heart had been torn in two that day. Walking away from her had been the most difficult thing I ever did in all my young years as an immortal. My parents had spoken about some of the things they'd endured over the centuries, some of the heartbreak that had befallen members of our family. Some of them didn't fare so well, taking their own lives rather than live a life without a mate. That made it all the more painful when they had tried to deny me my love in Falon. You'd think they would have understood. Instead, they claimed it was because of that suffering that they wanted to stop our union.

So we were lucky, very lucky, Gwen, Rick, Abeo, and I. We found love, and were able to help those humans make the transition into immortality so we didn't have to be alone. Now there was another generation coming and they would be immortal too.

There was a question I had to figure out: *Do we isolate ourselves?* What about the inner circle of friends and children? Do we bring them into our world? Do we expand? What dangers would that incur?

What sombre thoughts for a day like this! I chastised myself. I was supposed to be thinking about the holidays and what we were going to do. Our house wasn't large enough to have everyone over for dinner, but I hated asking Rick and Lora to be the hosts all the time. Perhaps Margaret and Abeo could? He travelled so much. *That reminds me, I need to speak to him about the project.*

I should really ask Falon if she would like a larger house for entertaining. It's not like we can't afford it. Perhaps now that our friends had such luxury homes, she'd agree to something we could grow into. Getting up and putting out my cigar, I walked into the hall and looked for Falon.

"Falon? Where are you?"

"Yeah, upstairs folding laundry, hun." I ran upstairs. "What's up?" she asked me.

"I think it's time we get a bigger house," I said.

"Why?"

"So we can have large parties too."

"Are you jealous?"

"No. Well, maybe. I don't know. We really don't have the space for that many, do we?" She looked at my face at that moment. "Oh, that's the point isn't it. You want a bigger house because everyone else has a bigger house."

"No, not because everyone else does, because I wanted one in the first place hoping we would have kids."

"That is a different discussion. One I'm willing to have, just not right now while I'm folding laundry. Okay, let's look at houses in January."

My face must have changed because Falon giggled, put down the towel she was folding, and came to stand in front of me. She hugged me and laid her head on my chest.

"It means that much to you, eh?"

"I guess so. I always wanted a big house with lots of bedrooms for a large family, and a big back yard. I tell you I would have purchased the house Rick bought if he had not."

"Really? We'll need a housekeeper to help with a place that big."

"Already thought of that."

"Mr. Chisholm, what have you done?"

"Nothing, I swear. I've done nothing, yet. But I have been planning."

35—Celebrations!

Lora

I was decorating for the holidays. My celebration wasn't Christmas, but Yule. It happens at the same time but it's much, much, older. Traditionally, Yule was a celebration of Winter Solstice, the turning of the seasons and of new life to come. A big feast was made for all to participate in. It has since been hijacked by many cultures.

Holly was a sacred plant for Wiccans, because it stayed green all year round. Red and green were the colors of Yule, along with white, silver, and gold. So I was decorating everything in those colors. Rick had pulled out the big tree again, and Anita and I were having fun stringing lights and hanging ornaments. She helped me create beautiful boughs of pine for the staircase and we wove lights throughout.

The artificial tree stood twelve feet tall, but it was narrow at the bottom, which was perfect for not taking up the whole front hall. We still had room for the table and flowers in the center. The tree was nestled in the circle of the stairs, looking like it was being hugged by light.

This year for the holidays, I was going to experience a Cuban Christmas for the first time. Anita was preparing all the traditional foods. Since my kids wanted some of our foods too, we were combining everything into a new tradition for us. Turkey with my stuffing and mashed potatoes, plus a roasted pig with black beans, rice and garlicky yuca. It was going to be a spectacular dinner. We'd have so much food, I'd need help eating it all. *Time to invite friends!*

We were also all gearing up to the official opening of Justin and Rick's new restaurant. New Year's Eve was going to be a huge party. The soft launch that started in October had gone perfectly, and their place is perfect. I loved their new menu too. But the two of them could really use some rest and relaxation.

They were thinking of shutting the restaurant down for a few days at Christmas to get ready for the big day. It was generally unheard of to close a restaurant during this season, but they wanted a hard line between the soft launch and the official opening. The media had been invited for a tour the day before the opening, so Justin wanted everything perfect.

Christmas was in a few days. The kids were off school now, and getting more excited every day as things in the house got busier. I needed to go shopping with Anita for food.

"Anita, when you have time, let's go shopping today for the feast. I want to make sure we get a large turkey," I called out.

"Si, Lorita, I should be ready in about thirty minutes."

Our first stop was to a farm outside the city that sold animals directly to customers. They selected a thirty-pound turkey for us and a thirty-pound piglet. They did the slaughtering for me, because, frankly, it wasn't my thing. Anita had volunteered, but it made me queasy. Not enough to stop eating meat though! Once the animals were dressed, and packaged for us, we took them home immediately to get them into the second fridge. Then we went to get all the accessories for dinner.

"How many potatoes do you think we should make?" I asked Anita.

"One per person and one for the pot."

"Got it: a ten-pound bag should be good." I also picked up a dozen sweet potatoes, ten heads of broccoli, two dozen ears of corn, and a case of twenty-four jellied cranberry sauce.

"Lorita, we can make cranberry sauce."

"Yes, I know, but my kids and I don't like the berries in the sauce, so the canned stuff is easier."

"Tsk, tsk. I will go and get a large bag of rice. Any preferences, Lorita?"

"I've always been partial to Basmati rice, myself."

"Good choice. And I will get the black beans and spices I need."

"I'll go find plantain bananas. How many do you want?"

"Two dozen, please. I also need yuca, a root vegetable, and garlic. A whole rope if they sell that here. If you cannot find the yuca, I know of a Cuban grocer we can stop by."

"Meet you by the checkout!" We went off in different directions. I found the plantains and garlic, but no yuca. Then I picked up sausage, apples, Spanish onion, pine nuts, frozen cranberries, and breadcrumbs for the stuffing. We already had the spices I'd need in the kitchen. Fifteen minutes later, I found Anita at a cash register, waiting in line. Luckily, no one was behind her.

Anita was cooking for the next two days and I made the stuffing up in advance too. Christmas morning was busy with the kids, and they had the whole day to play with all the gifts they got. We're having the big party the day after, to give everyone Christmas with their families.

The following morning, Anita was outside on the barbeque getting her piglet ready to roast while I was dressing the turkey with stuffing and getting it ready for wrapping. I helped Anita with the pig because it was heavy to lift onto the flames on her own. She helped me wrap the bird and get it into a roasting pan and into the oven for the same reason. They would be cooking for most of the day.

By 4:00 Christmas day, our friends started arriving. They all brought small gifts, so I asked them to put them under the tree, where they found gifts for them too. We all collected in the family room around the fireplace. Rick was being a barkeep, and invented a toddy for the occasion. I wasn't drinking, but I didn't tell anyone why.

When Anita told us all the food was ready, everyone piled into the dining room and found a place to sit. Along the long side tables were plates of food sliced, prepared, and presented like a professional chef would. Anita was priceless. I was glad her cousin, Carlos, had decided to stay after the wedding as well. The two of them worked well together, and the catering business was starting to pick up steam. Carlos was booked most weekends now, so it was nice he had reserved the holidays to spend with Anita and us.

Once everyone had a seat, I wanted to say a toast. I stood up at the end of the table beside Rick and looked down at the very long table. I felt like it was a movie. I took a moment to gaze at all the faces I saw there—old friends, new friends, family—and tears formed in my eyes and my heart skipped a beat. *Gosh, I was so lucky. How did I get so lucky?*

"Dear friends, thank you for coming to share this day with us. It warms my heart to see everyone here. I want you to know that Anita and her cousin Carlos did all the work preparing this feast for us, and I want to especially thank them for an exemplary job."

"Carlos, if you ever want a position as a chef, come talk to me," said Justin.

"*Muchas gracias*, Justin," said Carlos, nodding his way.

Everyone clinked glasses with their neighbors and said, *Salut*!

"So without further ado, we'll start at this end of the table and go through the beautiful buffet!" Rick stood and started the line and I returned to my spot on the opposite end. He handed a plate to the next person and let them go first. When everyone else had gone, he and I went and served ourselves. There was still so much food!

"Please take seconds and thirds!" I pleaded with everyone. They all laughed.

"I know I will! I'm always hungry!"

"Are you pregnant, Lora?" asked Mark, sitting on my left.

"I hope so, but shhh, I haven't told anyone yet."

"Oh, I'm so happy for you. That's so exciting!"

Dinner was amazing, and the men almost cleaned out all the food. Three helpings later, people were pushing back their chairs, holding their stomachs and groaning.

"Oh, I'm so full," said Mark. "But my taste buds are very happy right now."

"So am I," said Andrews. "If I try to eat anything else, I think I'll be sick."

"That's as it should be!" cried Anita. Carlos and Anita had big grins on their faces, pleased that people nearly finished all the food. There would still be leftovers for a few days, but their efforts were a huge success.

"Kids, please help Anita clear the dishes from the table and stack them in the kitchen neatly!" I called after them as they grabbed plates and walked out.

"Shall we open gifts?" I asked. In response, everyone moved into the family room. We brought in more chairs for people and arranged them around the room so everyone could speak to anyone.

Rick disappeared for a few minutes and came back wearing a Santa suit, doing his Ho Ho Hos. He loved playing Santa. We had gifts for everyone who came, something personal to mark this day in an ornament to hang on the tree. For our part, we got lots of wine and decor for the house. The rule was not over fifty dollars. The kids had finished the dishes with Anita, and wanted to watch a movie.

"That's a good idea. All those who would like to watch a movie, waddle toward the theater room and select a seat. Rick and I will bring in refreshments."

"Oh, no more food!" cried Gwen.

"What about coffee and liqueurs?"

"Not for me, thanks," said Margaret. "No, I'm not pregnant again, I think. I just can't put another thing in my mouth."

"Really?" asked Abeo. Margaret blushed on cue, and Abeo squeezed her hand.

"I will have coffee," said several people. So I set up the coffee service on the table in the back of the theater, which made twenty cups of coffee in a spigot carafe. I also brought out a regular coffeemaker to make a pot of tea.

It was a toss-up between a Marvel movie, an Indiana Jones movie, or a comedy. Marvel won out, and the movie *Endgame* was put on. While everyone was focused on that, Rick and I snuggled in the back on a two-seater we had added to the room.

"It's a good thing we expanded this room to have thirty seats," I murmured, looking at all the people in there. We had removed all the oversized recliners and replaced them with used theater seats. We got an amazing deal on ebay. So we could fit six across a row instead of four.

"You know, you have made a wonderful home for us here with all our friends," said Rick. "I want to thank you and tell you how much I love you."

"It's because of you we have this home. I'm grateful on behalf of my kids and I, thank you," I said. "I love you too with all my heart. I have a gift for you."

"Mmmm?"

"We're going to have a baby."

A second slipped by before Rick's eyes opened wide and the biggest goofiest grin split his handsome face like a hatchet.

He jumped up and grabbed me and spun me around and cried out, "I'm going to be a father! Again! Just wait 'till I tell my grown kids the news!"

Everyone was congratulating us as he got down on his knees and laid his hand on my belly. In the softest voice, he spoke to his child, making it a promise to love it forever. The tears were falling freely down my face at this point as I gazed down at my amazing man.

The others were standing around us and clapping us both on the back, and my kids were jumping up and down with joy. Little did they know, they would be getting an immortal sibling. And we needed to tell them. But that was for another day. Right now, I just want to enjoy this moment.

Falon was looking at me from across the room with a secret smile on her face. She nodded to me, so I think she had a bun in the oven too. I would hate her to be the only one without.

36—L'Escalade

Rick

L'Escalade, which had its soft launch in October, has been well received in Montreal. Still, we had changed the menu from the fare we served in Atlanta, because the clientele in Montreal was more European, and accepted more exotic fare. However, we hadn't stopped serving our signature dishes that made us successful in the South.

Growing pains aside, the chefs we had on staff now were excellent and could manage the kitchen properly. Justin and I simply had to be present on a regular basis to make sure everything stayed that way. With the holiday season underway, our goal was to have a grand opening on New Year's with an epic party to put us on the map here. The media has been invited for a tour and sampling of the menu for two days before. So we shut down the restaurant. *I know, gasp!* Just for three days: Christmas, Boxing Day, and the day after. That gave us a day off to spend with friends and family, and a couple of days to decorate the restaurant to fit the epic nature of a grand opening.

Media day saw every news crew in the city come, cameras in tow, for the tour. We showed them everything, kitchen, bar, lounge upstairs, and the dining room of course. We let them in on some of our future plans with the lounge, and then sat them at their tables for the tasting. We went with a tapas format, giving each person one bite of each dish so they would be able to get through the whole menu. Plying them all with plenty of spirits and wine went along with that. And Chef Marcel knew just how to pair each dish with the perfect wine.

The reviews the next day were glowing: "Best new restaurant in Montreal!" "Book your reservation NOW for this place, because you won't be able to get in later!" "Chef Marcel is a genius with his food design!" "Congratulations to Chefs Justin and Rick, owners of the new L'Escalade in Old Montreal, on another world-class eatery!"

"Justin, I owe you all the gratitude," I said, reading the reviews. "You've been the guiding hand designing and organizing this venture. You have done an amazing job, brother."

"Well, we've done this together, bro. Without you, I wouldn't have been able to start our restaurant in Atlanta. I'm just so delighted that it's working so well."

"What will we do next?" I asked.

"Let's get through the grand opening first, eh?" Justin asked, then smiled. "I used 'eh' like a native! I'm being Canadianified!"

"That's not so bad. There are an astounding number of good things here."

"I know, Greggory is one of those good things," said Justin."I think I have a crush on that handsome man. I want to eat him every time I see him."

"Have you formally asked him on a date?" I asked.

"No! I've been nervous too," said Justin. "I'm not sure why."

"Maybe it's just that so much is happening. Wait till after the opening. You'll have the space and time to relax and get to know each other."

"You're right. Maybe I'll ask him to be my plus one for the party."

"Good idea."

The New Year's Eve plan was similar to the party two years ago: two sittings, with dancing, and giveaways. Everything was in place, all we had to do was execute it. The difference was that Justin and I had no intention of working that night, it was going to be all the staff. Lora and I planned on being guests that evening at the second sitting. Justin was going to be a guest plus one for the first sitting.

Lora and I got to the restaurant early. The first sitting hadn't finished and the cars were packed on the streets. The valet parking was having difficulty finding places for all the cars. So I made a note to myself to find parking nearby that we could use for guests. Once inside, I was happy to see the decor was elegant and gorgeous. I had worried a little when Justin left the decor to the staff. But they did an exemplary job.

We walked around the tables to greet some of the guests. Who did we see at a cozy table by the window? It was Justin and his plus one, Greggory. They made a cute couple. By 9:00 people were leaving and the restaurant was being cleaned up and reset for the second sitting at 10:00. Lora and I spent our time sitting with Justin and Greggory. Once things were ready, we took over their table. Greggory left, but Justin went back to the kitchen to make sure everything was ready to go.

The meal was perfectly prepared and served. The champagne was chilled and so was the white wine. The red was at perfect room temperature. There wasn't anything I could complain about. The servers were attentive and the wait staff bussed the tables efficiently so that no one sat longer than five minutes with dirty plates in front of them. Everyone really knocked it out of the park. I sent Justin a message to tell him that we needed to give the staff a sizable bonus for doing so well.

I checked the bar mid-way through the night, and the tab was very healthy. Not as big as it was in Atlanta, but healthy. Midnight was twenty minutes away, and the staff was rolling a trolley up to the stage with the prize draw on it. Once the clock turned over, they would draw three names from the bowl for three prizes.

Three, two, one, Happy New Year! We were jumping up and hugging and kissing the people we were with. Justin came back on the stage and asked me to join him.

"Ladies and gentlemen, Happy New Year, and thank you for celebrating with us, on our first year here in amazing Montreal." There were whistles and cheers from the crowd.

"Right now, we have three prizes to draw, so please take your seats and get your tickets out and we'll pull three lucky winners. The prizes are gift boxes that you can choose from." One of the servers brought out a trolley with three gifts wrapped in festive metallic paper.

"Our first winner is … Mr. Stephen Knight! Is Mr. Knight here?" I asked. "Come on up to the stage sir."

A gentleman jumped up in the back of the restaurant and worked his way forward.

"Thank you! Wow!"

"Sir, go ahead and select a gift." He picked up the middle one and ripped it open, "It's a dinner for two here at L'Escalade for five hundred dollars!" A woman squealed somewhere in the audience.

As the man made his way back to his seat, I drew the next name.

"Our second winner is … Mme Sophie Morreaux! Is Mme Morreaux here?" Justin asked. "Come on up to the stage, madam."

A table by the windows got excited when a lady stood up and hopped to the stage.

"Oh merci! Merci! Merci!"

"Go ahead and select a gift please," I said. She chose the third package all wrapped in pink and white. When she opened it, she was smiling like crazy.

273

"It's a beautiful bottle of very expensive wine and some glasses to share it. Thank you."

"That is a three hundred dollar bottle of 2018 Cabernet Sauvignon!"

"And finally, our third prize is for … Mr. Sheffield. Come on up for your gift."

A man in his fifties wearing a tux came to the stage to open the gift. When he unwrapped the ribbon carefully, and peeled back the paper, a note fell to the floor. I instinctively bent down to pick it up and my face blanched as I opened the folded piece of paper. I froze, staring at the slip of paper in my hand. I could hear Justin saying, "What is it, Rick?"

I looked up. Everything seemed to slow down. I glanced at Justin and he saw my face and his smile dropped instantly. I glanced at the tables, and people were cheering unknowingly. Mr. Sheffield was still opening his gift, which was a selection of expensive scotch and whiskeys from around the world, valued at four hundred dollars.

I could hear customers shouting congratulations to the winner. Justin was staring at me with a blank look on his face. I glanced at my wife, and she knew instantly something was very wrong. I watched Lora stand up and start walking to the stage.

"Um, ladies and gentlemen, please be seated for a moment. There seems to be a problem that we need to address immediately." I shoved the slip in my pocket. "Mr. Sheffield, please take your seat. We'll be back in just a moment."

I grabbed Justin's arm and started moving to the back, to the office. Lora was following us. She was practically running down the hall after us.

Once the three of us got inside the room, I slammed the door. I pulled out the slip of paper and read it to myself again. Then I showed it to my business partner and my wife.

THERE IS A BOMB IN THE RESTAURANT

AND IF ANYONE LEAVES ALL WILL DIE

I watched as Justin absorbed the message, then he crumpled on a chair with his mouth dropped. "What the fuck are we supposed to do?" he cried.

"Oh. My. God," said Lora. "Oh my God. Oh my God."

"Should we call the police?" I asked?

"I would," said Lora. "It doesn't say anything about the police, only leaving. Should we lock the doors?"

"If we do, we'll have to tell the customers why they can't leave. That will cause a panic," said Justin.

"I don't see a way around that. What about calling the police first, and telling them, then asking them what to do?" I asked.

"Let's do something!" said Justin, starting to panic.

"Calm down, Justin. Panic won't help us." I picked up the phone.

"911, what's our emergency?"

"Hello, my name is Rick Benal. I'm one of the owners of the L'Escalade restaurant on St. Paul Street in Old Montreal. We have just received a bomb threat."

"How was it delivered?"

"It was a note in the prize bowl."

"Do you think the threat is credible?"

"Who am I to judge? The note says there is a bomb in the restaurant and if anyone leaves we all die. What do we do?

"We will send a bomb squad and fire department. Try to keep your customers as calm as possible, lock the doors so that if it's a real threat, that won't be an excuse."

"Okay."

"They are dispatched now and will be there in a minute."

"Thank you."

"Someone stay on the line with us please."

"I will do that," said Lora. "Hello, my name is Lora. I'm the wife of one of the owners."

"Justin, go lock the back doors. I will go lock the front."

"All right. Then I'll meet you back on stage."

"Folks, can I have your attention please. Could everyone take their seats, and could we bring up the house lights, and kill the music? Hello again, my name is Rick. I need to explain something, and I need everyone to remain calm and in your seats. We have received a bomb threat. The police, bomb squad, and fire department are already dispatched and they are arriving now. The bomber told us no one could leave. So we will obey him for now. The bomb squad is coming in and will ascertain if there is indeed an explosive on the property." I took a deep breath.

"Folks, you can help. Gather all your own possessions. Check that they haven't been tampered with. If you find anything you don't recognize, anything at all, leave the object where it is and clear the immediate area around it. No one touches anything suspicious."

At that, everyone gathered up their belongings and put them on their tables. Thankfully, table service had been finished and the tables were relatively clear of dishes. So everything went on the tables. I looked at the trolley that had been brought into the restaurant for the draw. I had a bad feeling about it. I dared not look under the cloth, but I had to.

I gently lifted a corner of the tablecloth, looked under, and saw blinking lights. Releasing the cloth, I got everyone to clear the space around the stage and trolley as far as we could go. People picked up their chairs and went to the farthest point in the restaurant and sat down again.

Lora came running into the room. "Rick, the police are ready to come in."

"Tell them I found the bomb. It's this trolley. So the doors may be okay."

"Rick says it's a trolley we used for the draw. Uh huh, uh huh. Okay."

"They are going to use special detectors to see if there is anything boobytrapping the doors before they come in."

"All right," said Rick. "People, please move away from the doors to give the police some working room."

A tense five minutes was spent while we watched the police use some device to scan the door lock, doorframe, and door itself for any boobytrap. When cleared, the bomb squad men entered with a robot. A regular dressed officer came in with them and came to speak to Justin and Rick.

"Do you know of anyone who would want to do this to you?" asked the officer.

"No."

"We just had our soft launch in October."

"Do you have any difficult staff who may have a grudge, someone fired recently?" ask the officer.

"I don't know. I don't think so. They're all new," I said.

"Maybe. I'd have to confirm with the chefs," said Justin. He went to speak to the chefs and came back a minute later. "Apparently someone was let go a couple of days ago and wasn't too happy about it."

"Are all your staff on duty for this event?" asked the officer.

"Yes, we have a full staff complement tonight."

"Except for the cook who was fired, and another who called in sick."

"Okay, I'm going to go speak to your staff," said the officer. Justin showed him back to the kitchens.

Meanwhile, the robot was sitting in front of the trolley and the specialists were discussing what they were going to do next.

"Lora, can you do anything? You know, magical?" asked Rick.

"Hmm, let me think about that." She pulled out her phone and opened her grimoire and started scrolling through the different spells. "I may have one to contain a blast or energy outburst."

In the meantime, the police were still checking everywhere for triggers or other devices. Our patrons were stuck in their seats with nowhere to go. Tension was starting to build. People wanted out of the restaurant.

Finally, an officer came in and told everyone that there were no other devices. Once the bomb squad finished their examination of the trolley, they would be able to leave.

So far, the customers had been cooperative and quiet. A thought passed through my head to give them a drink like they do on airlines when the turbulence gets scary. But as the thought formed in my head I discarded it. The last thing we needed were drunk patrons. Looking around at their faces, it did seem as if the scare had sobered them all a bit.

Justin was standing by my side again with Lora. We were watching the bomb people. In the meantime, the fire department had started coming inside to see if they could do anything.

"Hey, Rick, when can we leave?"

"Like the officer said, soon. As soon as the bomb squad says we can move."

"Mr. Benal?" asked one of the bomb squad guys. "Can we speak to you?"

I walked close to them and asked them what was up.

"Well, we've determined the type of explosive the bomber has used. It's C4, and enough of it to demolish this entire building."

"Can you defuse it? Remove it?"

"We can try to defuse it. Removing it would be ideal, but there is no way of looking at it now, if there isn't a booby-trap on it."

"How is it supposed to detonate?"

"It seems to be a mercury switch, which would activate as soon as the bomb moves."

"Why didn't it explode when we rolled into the room here?"

"Likely because it was a two-step switch. Move once to activate, move again to explode."

"What do you suggest?"

"We need to uncover more of it to find out if there is a remote backup."

"What if there is?"

"Then we are cooked, sir. It's unlikely that we would be able to disarm it."

"Let us work a bit more, maybe we can find something we can use."

Ah, mon dios!

"Can I at least get people out?" I asked.

"Yes, start evacuating patrons quietly and carefully with as little commotion as possible. Do it one table at a time. Have them remove their phone batteries first because people try to cheat thinking they know better."

"Okay," I said.

"Ladies and gentlemen, I'm sorry your festivities have been cut short, but the bomb tech believes he can safely disarm this device here inside the building. Before he does that, I need everyone to turn off their phones and remove the batteries."

"Justin, go tell the kitchen staff, please."

"Once you have done that, please carefully stand without moving any of the tables. We're going to ask you to evacuate table by table carefully." The first few people stood waiting. I directed the tables closest to the bomb to go first. One woman flung her designer coat around, nearly hitting the cart. We all held our breath, watching in horrified slow motion as the coat's edge swirled out from her and swept past the trolley, missing it by mere inches.

I think I wet myself at that moment.

"Please folks, be more careful! That nearly made contact with the trolley." The woman threw me a contemptuous look but made an attempt to walk carefully between the tables. As each close table emptied, I felt my tension go down a smidgen, only to ratchet up again when another table stood and started moving.

Everyone appeared to do as they were told and in a somewhat orderly fashion. When they got to the back, the customers couldn't leave because the police hadn't cleared the doors yet. So people were piling up and getting anxious. When someone knocked a glass off a table, it exploded on the floor. The crowd reacted like a flock of starlings and dodged as one entity away from the sound, knocking over chairs.

That created even more anxiety.

The police and fire were letting people out now. As they shuffled out of the restaurant, the police took them to a building across the street and wrapped them in blankets. Officers took statements from everyone just in case something popped up.

"You know," said Lora, "the note was slipped inside the wrapping of the gift prize for the second sitting. Who would know to do that? It would have been a random person that opened that gift, but the bomb is on the trolley. So who is it they're targeting? Would they be part of the kitchen staff now?"

"I don't know, but it's worth telling them when we get out of here," I said.

I watched as the robot carefully unwrapped the trolley and exposed the bomb underneath. There were gasps from the customers as they saw the blinking lights revealed. It looked sophisticated with lots of wires and lights, but I don't know anything about explosives. I heard the bomb guy muttering under his breath, and I sharpened my hearing and listened to him.

"Okay, first find the ground, there it is. Next it goes to a switch, there is the mercury switch, is there another, no I don't see you, so what did you do? Ah ha! There you are and you're not remotely set up, that's good, so a phone call won't set you off, good girl, we're just going to have a little dance here, let me see your good side, that's it, nice and slow, you can show me, there you are. That's the one. We can end this."

"Bomb Unit One to Lead, come in."

"This is Lead, over."

"I can defuse this bomb but we cannot move her. I suggest we evacuate all personnel and then let the robot and her dance, over."

"Roger that. We have determined there are no triggers on the doors, over."

"Roger that. All cell phones are off and batteries removed. You can go ahead and jam. I'll make another check for a remote active switch, over."

"Roger. Shutting down cell frequencies, out."

I watched the last customer go out the front door. Then all the wait staff, kitchen staff, and anyone else from the back, came out front to leave. The place was almost empty, but my nerves were raw with anxiety.

Lora and I found our coats and started to get dressed in outer clothes when a blinding flash came from the stage. Then a wall of air knocked us over, followed by the loudest noise I'd ever experienced. It deafened me.

The next thing I knew, there were three tables flying toward me and Lora, and it was all I could do to stop them from hitting her.

The concussion from the air blast knocked everyone sideways, and we all ended up flattened against the wall with debris flying at us. I managed to grab a table, tip it on its edge, and hide some of us behind it. Thank God for my immortal strength and speed, or we would have all been decapitated.

I looked behind me. The fireman that had been standing at the door had been cut in half.

Most of the staff that had been standing there were on the floor with gaping wounds. Justin was nowhere to be seen. He had been beside Lora. I frantically looked everywhere.

I finally saw him, buried under a pile of debris. I had no idea if he was alive or dead. The entire front of the building was gone, the walls, the floor, the windows, some of the ceiling from upstairs, which was Justin's living quarters when he was in town.

I was in shock. My ears were ringing, and my head was aching. Shaking like a leaf in a gale, I knelt down holding Lora, not able to do anything.

A tiny part of me realized that Lora was limp. I looked down at her finally, tearing my eyes from the horror I saw all around me. There was a gaping hole in her neck, and her body was pumping blood onto the floor.

I tore off my tie and wrapped it around her neck to stop the bleeding. Then I bit a hole in my own arm and made her drink my blood. I don't know why. It was just an instinctive action. I was born this way, she was made; it seemed like my blood should be stronger.

I watched as her neck slowly started knitting back together. The flesh had almost closed by the time the EMTs found us in the rubble. Her head was no longer nearly coming off, but she was still gushing blood. The EMTs asked me if I had any injuries. I didn't think so, but it didn't matter. I insisted they take Lora first.

Dazed, I walked out of what was left of the restaurant into the street. I was told they would take her to the new, huge Montreal hospital, and I told them I would follow.

Once outside in the street, I witnessed the devastation of the explosion. It had broken windows up and down the block and across the street. A voice in my head wondered if my insurance would go through the roof, but I dismissed it. What mattered was finding Justin, and seeing what the casualties were.

The customers the police had collected inside the building across the street were now being moved quickly, some with injuries because of flying glass. Ambulance after ambulance was showing up, sirens blaring and lights flashing.

Walking over to the fire chief, I gave him my name and asked him how bad it was.

"Sir, were you in the explosion?" ask the fire chief. "Medic, come over here and look at this man. He's covered in blood, he may be injured."

"No, no, it's not mine, it's my wife's blood, and she is on her way to the hospital already. I'm one of the owners of this restaurant. My partner was in the building, but I haven't seen him come out yet."

A medic arrived with a bag. "Sir, come with me and let me at least check you over." She pulled me along with her over to the ambulance. The medic then forced me to sit down while she took my blood pressure and did a cursory look over me. "Sir, you were in the explosion?"

"Yes, but I managed to get a table as a shield in front of me and my wife. Unfortunately, the shrapnel still injured her. I'm okay though, this blood is not mine."

"Sir, you may have a concussion, so I'd like to send you to the hospital as well."

"No, no, I have to stay here and see that everyone is rescued."

"Sir, that's our job. You don't have anything to do right now but recover." They laid me on a stretcher and strapped me in. With little effort I could have freed myself, but I had no incentive. I was numb. I couldn't think straight. All I could see was the explosion happening in front of me over and over again. So I let them pack me into the ambulance and we traveled to the hospital.

"Hey, where are you taking me?" I asked the EMT sitting in the back with me.

"You're going to MUHC."

"Are you sending all the victims there?"

"Yes, it's the closest one. Unless they are full, which they will notify us before we get there."

"Did you see how many got clear?"

"No sir. I'm afraid I didn't. I know there were some firefighters inside, and some staff members still inside, but other than that, I don't know how many."

I closed my eyes and just felt the sway of the vehicle speeding through the traffic and running lights. When they stopped at the emergency door, I was swiftly taken inside.

"Thirty-five-year-old male, concussion, contusions, doesn't appear to be bleeding. BP is 135 over 90. He claims the blood is his wife's. He was inside the restaurant when the bomb went off."

"Okay, thank you. Put him in bay seventeen."

They transferred me to a gurney and I was suddenly moving again. Then the bed stopped and an army of technicians and nurses suddenly appeared at my bedside, hooking me up to all kinds of machines. In the back of my mind I remembered that they couldn't figure out what I was, but my brain was still in pieces and I couldn't really form coherent thoughts.

"My wife, my wife..." I tried to speak.

"Yes sir, what's that about your wife?"

"My wife was brought in too."

"What's her name, sir?"

"Lora, Lora O'Reilly. She's a petite woman with long black hair and green eyes."

"I'll look for her for you." The orderly stepped away.

I heard someone making a fuss at the desk, and focused my hearing on it to see if it was about Lora.

"My name is Mark Chisholm. Rick Benal is a very close friend and his wife is my wife's sister. Where are they? What is their condition?"

"Sir, only immediate family can be let in, I'm sorry. But if you take a seat in the waiting room, I can have a doctor give you an update."

"Fine, come on, Falon, we'll go to the waiting room."

"Falon," I croaked out. "Falon … it's me…"

"Wait, Mark. I heard something," said Falon.

The next thing I knew, Falon and Mark were standing beside me, and I heard her sob in shock.

"Oh, Rick, oh my God, are you okay? Were you hurt?" asked Falon.

"No … not my blood."

"Do you know if Lora is here?" asked Mark.

I nodded, because that felt easier than speaking.

"Okay, I'm going to walk around and see if I can find her," said Falon. "You stay with him please."

"Justin…"

"I'll look for Justin too."

"Man, you scared us. When the news broke that there was a bomb scare at the restaurant, we started driving into town. We were about six blocks from the place when we heard the boom. We parked about five blocks away, and walked in. There are so many broken windows along the side streets, it's amazing. It must have been a pretty big bomb."

I nodded again. "Big … very." Mark took my hand and just sat with me. It felt better to not be alone. But I was getting confused and hazy. I had been numb and clear-headed before. But now the enormity of what just happened was settling in.

"Wait, how … know?"

"How did we know?"

I shook my head. "Know bomb … how bomb."

"Umm, I'll take a wild guess, how did they know the bomb was there?"

I shook my head.

"How did they know the bomb would work?"

I shook my head again.

"How did they get the bomb there?"

I nodded.

"Hmmm, good question. I am going to get Andrews and his crew to investigate. This feels like a targeted job. But who would want to destroy you guys?"

I shook my head.

"Look, here comes Falon."

"I found Lora. She's got an injury to her throat. It seems that a piece of shrapnel tore out her jugular and she nearly bled out."

"Has she healed yet?" asked Mark.

"They stitched her back together and then bandaged it. If it's healed, they won't realize it yet."

"That's good," said Mark. "So we have to get her and Rick out of the hospital before they are discovered."

"Yes, Lora was conscious, and in spite of the blood all over her, she seemed to be okay. She was scared for Rick and I told her he was basically okay."

"Good. Rick, can you hear me?" asked Mark. I had closed my eyes and was listening to their conversation.

"Yeah, I'm here. Thank you for finding Lora."

"Do you think you can walk?" asked Mark.

"With help, yes."

"Well, we will wait until the doctor checks you out. We'll go and sit down and come back after that, okay?"

"Yup."

I closed my eyes again, listening to the humming of the machines and the scurrying of people back and forth. It wasn't too long before a doctor was poking me.

"Hello, Mr. Benal, are you with us?" asked a voice I didn't recognize. Opening my eyes, I saw it was a doctor.

"Yes, I'm here."

"Mr. Benal, you're in the Montreal hospital. Do you remember why?"

"I … I … I was in an explosion," I stammered.

"That's right, Mr. Benal. How are you feeling?"

"Woozy."

"That is probably due to a concussion. We think you may have been hit in the head with a heavy object. Can you remember anything?"

"I remember a table flying toward me. I used it to shield my wife and myself."

"That's very brave of you, Mr. Benal. It probably saved your wife's life. Yes, I do think that you have a concussion, and we should probably keep you for observation. However, the incident has brought in too many patients, so if you have someone who can watch over you carefully, we can let you go."

"My friends are here. They can take me home."

"Excellent, then I will prepare the paperwork for you to leave, Mr. Benal."

"Can I take my wife home too?"

"I will check on her for you. What's her name?"

"Her name is Lora, Lora O'Reilly."

"Oh yes, she is the spunky one. I think she can leave too, but let me verify that first."

The doctor went to check on Lora's chart. Mark came back to my bed, and was standing there when the doctor returned.

"Good news, Mr. Benal. Lora is good to go as well. You two were very lucky tonight. Happy New Year!" said the doctor.

"They're letting us both leave," I said to Mark.

"Falon will go and get Lora. I will take you," said Mark.

"I still haven't heard about Justin."

"I will keep my eyes and ears open for you," said Mark. "But my priority is to get you two out of this hospital, now."

It only took another fifteen minutes before the nurse came back with the discharge papers and instructions for the next seventy-two hours.

"Remember, light sleep, wake up every hour or so. Drink lots of water."

"Thank you, nurse." I got into the wheelchair that was waiting for me, and Mark started toward the doors. Falon and Lora were already there waiting.

"I'll go get the car. Wait here," said Mark.

"Lora, I was so scared for you," I said.

"I know … but let's wait till we're out of here to speak freely."

Once in the car, we hugged and cried and hugged some more. I related the story to the three of them of what I experienced, including Lora's neck being torn out, not just her jugular.

"We were lucky it took a while for the EMTs to find you. Had they seen her neck in its original state, it would have been dangerous to you both," said Mark.

"Indeed. That is the reason I gave her some of my blood. I hoped that the added immortal blood would help her heal faster, and it did."

Epilogue

Rick

We arrived at our house. Anita and the kids were standing at the front door all wearing expressions of being very scared and worried.

It was clear from their faces: they must have found out about the bomb. We hadn't called them at all. I had been too busy keeping Lora alive, and then we were in the hospital. Anita and Minni must have seen it all over social media and they had told the boys there had been an incident. They were all so scared, and looked like they had expected us to not come home.

When Lora and I got out of the car, the relief on their faces was visible. Minni started crying as she ran toward us, neglecting the fact that it was cold and she wasn't wearing a coat. She ran into Lora and threw her arms around Lora's waist and clung to her, sobbing.

Pascal and Trent ran too, and were hugging Lora around her lower body, also crying in relief.

"Mom, I was so scared," she said once the hiccups ended. "Wait, why are you covered in blood?" she asked when she pulled away from her mother and saw the blood covering her clothes all down the front. It looked very gruesome, and indicated there was a horrendous injury.

"It's okay, Minni, I'm fine, I'm fine, we're fine, it's going to be alright. Boys, we're okay. Come into the house before we all freeze. We will tell you what happened, together."

"Anita, we'll explain," I said, when I saw how confused they all were.I placed my hand on the back of Anita's shoulders and led her back inside, while Lora held her children's hands.

Lora and I looked at each other.A meaningful message passed between us.

It was time.

Time to explain what we were.

Time to let them know what they could become.

Excerpt from Immortal Generation, Book 7

1—Tell the Kids

Lora

The last seventy two hours have been frightening. First a bomb blew up the new restaurant, landing in a hospital and risking exposure, then finally having to tell Anita and the kids who and what we were.

But first the bomb. At the apex of our New Year's Eve party, we received a bomb threat, delivered in a very strange way: It was a slip of paper inserted inside the wrapping of the gift box given to one of our guests. How that slip got in there, we don't know. How the bomb got in the restaurant is also a mystery.

Putting the mystery aside, we called the police, and they dispatched a bomb tech and the fire department. We were assured they could defuse it. So we started evacuating the restaurant into the cold January morning. Just as the staff was leaving, the bomb exploded, sending shrapnel and furniture flying in every direction. A table had flown toward Rick and I and hit Rick on the head, and I got hit by a huge shard of glass in the neck. Rick apparently managed to take that table and use it as a shield for us protecting us from more damage.

The resulting slaughter of most of the staff and a few firefighters was nothing short of a tragedy. To make things worse, Justin was missing. We didn't know where he was in the restaurant when the bomb went off. The police had taken over the scene. The fire department was using dogs to find bodies, which was sorrowful and gruesome. Our dear chefs lost their lives, and that was a terrible loss of talent and life. Most of the wait staff was gone too, some of them who were standing up against that wall, managed to escape the worst damage because everyone fell on top of them.

Sadly one of the firefighters who was helping people get out was cut in half by a pane of glass from one of the windows. The news cast taped footage of the damage to the neighboring heritage buildings. It was just a crime to see and will cost even more to repair.

Memorial services were being announced for various victims, and Rick and I planned on attending most of them if not all. But we still had no word about Justin. The wreckage was nowhere near the point of being removed. They were still investigating the bomb. We were told it could be months before Rick could think about rebuilding. He had already been in touch with his insurance. They were going to cover them, at least that much was ascertained. We don't know to what extent yet.

The bombing had held the news cycle for the last three days, but there was so much more for them to dig into, I expect it will be another week before they tire of it. We'll know when they get down to doing a bio on Rick ... that will be close to the end of the public scrutiny. At least one good thing has come out of the investigation so far: The police have cleared the owners of the restaurant, aka Justin and Rick, of any wrongdoing. They were called victims of a terrible crime, and that they would get to the bottom of it as soon as they could.

I had a huge question though, just how did the media find out about a bomb in the first place? Mark had said they heard the story on the radio and jumped in the car and got close enough to the restaurant to hear the explosion. So how did the news know about it in advance? Was that cook involved? Did the cook who called in sick have anything to do with it too? Why?

At least we would be clear of lawsuits from building owners. So Rick sighed after that announcement.

Next was the talk we had to have with Anita and the children. When we got home, they were reasonably shocked that we were basically unscathed. They had heard that we had been inside the restaurant and in front of many of the others at the time of the explosion. So, of course, they were terrified we had been injured seriously, or worse.

Mark and Falon stayed with us to help with the explanation and as support.

"Come on kids, let's get inside out of the cold," I had said to them as they clung to us on the step when we got home.

All eight of us went inside, Mark lit a fire in the fireplace and we all sat down together.

"Anita, kids, we need to have a conversation," started Rick. "I need to explain to you something about myself, your mom and our friends. It's not a bad thing, not at all. But it is a secret thing."

"Ricardo, how are you okay?" asked Anita. "How? They said you were right inside the restaurant when the ..."

"Everybody take a deep breath," said Rick. "We're all okay, not a scratch on us. We're not dying, and not going anywhere. Okay? Now, I'm going to tell you a true story."

"Once upon a time, an alien race came to Earth because their home was dying. When they got here, they found humans. Eventually, the aliens and the humans had babies together and some of them became magical, like your mom. Today they are called witches, but back then they were considered very special people. Others live very long lives, so long in fact that the humans came to think of them as immortal because they lived longer than the memory of most people.

"The aliens looked like humans, which helped them have babies together, but they had some hidden differences. One was, they had fangs which they used to use for hunting. But on earth, they didn't. Because they were predators, like our big cats, they had a better sense of smell, could see much better, and could hear much better. This of course helped in hunting.

"I am the descendant of one of those immortals," ended Rick. He fell silent, looking back and forth at the four of them. Their faces showed they were each processing what he had said. Some had widely dilated pupils, Anita was squinting. My youngest looked a combination of intrigued and scared.

We waited for the onslaught of questions that would inevitably come. Minni was first.

"We know mom is magical, is that how, mom? Is that how you guys survived?" asked Minni.

"Good question Minni. As it turns out, yes. I have been tracing my lineage backward, and I discovered that the magical ability I have inherited through my family line, originally came from these immortals."

"Are you immortal now?" asked Minni, drawing the right conclusion.

"Yes, but that is because Rick has changed me. I was born human, just like you."

I could see the wheels ticking over in their heads as they processed what we were saying. In many ways, our kids would accept this story much more easily than Anita will.

"Does that mean I can be changed too?" asked Minni, again a leap in understanding.

Good girl, I knew you were smart! "Yes it does."

Anita had remained silent through all this, as she listened to the kids asking questions, and our answers.

"Rick, can we see your fangs?" asked Pascal.

"Of course. I'll show you," said Rick. He slowly elongated his fangs, as my sons were saying things like awesome and cool! Anita was gasping in shock. When his fangs reached their maximum length, he purposely spoke to sound silly and break the tension.

"Noo you thee thath I cannoth thpeath very dell dith my theeth like thith," I lisped.

"Rick you sound like Sylvester on Tweety Bird!" They all laughed out loud. He let his fangs retract then so he could continue.

"Now there is more to this. When I say we're immortal, I mean long-lived. It does not mean we don't, or can't die. It really just means we live a very, very, very long time."

"How long?" asked Trent.

It was Mark's turn to answer. "Well, for example, my sister Gwen is three hundred years old and I am one hundred and fifty years old."

"Wow! Really? What's it like to live so long?" asked Pascal.

"I'll bet it can be lonely," said my daughter.

"Yes, it can be lonely," answered Mark. "We watch all our human friends and acquaintances die. We don't usually allow ourselves the luxury of becoming involved with humans, because we have to leave before they discover our secret."

"What secret?" asked Trent.

"That we are not human," said Rick. "We can never tell anyone that we are not human. We cannot tell even our bestest friends. Because it would be very dangerous to us if the human world knew we existed."

"What would they do?" asked Trent.

"I fear that they would keep us in cages and experiment on us," said Mark.

"You mean like in the movies?"

"Yes, just like that."

"Now, there is one more thing about being immortal that is relevant right now," I said. "We heal very quickly. Only the most serious injuries, like losing our head, will kill us. Other injuries we heal."

"Is that why you and Rick appear unharmed?" asked Anita, speaking for the first time.

"Yes, that's exactly why. We can show you," I said. "If you want to see."

My kids were all excited about that, Anita not so much, but she wanted to witness it for herself.

So I took a sharp pocket knife from Rick and in front of them cut a deep gash into my arm. They all screamed together, and watched as a drop of blood fell to the floor, but then the cut started to knit back together until it had disappeared altogether.

"Wow!"

"Amazing!"

"Oh my gosh!"

"Ah mon dios!"

They all sat silent for a minute. Then an explosion of words came from their mouths.

"When can I be changed?" asked my daughter.

I looked at Rick and Mark. We hadn't talked about this yet. But according to Abeo, it would not require sex, so that was good.

"How about this: let us speak to another immortal who knows more than we do, and when we get the answer, we will tell you."

They all spoke at once of course.

"Wait! Anita, you have a question?"

"Is this condition inheritable?" she asked. "When your baby is born, will he be immortal?"

I looked at Rick and he nodded. "Yes, Anita, he will be born immortal. But he will not have all his adult characteristics."

"Then I request to be changed, so that I can continue to care for the next generation," she said.

Tears formed in my eyes, this woman was amazing. She lived her life — more than fifty years caring for another family. And she wanted to keep caring for their future too.

"Of course you can. Anita, it would be our privilege to bring you into our family."

"You need to understand, mama, that when you change, your appearance will also change. You will become young again."

"Alabado sea Dios."she murmured. Rick chuckled.

"What did she say?" I asked.

"Praise be to God!"

"So let's recap," said Minni. "You're immortal with my mom and Mark and Falon? You all heal very fast. You all have incredible senses. And we can become like you?"

"You can add Gwen and Robert as well as Abeo and Margaret and all their children," I added.

"So basically, everyone who comes over here is immortal?" asked Trent. "Cool!"

"Is there anything else we need to tell them now?" I asked Mark.

"No, that's about it for now. Kids, Anita, if you have any questions, ask us. Anytime. Okay?" said Mark.

The kids got up and animatedly talked with each other as they went up to their rooms. Anita stayed sitting there for a few minutes quietly.

"Ricardo, I would like to do this as soon as possible. What do I have to do?"

"Mama, we need to give you a few injections. I'll ask Abeo what he thinks the dose should be and how many. We can get started on it as soon as you're ready."

"Gracias, Ricardo."

What's Next

The next installment of the Immortal Stories is ***Book 7 - Immortal Generation***.

- A massive investigation starts looking into the motive, means, and perpetrator of the restaurant bombing.

- Lora and Rick finally explain everything to their kids and Anita.

- Lora starts working with the rescued witches.

- Andrews uncovers a New Orleans connection to the bombing.

- Minni invents an important life-saving device.

About The Author

Linda Ashton Trott

Ms Trott, a native of Montreal, Canada, currently lives in the nation's capital with her husband of twenty-four years, their four cats, and eight Japanese Koi.

When not writing, Ms Trott can be found in their backyard relaxing by the pond or editing her husband's stories.

Ms Trott has always had an interest in all things supernatural, the occult, UFOs, aliens, and the paranormal. It seemed natural to combine one or more of these elements into a unique universe in which to tell interesting stories.

These are not children's stories. "It's funny, I never sat down with the intention of writing Adult books," Linda once said. "But here they are. I wanted to express physical love honestly without cutesy acronyms and vague names."

These stories contain explicit language and hot, steamy sex scenes that will leave you panting.

Books In This Series

The Immortal Stories Series

The Immortals are a race of beings that came to Earth many tens of thousands of years ago. Their stories stretch across time and have become woven into the history of humans. Their society is hidden from humans even though they live among them. Forbidden from developing romantic liaisons with humans, some break the rules and form close bonds and get married. But this always comes with consequences.

1 - **Immortal Desire**

One immortal and one human.

As Zisis's world collides with Falon's, she is left to cope and deal with the blowback. Their love affair is erotic, passionate, and stirs the soul, but it is ill-fated. This is a story of romance, heartbreak, hardship, and survival. The sex is hot and steamy, the highs euphoric, and the lows devastating.

2 - **Immortal Fulfillment**

What a twist! What has Mark done?

After a nasty life twist has her rethinking a relationship with her Texan, Falon needs to decide which direction to go. Is she back to square one? Certainly not! Between hurricanes, hot tub invites, and road trips with hot, sexy guys, there is plenty of action and adventure.

3 - Immortal Peril

The Family is NOT happy!

Lora meets Rick, a talented dessert chef in an up-and-coming restaurant in Atlanta, Georgia, while visiting her best friend, Falon, who is on contract work there. Lora and Rick hit it off in ways she can't believe—one hot weekend in Miami and she can't get him out of her mind. So, when invited to Atlanta again, this time by Rick, she doesn't hesitate!

When Mark disappears without a trace, Falon is left to find out what happened.

4 - Immortal Victory

Out of the fire and into the frying pan!

Falon gets out of one problem only to find herself in danger again. An ancient enemy is targeting the immortals and will stop at nothing to eliminate them. Dodging assassins and traps, Falon decides to end homelessness, one person at a time.

Her BFF Lora discovers that true love sex generates magical energy while she looks for her ancestors.

Gwen finds a partner in Andrews.

5 - Immortal Hunt

Having just survived a coordinated attack from an ancient enemy, the immortals rejoice and celebrate their success. Attention turns toward locating their ancestors when a news item catches Lora's attention and gives her a very important clue to finding them. The immortals are off on a great adventure to distant places. Pirates, witches, time travel, spooky castles, and volcanic caves are some of the encounters happening this time. Don't miss out on the adventure!

6 - <u>Immortal Nexus</u>

New is old, and old is new

Surely, saving a coven of witches from a pocket dimension would be a highlight in life. But it's not. The immortals return home to everyday life; family, moving, school, raising teens, and of course, spicy lovemaking.

We meet a new character with a deep past. And when a new couple moves in across the street, Falon notices some familiar characteristics. She makes it her mission to meet the new neighbors.

Family matters are front and center in this story. The close-knit group of immortals is becoming a family, and some stories need sharing like Andrews' tale of being hired by aliens.

Justin and Rick finally open the new restaurant. It was a New Year's Eve celebration with a bang!

7 - Immortal Generation — Coming 2023

Short Stories

<u>First Contact: An Immortal Origin Story</u>

The Immortal's Origin Story started 33,000 years ago, when they arrived on Earth. *First Contact* follows the story of how the immortals meet the first humans and what happens when they interact and live together.

Praise for the Series

What are readers saying about this new series?

"Yet again I've got an ARC for this author and I've got to say that these books just get better and better. I loved this one [Book 6] and it is my favourite so far out of the series. There is now so many new people with there own stories that I don't think it will get boring any time soon. My favourite couple were Falon and Mark but I have quickly fallen in love with Margaret and Abeo and I didn't see the twist and turns right at the end. Brilliant book by a brilliant author."

*... Sam ***** Amazon*

"Linda Ashton Trott has a real gift for crafting intricate sex scenes that are highly charged and also entirely believable. She really brings you into the bedroom in a joyful way. The will-they-or-won't-they story keeps you wondering, right up to the plot twist at the end, which sets readers up for Book 2."

*... Amy **** Amazon*

"Ohhhhh! This book was good! Hot hot scenes with enough of a story in between to keep you hooked. We all need to become

Leopard Ladies! Nice quick read. Can't wait to read book 2 of the series!"

*... Josée **** Goodreads*

"Brilliant book loved the storyline and I couldn't put it down once I started. I loved the characters and got really absorbed in to their lives and feelings.

all I can say is Wow I loved every part of it (#3). I'm really sad that the book ended the way it did as I wanted to carry on reading and finding out what was going to happen. I love this series and all the characters. Hopefully there should be another one."

*... Sam ***** Amazon*

"Picking up where the first book ended, this installment of the series was the heroine's journey of self-discovery in order to make the right decisions for her, something I really enjoyed!

This book was sexy, fun and the character development was great! Ioved how the heroine slowly took back control of her life and found empowerment in her spontaneity."

*...Nikita **** Goodreads*

"wow! amazing, fast paced and enthralling new world! Wonderful characters that charmed me from the beginning. Honestly this was a wonderfully perfect read to help me escape from the world for a bit.

Amazing (#3). I love this world and it's characters. Great storyline and well written. This series has been amazing to read. Definitely need to pick them up."

*... Naomi ***** Amazon*

"Yet again I'm absolutely totally blown away by this book (#4). I love the characters and the story line. Linda has written a fantastic book with steamy scenes that I didn't think were possible but brilliant. I loved the fact that we're now starting to see smaller named characters have a bigger role. It's very well written and can't wait to read more of the series."

*...Sam ***** Amazon*

Being an Indie Author

I've chosen to publish independently. This means I don't have the big machine of a traditional publishing company behind me. Reviews are very important on Amazon because they determine how visible you are in the marketplace. That makes your review, and every other review I receive, the most important tool in my marketing toolbox. If you've enjoyed reading this book, please consider spending a few minutes leaving me a review on Amazon. It doesn't have to be long.

Thank you!

See my website at www.lindaashtontrott.com to join the mailing list. You will not be inundated with mail, I promise! It will let you know when the latest book is released and if there are freebies.

Visit my Amazon author's page at
https://www.amazon.com/~/e/B09TG29J19